John McCabe is a geneticist who lives and works in Birmingham. *Paper* is his second novel.

Paper

John McCabe

BLACK SWAN

PAPER
A BLACK SWAN BOOK : 0 552 99874 5

Originally published in Great Britain by Granta Books

PRINTING HISTORY
Granta Books edition published 1999
Black Swan edition published 2000

1 3 5 7 9 10 8 6 4 2

Set in 11pt Melior by
County Typesetters, Margate, Kent.

Black Swan Books are published by Transworld Publishers,
61–63 Uxbridge Road, London W5 5SA,
a division of The Random House Group Ltd,
in Australia by Random House Australia (Pty) Ltd,
20 Alfred Street, Milsons Point, Sydney, NSW 2061, Australia,
in New Zealand by Random House New Zealand Ltd,
18 Poland Road, Glenfield, Auckland 10, New Zealand
and in South Africa by Random House (Pty) Ltd,
Endulini, 5a Jubilee Road, Parktown 2193, South Africa.

Printed and bound in Great Britain by
Clays Ltd, St Ives plc.

P-a-p-e-r

Abstract

Science, seen from the inside, is like the grass in the teeth of a rake. On the face of it, a rake is useless. It has ten or so slender teeth, widely spaced, wider in fact than the blades of grass it is used to collect. It cannot rake anything without the presence of many many blades of grass. This might sound self-evident, but if there were say twenty blades of grass needing collection, a rake would be useless. What a rake relies upon is one blade of grass attaching to one of its teeth, catching the weight of another blade and so on until each blade is caught up in an interconnecting mass, self-supporting and self-raking. In essence, it isn't the rake that does the raking, it is the grass. In the same way, science is one idea supporting another idea which in turn supports another and so on. Each idea on its own and without entanglement in all the others is useless. Puncture holes in this structure and ideas drop between the rake teeth and everything falls apart at the seams.

I realized from my time spent in laboratories that science is ultimately leaky. Science is leaky because people are leaky. And science, in a laboratory, is nothing more or less than people. This realized, many things stop making sense. Having witnessed and, on many occasions, contributed to the fallibility of science, I came to question absolutes. One such absolute which is always bandied about is the indisputable nature of forensic evidence. Tell your suspect that you've done DNA testing and you threaten him with the infallible world of science. That's if he's never worked in science. Tell *me* you've profiled my DNA and I will tell you to fuck off. A laboratory technician in a windowless building will have extracted or, more likely, attempted to extract DNA from a hair follicle or a few cheek cells or some other such sample of microscopic dimension for fingerprint analysis, while he dreams of the weekend, frets about the car's MOT, phones his girlfriend, listens to the radio, looks at his watch counting down till lunchtime, calculates how many days till pay day, jokes with his colleagues and stares back at the ninety-six tubes in front of him and wonders which one he put your DNA in.

So, through the nature of my predicament, I endeavoured to put forensic science to the test.

At first, I realized that I was in an impossible position. To silently slip away, to move city and to leave no forwarding address, to change my name, to live my life in silent, isolated terror, these were the only options open to me. But this is what they wanted. And as I sat through long solitary evenings, I came to realize that to slide gently out of view would be to run away. After all, you don't just do DNA tests to corroborate what you already know. No, you do it to make people nervous. You do it to flush people out of the woodwork. You put the word round, you announce it, you make sure that everybody hears. You do it because you know that the one guilty person among the cohort of innocent punters you test believes that science can't fail and that forensics is infallible. The average man is going to feel the black magic that is genetic testing start to prick into his skin. The average man is going to panic. The average man is going to run away, and, in doing so, confess his sins as surely as he would have done by going to the police and giving himself up. The average man cannot win under such circumstances.

But I am not the average man.

And as I thought about the inevitability of testing a large group of people and hoping that one of them will run out from the protection of the throng, I began to see that my only chance was to stay firmly in the thick of things. I thought of the African plains, and of lions attacking only at the periphery of the herd, watching for hysteria, waiting to single out the lone, frightened ungulate who thinks they're in with a chance if they can just make a dash for it. So I decided to nuzzle my way into the centre of the pack using my wet nose to force my way in. Clearly, I could only stay camouflaged for a finite period, and that period might not be particularly long, but I would play them at their game while I could, all the time trying to think my way out of the cul-de-sac circumstance had forced me down.

Introduction

Care in the
Scientific Community

It isn't until you start work that you really come to appreciate just how many nutters there are in the world. The fact that most of them are gainfully employed comes as another shock, though invariably with nutters, it's almost impossible to divine what they're actually employed to do. That there are so many unhinged people lurking in the corners of laboratories the world over is testimony to the fact that Care in the Community is alive and working in science. Lunatics will always end up in institutions at some stage, it's just that these days a fair proportion of them end up in scientific institutions. In Dr Darren White's department at the Sheffield Institute of Medical Diagnostics, there were three official nutters and around thirty unofficial ones, out of a total staff of thirty-four. Darren generously awarded himself the benefit of the doubt in such matters. The insane were free to come and go as they pleased, were largely without responsibility, and were almost impossible to get rid of. The reason for this was that fellow scientists got distinctly nervous about the concept of sacking people with personality disorders. This would be employment suicide. After all, when

15

you live in a glass house you aren't exactly desperate to throw stones around the place.

One class of sociopath prevalent throughout the scientific world is the Tea Break Terminator. Predominantly male, dull or irrelevant or both, bordering on the autistic in their approach to human relationships, and always, always interested in computers, TBTs waltz into coffee rooms the world over and empty them of people. The Institute suffered badly from one such case. And geography was no safeguard, Darren mused, blowing gently across the temporarily corrugated surface of his coffee and noticing for the first time that the TBT at the far side of the room was peering over at him. Darren took a small nervous sip and glanced at him again, discovering to his horror that he was in imminent danger of being trapped. He looked quickly back at his coffee, keeping the mug in front of his face and praying he had been wrong. Darren glanced up one final time to make sure, and this was his mistake. The Tea Break Terminator pounced.

'Do you know the Windows 98 wallpaper logo looks like an inverted crucifix viewed from its lower side?' he imparted as an opening gambit.

Darren grunted. Any more commitment to the conversation and it would all be over. He was aware that his colleagues were edging away from him. There was no solidarity when it came to such matters.

'Yes. Got it off the Microsoft Antichrist web page. More mailings than for Clinton. Two more sites. Both opened today. Well, one yesterday and the other this morning.'

Darren grunted again and took a heavy swig of coffee. A couple mouthfuls more and he could make an honourable retreat from the canteen. However, he had made another bad mistake, and knew it. The grunt had sounded faintly inquisitive. This could be costly. Other staff continued to recede. TBT seized his chance to capitalize upon Darren's apparent interest. 'Gates. Bill Gates. Now the least popular man on the planet. Seventy-two thousand, one hundred I think. From all over. Everywhere. Can't move for them. Slows everything else down though, that's the problem. Servers weren't designed that way, you see, working in parallel data streams.'

Darren glanced around the room. There must have been four or five other members of staff all closer to the nutter than he was, and all of them relieved to have escaped. In fact, as he looked more carefully he was aware that they were visibly delighting in his discomfort.

There was a set protocol here and Darren had ignored it at his own peril. One. Appear busy or preoccupied or deep in conversation. Two. Avoid eye contact. Three. Wait until some other poor sod has been latched on to. Four. Sit back and enjoy their misery. And Darren had done this many times himself. TBT continued, oblivious. The floodgates had been opened and whether or not anybody was remotely interested, he was going to talk.

'Found a number plate by the roadside. Stopped to park and there it was, just lying there. On the pavement it was. K286 YBF. Black on yellow. Midlands area circa nineteen ninety-two, apparently. Not yours, is it?' Darren shook his head. 'Or anybody you know? On West Street a couple of doors past the dungeon shop . . . Still in good condition. Cleaned it up now and it looks a lot better. I'd use it myself only my car's already got number plates . . .'

As TBT continued to drone and Darren to unhappily survey his smiling colleagues, he cursed the thin level of humanity apparent in the department. It wasn't that

its staff were in any way unfriendly or distant, just
that there was a tangible lack of togetherness. They
needed a common focus. Several weeks ago, he had
taken the initiative and tried to liven things up himself. He had planned a campaign of intrigue, of
conjecture, of discussion. Operation Make Work More
Interesting, or 'Mwimi', as Darren had christened it,
coining the sort of catchy acronym that you always see
in marketing and which never catches on, started
gently. There was no storming the beaches or agent-
oranging the forests. It was an operation of subtleties, a
snowball-rolling-gently-down-a-hill-and-taking-every-
body-along-with-it sort of operation. First, the teaser
campaign. Mwimi kicked off with odd shoes. Two
more days of minor adjustments (an inside-out shirt,
V-neck sweater worn back to front) went without com-
ment. Day Four saw the first in a series of Different
Hair days. Darren started with a wet look, which gave
the permanent impression that he'd just been rescued
at sea. No-one commented. Day Five, Friday, brought
forth a curiously slicked-back kind of look. Nothing.
Darren continued to mull over the details of his failed
campaign as TBT paused for breath and then continued with renewed and unshared enthusiasm.
Darren had abstained from shaving over the weekend
so that by Monday, Day Six, Strategic Shaving could
come into glorious, or more likely, not so glorious,
being. For, somewhere along the line, Darren felt he
had been let down by the nature of his beard growth.
He had, as a consequence, a very real fear of being kid-
napped, washed up on a desert island or lost on a
remote expedition. This wasn't for safety reasons –
most days he didn't particularly care if he was alive or
not – nor because these were scenarios which were
especially likely to involve him. He was just about as
likely to die from excessive sexual intercourse as to be

abandoned on a deserted island for a significant period of time. No, the real reason for his fear was his substandard beard production. Any crisis that could potentially deprive Darren of a razor for longer than three days was a crisis to be avoided at all possible costs. What he dreaded most were the TV pictures you see when the three hostages are released after six months' captivity, or when the marooned sailors are interviewed about their ordeal, or the lost expedition is found again by the world's media. This is when the saved men walk out, blinking in the sunshine and the flashbulbs, long, thick, luxuriant, overgrown beards leading the way. Think of Terry Waite, think of Brian Keenan. Darren tried to imagine himself stepping out into the press conference, released after months of captivity, with a gingerish, patchy, wispy sort of beard, which looked as if it might have grown over a careless weekend, or been stolen from a passing old lady. He thought of W.G. Grace striding out to bat with a thin, translucent, straggly chin growth. Of course, Darren was no W.G. Grace, for a number of reasons. He was alive, for a start, and the sheer tedium of cricket frightened him. But a beard is a beard, and half a beard is nowhere. Moustache-wise, he was OK. He had no complaints in the moustache department. Should he ever consider a change of sexual orientation, he would be quids in. Chinwise was still OK, but only OK. It started fairly promising. The first day's growth was as straight and stubbly as any man might wish for. From here on in, however, it seemed to give up the ghost, evidently a little too self-satisfied with the first day's progress. It started to thin and change direction. It got a bit excitable. It headed out like a bunch of optimistic weeds and then quickly shrivelled in the midday sun. It became more and more ginger, as if he had a secret red topsoil hiding in his chin. So by

Day Six, Monday, which saw a spiky kind of hair styling, Darren had managed the merest suggestion of a straggly goatee beard and had elicited the first raised eyebrow of the campaign.

'Hey, Dazza, what the fuck d'you call that thing?' Gavin, one of the huddled research associates, asked.

Darren had experimented throughout his adult life with a series of grisly Darren-related half-words such as Daz, Darro, Da' and even, on occasion, Dazza, but with little success. There was, he was forced to concede, no easy alternative to his Christian name. Daz was bearable, Darro OK, depending on the circumstances, but it was downhill from there on in.

'You'll see,' he answered enigmatically.

'I can barely see fuck all now,' Gavin replied.

Day Seven was a rest day on the Strategic Shaving front, but was a blow-dried day on the hair front. Zero. Day Eight was the long-anticipated Hair Normal, Moustache Day. Darren had shaved his chin and neck and sideboards, mildly grazing three or four hairs as he did so, but left his more impressive top lip region to do its own thing. This time, there was a more eager curiosity.

'You want to get yourself down The Oboe with a 'tache like that,' Gavin suggested.

'Oh yeah, you'll be right popular down there,' Mike, a less than illustrious lab technician, agreed.

Of the three males including Darren who regularly shared break times at the Institute, Gavin Viner and Mike Stewart were widely regarded, at least by a two-thirds majority, to represent the wit of the coffee room. As the sizeable minority, Darren was unable to argue with the statistics of the situation, though had grave doubts about its authority. However, wit or no wit, Gavin and Mike were at least interested and had, momentarily, stopped discussing real ale.

'Turk's Head as well,' Gavin continued.

'Turk's Head? It isn't, is it?'

'Oh yes. Apparently, of course.'

'Aye, but mind, Daz, there's one thing you should never say in a crowded gay bar if someone's trying to squeeze past your table,' Mike said.

'Yeah?' There wasn't much in the way of question in Darren's reply, as he awaited the inevitable.

'Yeah. Never say, "Can I push that stool in for you?" as they squeeze past. Could get you in all sorts of trouble.'

Darren sighed and shook his head while a couple of the technicians and, he noted, a couple of staff who should have known better, chortled to themselves. Gavin and Mike soaked up the glory of what was, admittedly, not one of their worst efforts, and Mike even repeated his punchline for the benefit of one late-comer, and then again for someone who didn't get it, and then one more time for luck, stringing it out for a good couple of minutes or so. Gavin also enjoyed a deal of the attention, attempting a couple of follow-on gags on the back of the success, each one of which was in turn weaker and given less of a welcome. Gavin was of particular irritation to Darren, though Mike was hardly blameless in this department. Whereas Mike was a technician who had settled for being vaguely technical and very little else, Gavin was the worst sort of person to have working in a satellite department of a hospital. He was a failed medic, someone who had managed the science but had been unable to cope with the unwell. Taking the hospital's medical staff as a whole, this would have been by no means fatal to a medical career, but apparently things had become fucked up at some stage during his training, and Gavin now worked within spitting distance of the hospital which had precipitated the demise of his medical aspirations. This was not particularly uncommon: the Institute, as with other hospital-associated buildings, saw ex-medics washed up on its sandy shores with relative frequency, as if by working in association with or close to a hospital, they lived perpetually on the verge of being doctors.

Darren had left the coffee room, provoking a couple of wolf whistles as he did so. It hadn't really been the kind of attention he'd wanted his teaser campaign to attract, and he had ditched it there and then. TBT cleared his throat and looked over expectantly in Darren's direction, as if awaiting a reply to some extended monotone of nonsense or other. Darren remained silent and stared back into the sticky carpet, trying not to catch the eyes of his smiling colleagues. One irrefutable truth of the time he had spent within the Sheffield Institute of Medical Diagnostics was the general lack of respect he had managed to engender from the people he worked with. He had often pondered whether it was better to have respect from people who know you or from people who don't know you. Certainly, he had neither and both were out of the question. Outside work, his doctoral title occasionally made the bank less patronizing, but that was about it, and even then he felt a bit of a wanker for insisting on it. Inside work, most of the staff appreciated that he had minimal jurisdiction over anybody and acted accordingly, which made him feel inadequate too. All in all it seemed that he had merely gained two opposing conflicts of identity and precious little else out of having a doctoral title. Still, had Darren been forced to give it up, he realized he would now feel naked without it. He grunted at TBT and headed back to the lab. Although safe for the time being from TBT's clutches, eagerly anticipating his return was another of the department's acknowledged lunatics. Mormon Dawn, as she was unanimously known, had for some time, Darren suspected, been trying to inspire him towards a nervous breakdown. And her techniques so far had been ruthlessly efficient.

Bug Eyes

Darren entered his lab, sighed and sat down. From his bench he could only see one other person, and as this was Mormon Dawn, this was often one person too many. The trouble with Dawn was that she had Sayings. Her favourite Saying at the moment was, 'It can't be bad. It's gotta be good.' She would say this fifty times a day. Occasionally, she switched between Sayings, but 'It can't be . . .' had been the mantra now for about six weeks and seemed in no danger of going out of fashion. And every time she said it, Darren felt a hammer blow of inevitability crack against his skull.

Dawn looked over from her side of the laboratory and opened her mouth. She was a researcher with a Ph.D. like Darren, only slightly younger and less senior. Darren knew what was coming. She grinned at him, like she was burning with secret knowledge. 'Can't be bad,' she said. Darren awaited the inevitable. She drew it out. Maybe it wasn't coming. She was still grinning, dry pink gums and long ivory teeth staring out at him, bug-eyes magnified through her glasses. He got up from his stool and tried not to panic too soon. He was all right. He sat down again. She let him believe he was safe. Then she delivered. 'It's gotta be good,' she mouthed.

Introduction

One more time. One more time and I will kill you, Darren whispered to himself.

Dawn was up to her eyeballs in God. Darren was up to his eyeballs in boredom, defeat and guilt. And he had a grating, slowing, consuming, brain-squeezing hangover. It had to be good for her. She was a Born-again, a Mormon. She saw the light eighteen months ago and had been sunny ever since. Fair enough. But if she told him one more time, just once more, it was going to be very bad for her.

The next day, before Darren had even had a chance to open his lab book, Dawn looked over at him from her bench. 'Can't be bad,' she smiled. Darren got up and headed for the door. Five paces, four, three, two, one, the handle, turn it. Quick. He pulled the heavy white door. 'It's gotta be good.'

He stopped. 'What?'

'It can't be bad.' She was grinning again. 'It's gotta be good.'

'What has?' He turned to face her.

'What has what?' she asked.

Darren took a couple of paces forward. '*What* has got to be good, exactly?'

'Can't be bad. It's gotta be good.' She was grinning uncomprehendingly.

'And just what do you mean by that?'

She was faintly quizzical, around the eyes. Her crowded mouth continued to smile. 'It's gotta be . . .'

He took another step forward. He was nearly in her face. Up close he almost expected to see the wooden join of her ventriloquist mouth. 'No. It doesn't.' He was shouting. 'Nothing does. Nothing ever has to be. That's the point. Can't you fucking see? Can't you see anything?' Darren was about to erupt. He looked away. He was overreacting. She had stopped smiling and was regarding him with a curious sort of pity.

'You all right?' she asked.

I am calm, he said to himself. He closed his eyes. Calmer. Fitter. Healthier. He gripped his temples with the thumb and middle finger of his left hand, the palm obscuring his eyelids. 'Sorry. Yes, I'm fine. Sorry.'

'Sure?' she checked.

'Yeah. It's just . . . no, everything's OK. I didn't mean to . . .'

'No problem,' she said.

'Things sometimes . . .'

'Not to worry. It's all right. Everything is all right.' Darren opened his eyes. She was grinning at him again. 'Can't be bad,' she said. You can't do this to me, Darren pleaded under his breath. Please, you can't do this to me. 'It's gotta be . . .' He walked out of the lab, heading for the canteen before she could finish.

Swallow

The policeman asked my name and I told him. He wanted to see some ID and so I showed him my driving licence. Satisfied, he said, 'If you'd like to come along with me, sir. We won't take up much of your time.'

I followed his creaking shoes up one flight of stairs and down a short, cheerful corridor. The station was surprisingly plush, carpeted even, and not in the least how I had imagined it over the long long weeks since the letter had arrived. My mouth was bitter, more bitter even than I had expected. The policeman knocked on and opened a door in one practised movement, and ushered me inside, where he nodded in the direction of a plain office chair. I sat down and tried desperately not to swallow. This proved difficult. It was like being at the dentist. As soon as you are told you can't swallow, it becomes the one thing you have to do or else you will die. The sergeant left the room and closed the door. I tried tilting my head forward, but my salivary glands seemed to have got the message that I couldn't swallow, and pumped more and more of their thin fluid into my mouth, swilling the acidity over my tongue and around my cheeks in an act of watery defiance.

On the desk a couple of feet in front of me lay

several small clear plastic bags with self-sealing ends, two plastic beakers containing pink fluids of a possibly antiseptic origin, a few scattered sachets housing alcohol-soaked swabs, and a kidney-shaped metal dish of the sort that bullet fragments habitually ding into in films. Instead of shrapnel, the dish housed twenty or so syringes with matching needles, and a couple of what looked like cotton-wool-tipped ear buds. I shivered as I regarded the dry buds that would scrape the inside of my mouth and then glanced out through the window which dominated the small functional room. The sky was blue and people outside would be feeling variously glad to be alive. This wasn't at all how I had pictured things. It should be raining, at the very least, with distant peals of thunder and alarmingly close stroboscopic lightning. The window was partially shielded by a blue, vertical blind, which looked as if it might actually perform some sort of function, rather than simply hanging there tangled and useless like normal blinds. The door behind me opened smartly and a woman in incongruous civilian clothing breezed in. She was edging fifty and looked as though she would be considerably happier pottering around her garden instead of being incarcerated in the police station carrying out her daily work. The woman asked me my name, scanned down a clipboard list and then scribbled something with the biro which was harnessed to the metal clasp of the clipboard by a length of off-white string.

'Any ID?' she enquired.

I showed her my driving licence. She scribbled again and I took the opportunity to finally swallow. This wasn't good. I had practised and reckoned I could manage almost five minutes without swallowing. Hopefully this would be my last. Get on with it, I said to myself. Come on.

Introduction

'And you have a letter from your doctor?'

I took the letter out of my back pocket and unfolded it for her to read. After twenty or so seconds she hummed to herself and then said, 'We don't see many like you, you know. Still . . .' I tried to focus on the back of my throat, forcing it to remain closed. Eventually, she handed the letter back, put her clipboard down, sighed and picked up a cotton-wool bud.

Cloudy Skies

Professor Graham Barnes's office was tacked on to the
far end of Darren's laboratory like some sort of peep-
show booth. From this vantage point, he was able to
survey the lab's variously working (Dawn) and pretending to work (Darren) inhabitants. In lieu of
working, Darren increasingly sat with his back to his
boss's office, a Gilson Pipettman – the Rolls-Royce of
pipettes – in his hand, transferring tap water back and
forth between two small plastic Eppendorf tubes. This
wasn't just normal skiving behaviour. There was a
reason for it. Darren had had an idea and didn't want
work getting in the way. Something had occurred to
him, something big. As he went through the motions of
endeavour, he would think, scheme, scribble and
dream as much of the day as he could. It wasn't, after
all, as if he was missing out on anything. There were
few distractions in the lab, and this was unlikely to
change. People rarely came or went. Staff got three-,
four- or, if especially unlucky, five-year contracts, and
generally stayed to see out their tour of duty. So there
wasn't about to be a mass exodus of dull people and a
mass influx of interesting ones. And this was the
reason he had initiated the spectacularly unsuccessful
Mwimi campaign.

As Darren continued to pipette water, he heard the shuffling noise behind him which usually pre-empted Graham's arrival, and so made a concerted effort to pipette more water and generally look occupied. Instead of his habitual dive for cover, Graham came over to Darren's bench.

'Darren, not sure, can't quite remember, did I tell you?'

Darren looked blankly at Graham and said, 'Tell me what?'

'Er, anyway, it's been sorted out for a few weeks now, maybe should have given you a bit more notice . . .'

Darren leaned forward slightly to protect the nature of his pretend work while Graham continued to evade the point. After a few more seconds, Darren tried to nudge him in the right direction. 'Hmm?' he said, raising his eyebrows.

'Yes. So tomorrow, in the morning, first thing I suppose, we should have a new member of staff starting here, with you and, and . . .' Graham nodded over towards Dawn's bench.

'Dawn,' Darren prompted.

'Yes, Mormon Dawn, well, tomorrow . . .'

'Right.'

This was news. Someone new in the lab. And at the bench opposite. He would now be able to see two people. A lot hinged on this. Dawn was a disaster. Another disaster and he would be surrounded. There was a fifty-fifty chance it would be a woman, a one in fifty chance that it would be an attractive woman, given the usual state of affairs, or lack of them, in science, probably a one in three chance that she would be single, and a one in, he gave himself a generous benefit of the doubt, say two chance she would fancy him . . . There was no arguing with the statistics of the situation – things were looking up.

Darren watched Graham shuffle over to his office and frowned. Working for Graham was like continually banging your head against a vague and unfocused wall. It still hurt, but you could never be quite sure of the actual moment of contact or see the part of the wall that you hit. It was a nightmare. Graham dithered and dallied, chopped and changed, digressed and delayed, umm-ed and ahh-ed, tutted and tsk-ed, yawned and stretched, and generally irritated and annoyed and vexed and irked and aggravated Darren so thoroughly that he found he could no longer even look at his boss without wanting to hit him. But the real irritation from Darren's point of view was that occasionally, through the all-enveloping haze of his vagueness, Graham was incredibly and frustratingly incisive. Just when you'd written him off as a has-been who had been put out to pasture on the professorial grass, promoted out of harm's way, he'd pounce and show you up for the intellectual inferior that you knew you were. For in academia, one stormy moment of brilliance under a long year of cloudy skies will take you further than a year of honest endeavour in the tepid sunshine. There was no doubt that as a person Graham was at the very least a gentleman, a man from a bygone era of doffed hats, opened doors and rain-coated puddles. He was fair and just and honest. In short, he was intolerable. For what your boss is like on a personal level is largely irrelevant to a working relationship. Work means the loss of personal feelings. You can't ever be true friends with someone you work for, or who works for you. *With you*, admittedly, may come close, but workmates are just that. Take away the work and you're not necessarily left with a mate. And the nicer your boss is, the more likely it is that you will grow to despise him. People clearly liked working for

Introduction

Adolf Hitler, despite his brutality and psychosis. Jesus Christ, on the other hand, was probably dreadful. How many days into working for Jesus would it be before His preaching, His omnipresence and His continual correctness would start getting on your tits? And this, for Darren, was one of the problems with working for Graham. Everyone who didn't work with him was taken with his demeanour of quiet English fair play. Everyone who did was frustrated nearly to the point of murder by him, and was spectacularly unable to convince outsiders that this English gentleman was in fact utterly useless and deserved, at the very least, to be shot.

Murder aside, Darren began to hope that Graham might just die of his own accord. While Graham made vague statements, retracted them, repeated them again and then contradicted himself for good measure, Darren peered into the whites of his eyes, searching for signs of glaucoma, listened to his breathing for symptoms of hyperventilation or bronchitis, watched his brow for sudden cold sweats of imminent heart attack and monitored his hands for the excessive shakiness of a wealth of early-onset and preferably fatal syndromes. In short then, homicide was out, but a sudden myocardial infarction would be most welcome. But, much to his dismay, Graham continued in rude health, Darren felt powerless, and his job and then his life became enveloped in the frustrating cloud of academic woolliness that surrounded his boss. This was of particular concern to Darren, as even the word academic, he was more than aware, had become a synonym for pointless. It was a bastardization, but it was there all the same, and as is usual for bastardizations, it seemed to ring truer than the original meaning. 'It's academic' should mean 'it's a point for conjecture' or 'it's hypothetical' or 'it's theoretical', but instead has come to mean 'it doesn't matter', 'it's irrelevant' or 'who cares?' And Darren, employed by an academic to work in an academy in the field of academic research was, therefore, mainly an irrelevance.

But he had to be relevant, somehow, and the world had to be pertinent. It just had, otherwise what was the point of anything? And so the idea had come to him a few weeks earlier, and he had started to try and make sense of the world, to let logic decide, once and for all. Life is an equation and equations are logical, so life must be logical. At least he hoped so. His days and nights therefore were devoted to this one aim – to explaining life in terms of logic. Darren's theory began to grow and multiply and divide and chop and change and generally go around in ever-widening and elusive circles, and as he drove home from the Institute early one afternoon, he surmised that there were two main premises to his hypothesis. First, everything in the world can be described in terms of an equation. As Darren drove his car, its inertia, the pressure in its cylinders, the ability of its radio to pick up far-flung stations, the inability of the cooling fan to remove any of the heat from the interior, the excitation of electrons buzzing around inside the green light he was approaching, the rate at which his neurones fired as a car from the right thought about jumping a red in the adjacent direction, the change in velocity of his car, the heat generated by his rapidly applied brakes, the energy needed to wind down his window, the force of contraction exerted by his lungs to scream 'Wanker!', the distance Darren's voice carried in the still, humid, closing air, the energy needed for the other driver to come to a complete stop and then unfold himself from his car, the friction generated between the soles of his large shoes against the melting road as he strode over towards Darren, the movement of air from

high pressure to low as the man's diaphragm con-
tracted, the frequency of the vibrations on his vocal
cords as he screamed 'Fuck you! Just fuck you!', the
slow rate of evaporation of the sweat from his forehead
into the defeating air, the velocity with which his fist
passed through Darren's open window, the change in
momentum of his head as it rocked sideways, the force
with which Darren's brain smashed around inside his
skull . . . Everything can be explained in terms of an
equation. So, as Darren sat in his car nursing a throbbing temple and cursing his luck with some fairly
unscientific language, the second premise came to him
in the guise of one of the all-time great clichés – it's all
relative. And it is. But more than that, everything is
relative because everything is related. Try to isolate
one thing from the whole mêlée of everything else it is
entangled in and you can't do it. Everything has some
relation to everything else. Everything. Mr Road Rage,
for instance, had just been to pick his daughter up from
school, only to find that his wife had done the honours
instead, and he was now running late to catch the bank
before three thirty, three fucking thirty, to pay in a
cheque that he had been waiting weeks for, a cheque
that would keep them in the black until pay day, but
only if he paid it in today, a cheque he had finally
received from his late aunt's solicitors representing his
meagre share of her will, an aunt who succumbed
eventually to the secondary effects of late-onset diabetes, one of the diseases Darren was researching and
which was generally occupying his mind as a green
Mondeo jumped a red light and was almost hit side-on
by a distracted scientist in a lacklustre Polo. But it
wasn't just diabetes that brought them, physically,
together. It was life. For life is little more than just one
big coincidence. And often a coincidence that you
could happily live without.

* * *

At home, Darren fingered the bubble wrap which surrounded the small brown glass vial containing a tiny amount of 7-chloro-1-methyl-5-phenyl-3H-1, 4-benzodiazepin-2[1H]-one. He squeezed the package and felt three or four of the bubbles succumb in rapid succession against the surface of the glass. He was shaking slightly and his temple was throbbing. Street name diazepam. In the absence of easily available chemical literature on the nature of the drug, Darren had reread a couple of Irvine Welsh stories. Jellies. Certainly not a stimulant, but Darren felt the need, the need to recede. He was frantic, and knew it. He had to lie back into himself, as if he was some sort of sofa, to relax, change down, let the ideas float on heavy eyelids, to slow almost to a stop, to let empty, idle thoughts permeate into the chaos of his mind and settle the indigestion of his brain like kaolin and morphine.

Living Solutions

Lie Number One. Laboratories are fresh, white, gleaming, bright spaces populated by studious beings in starched white coats and thick-framed glasses. Lie Number Two. Laboratories are humming, flashing, beeping, crashing arenas of endeavour stuffed with gadgets and machines and equipment and appliances and contraptions which spew forth into the bleached stillness a million unearthly noises. Lie Number Three. Laboratories contain any one of the following: huge fractionating distillers which hiss, boil and condense; bulbous flasks bubbling over with heavy vapours; gigantic V-shaped electrodes which point at the ceiling and encourage occasional arcs of lightning to crackle skywards between them; domed Van der Graaf generators with static electricity sparks standing out from their polished surfaces like punk hair; expansive banks of flashing lights and exposed circuitry with Catherine-wheel tape reels; ornate three-dimensional models of impossibly interconnected atoms forming delicate skeletons of molecules . . .

One of the most depressing things about working in a genetics lab is witnessing the reaction of genuine dismay which occurs when the uninitiated visit a laboratory for the first time.

'Oh. So this is what a genetics lab looks like then. I thought . . .' It usually tails off about there. 'I thought . . .' or 'But on television . . .' or, worst of all, 'I *hoped* . . .'

And it *is* a let-down. People want to believe that genetics is like some sort of science-fiction thing. They want to believe that it is some impossibly complex and breathtakingly exact form of magic. And maybe it is impossibly complex and breathtakingly exact, but it is still a disappointment when you enter a lab for the first time and see nothing more technical than row upon row of colourless solutions, sterilized racks of pipette tips, Petri dishes, opaque tubes, assorted pieces of paper, less than spotless benches, radios, scattered personal effects, cluttered desks, a couple of small tanks housing thin blocks of agarose and, if you're very lucky, maybe a small bench-top centrifuge or two. For genetics is accomplished more by solutions than by machines. Solutions are used to break cells open and precipitate their proteins, snatch their DNA, to clean it, dissolve it, assess it, cut it up into convenient fragments, to put it into other cells, to find out where genes are turned on and off, to amplify genetic material, to determine the code of stretches of DNA and so on. Machines help and are, at times, indispensable, but it's solutions and liquids that do the dirty work. And even with the best will in the world there's nothing particularly awe-inspiring about gazing upon row after row of bottles full of watery solutions.

To liven this situation somewhat, Darren decided one day to invent some new solutions for his shelves. He was struck by the inorganic nature of it all. Cold, clinical chemicals dominated his work space, solutions like sodium acetate, lithium chloride and tris borate, abbreviated semi-legitimately to NaAc, LiCl and TB, whose job it was to variously disrupt and damage living cells. It was a cellular war, inorganic invader against organic sitting target. Darren wanted to even the numbers up a bit. He filled six bottles with sterile water. Into each he put a small amount of a different bodily fluid, and christened the new solution accordingly. Bottle One, he called P15(s), '(s)' generally denoting sterility within laboratories. Bottle Two was BLO_2D. Three was 5PiT. Four was cUM. Five was (s)WeAt. And Six, which had an interesting hue when held up to the light, and a faint hint of froth on top, was Ph1(LeGm).

Several weeks into Darren's quest to find and answer one last great question of science in the twentieth century, he realized that however much of the clutter he deleted from his life, he was going to need some outside assistance to increase his capacity for learning. Alone, there was no way that Darren would be able to work enough hours or have enough insight without some sort of intervention. Flicking idly through a chemical catalogue one afternoon, he came across a section towards the back which caught his eye. Darren had seen it before, but not as he saw it now. Nearly everything can be purchased, semi-legitimately and with the correct licence, from a chemical company called Delta, which runs a controlled substance section in its catalogue so that researchers can assess the biological effects of drugs in animal models, and forensic departments can develop ways of enhanced narcotic detection. He opened the Delta catalogue and thumbed through its pages. They were all there, all the big players, albeit under partial pseudonyms, like tropococaine, pentobarbital and cannabiol, cheaper from the shelf than the street, and doubtless purer. He needed to find out which drugs would keep him awake and which might excite his imagination. Darren needed stimulants, sleep-evaporating uppers, drugs which would see him through wasted hours he might otherwise spend sleeping. While he was scanning the pages for likely candidates, it occurred to him that the worst, most harmful, most addictive drug of all is adrenalin. It is also the least enjoyable, but, ultimately, or transiently, all drug roads lead to or pass through adrenalin. Even waiting for a spliff to be passed can mildly race your pulse. Darren decided he would order some adrenalin as well, while he was at it, to put his theory to the test. Ten millilitres seemed like a sufficient quantity.

A week or so later, Darren got a call from the Neurogenetics department concerning some packages for a Dr Jeffries which had erroneously turned up in their section. He went along to pick them up on Dr Jeffries' behalf. Not, of course, that Dr Jeffries knew anything about it. After all, if you're going to order something illegally, it's always best to do it under someone else's name, and even better to use the name of someone who has recently left the department, and even better still someone now working in Brisbane, and even better than that, he congratulated himself as he headed towards Neurogenetics, to have them delivered to a department where your face wasn't known.

Neuro, as it was universally referred to, was another small department attached by invisible strings to the hospital. It was a pipette's throw from the Institute and housed twenty or so clinical and non-clinical staff of the preoccupied sort that you invariably saw wandering the corridors of research laboratories the world over. Darren knocked on the sturdy door of the department's delivery office, where packages housing multifarious tissues and consumables were dumped each morning by sweaty, affable delivery men. The door opened swiftly and Darren was confronted by a woman who, outside science, would be considered to be of fairly reasonable desirability. Within science, a woman like this was a no-holds-barred-ten-out-of-ten-Page-Three-stunner of the highest order and Darren, for a moment, was taken aback that she had obviously managed to slip through the rigorous screening procedure which sought to keep attractive females out of science. She asked him what he wanted. He was here to collect some packages on behalf of Dr Jeffries, he told her. She said there were quite a few. Darren tried to think of something to say. Nothing was forthcoming. He decided to simply open his mouth and let his brain do the talking, and see where he ended up.

Someone New

First Track of the Day: 'Blue Monday' *by New Order*

I saw someone I haven't seen before, today. I don't know whether he's new. It's so hard to tell – we're all so split up – but something about him was familiar. Maybe I've passed him in a corridor. I don't know. But his eyes shone like he was looking into the sun. Worried maybe that I shouldn't have worn quite so much blue today.

He came to collect an order, a new one, said it must have been delivered to the wrong department. Said he's Medical Genetics. This is Neurogenetics, I said. Looked nervous, sort of. I liked that. People here are so bloody arrogant. Waltz in and demand their orders. Are you sure you haven't seen it? they say. Should be here by now. You might have made a mistake. Won't you look again. But no, he was sheepish, apologetic almost. I liked that.

Said he might have a few more orders to collect from here. Swore a few times then said sorry. Something about giving out the wrong delivery address for a batch of reagents. I said that's fine, no problem. I'll look after you, Dr Jeffries. I'm not Dr Jeffries, he said. Who are you, then? I asked. Darren, he said. I'm Karen. Great, he replied. Well at least we rhyme, I said. He looked into my eyes when I said that. I blushed, then checked a few delivery notes, hoped he'd go. Just stood there looking at me. I didn't know what to say after that.

He's different. You could tell, just with a few short words. He is burning, on fire. I like that. It's there in his eyes. Green, I think, and almost yellow where they pale in the shadows of his pupils. Agitation in his face and mutiny in his eyes. Trouble. Darkish hair, maybe gelled or waxed a little. He is not tall, but also not stocky. This is important. I don't like stocky men. It's so primeval. It's just there, muscles and bulk, no mystery, no fine tapering bones, no angles. He's maybe a bit too skinny though. Should eat more, but not too much more.

When he left I checked through the order sheet. I will be seeing him again, several times. Has a lot of reagents on order. Some sound quite exotic. N-acetylmescaline. Amobarbital. L-amphetamine. Bromazepam. Methylamphetamin. And about eight others. All with Home Office approval. Dr Jeffries must have given them all the wrong address.

I've decided that I should ask him out. Happens every day in films. No stigma to single women asking men out any more. This is the Nineties. It's easy. Just look them in the eye and say how about a drink some-time? Yes, I will ask him out. Didn't see a wedding ring, so the chances aren't too dire. Late twenties early thirties and not married. A bit scruffy, looked like he sorts his own clothes out. May even be available. Late twenties early thirties and single. Might be something wrong with him. Too old to be respectably single, surely. Could be a bad bet. Dubious track record maybe. OK, I won't ask him out. A bit dodgy. Probably can't handle commitment or something. Did look a little on the wild side. Still single at his age. I mean, OK, I'm twenty-eight, but I've just had bad luck. And it's impossible to meet anyone stuck in bloody Neuro all day. No, think I'll avoid him when he comes again.

Initiation

'So, Darren, this is Simon . . .' Professor Graham Barnes thought he'd gone as far as he needed with the sentence, and refused, as was the norm, to go any further.

The professor retreated into his office and closed the door. Darren and Simon stood and half looked at each other. Simon introduced himself and confessed that he wasn't exactly sure what he should be doing. This was a good sign. People who know what they should be doing before they even start doing it are people to watch out for. Simon surveyed the lab, and as he peered at its less than gleaming surfaces, Darren took the chance to have a good long look at him. Aware of the scrutiny, Simon turned to face him, and Darren returned the favour by looking away and affording him the same opportunity. A short lull ensued while Darren struggled over what he should say in terms of introductory nonsense. It was just a matter of thinking of something relevant, something incisive about the day-to-day operations of the lab, something to put Simon at ease, something to make him feel he was joining an extended family of contentment in the workplace, one man one pipette, all problems shared, all resources pooled for the common interest of science and furtherment . . . Simon cleared his throat, opened his mouth and breathed in, as if readying himself to speak, but then just sighed the breath out. Darren decided to ditch the science and get straight down to the important stuff. He wanted to know, as soon as he could wangle it out of him, whether Simon was going to save his life. After all, a lot depended on him being halfway human. The laboratory was a waste ground of conversation and wit, and, lunatics aside, the department a vacuum of personality. One more oddball and he was surrounded. A real, proper, normal sort of person that you only find outside science and maybe he could live a bit at work again. Darren decided to take Simon away from the lab and give him a light grilling. But first, as was traditional for new members of staff within the Institute, the Initiation Ceremony.

'Drink?' Darren asked as they stood in the small kitchen which adjoined the low-ceilinged coffee room on the first floor.

'Tea, please,' Simon replied. Not a good choice. Darren smiled to himself and checked his watch while the kettle boiled. He had a quick glance up and down the corridor which served the communal area, and was delighted to see a small, harassed-looking figure approaching from the far end. The ceremony was about to begin.

Sitting down with their drinks Simon took a sip from his mug and screwed his eyes up. 'It's the water,' Darren explained. 'Tastes of metal. Christ knows what's in it, but it can't be very good for you. Still, does the trick . . .' Darren had, over the course of his employment, assessed a range of beverages for their ability to overpower the contamination of the Institute's water. Normal tea, as Simon's face had testified, tasted of iron filings. Earl Grey tasted of iron filings and talcum powder. Hot chocolate tasted like you'd accidentally eaten some foil with your Dairy Milk, and Ovaltine like you'd left the spoon in the cup. Nasty supermarket coffee, however, tasted like nasty supermarket coffee, which was at least a step in the right direction.

Simon risked another sip and winced again. As he did so, Darren watched the diminutive figure shuffle into the room and sit down muttering to himself. This was the third of the department's acknowledged nutters. In contrast to the irrelevancies of Tea Break Terminator and Mormon Dawn, however, Winning System, as he was universally known, was quite clearly very relevant. Winning System qualified under the Institute's strict guidelines as a nutter because no-one could face talking to him and because, through this, he had developed a system whereby he did no work at all. While everybody admired his scheme, they were still left with the impression that the one person who remained unconvinced by it was Winning System himself. This tended to suggest that scheme was too strong a word, and in fact the bizarre workings of Winning System were merely a manifestation of his dementia. Darren introduced Simon to Winning System and allowed the initiation to start.

'Simon is working in our lab,' Darren said to Winning System, 'and might need a hand with some paperwork. Do you think you might be able to spend some time sorting a few things out for him?' Winning System drew breath and Darren quickly stood up. 'You two have a chat about what needs to be done, and I'll catch up with you later,' he added, leaving the room and retreating to the adjoining kitchen area where he would be well within earshot.

This, then, was Winning System's winning system. Winning System was a compulsive talker, and probably breathed through his ears. The nature of his conversation was severely limited though, serving only to inform anybody who would listen, in incredibly painstaking and time-consuming detail, the exact reasons why he was too busy to perform the given task that they desired of him. Winning System therefore did nothing, and if anybody was ever brave enough to suggest some work that he might carry out, he would inform the poor sod over the course of maybe an hour just why he was too busy to be able to help them. Obviously it never occurred to Winning System that if he stopped explaining how busy he was he might actually be able to do something, but then again, why should it? He had, by definition, hit upon a winning system and there could be little benefit in changing it now. Darren listened with baited breath.

'It's like I said to Tony,' Winning System began, his momentum quickly building, 'I've no objection doing that for you. None at all. I'll do it, I said, gladly. Only too happy to. But if I get that done for you, who's going to do my job? I said. I mean, don't get me wrong, I'd work for free if I could afford it, as long as someone sorted me out for the basics, you know, and some holiday now and then, and board and lodgings and pension, and as long as someone else was willing to cover my end of things, I told him, and he said . . .'

The initiation would be a good test of Simon's metal – an encounter with Winning System should flush the dull out of anyone who had any dull worth flushing out. Darren peered through a crack between the kitchen door and its frame and watched Simon's nodding becoming less and less regular, his yeses less enthusiastic and his nos less sympathetic as Winning System continued to drone on, until yes and no deteriorated into an uninterested 'Mmm.'

'. . . that's not a lot of good to me, but that's not my problem I told him, I'm up to here with jobs that need doing the day before yesterday, you know, and it's no good telling me now that those things are overdue when they weren't even part of my itinerary, which, it just so happens, is full today and just about every day till Christmas when I'll finally be able to . . .'

Simon's 'Mmms' gave up the ghost altogether, as he stared at Winning System, seemingly transfixed by the enormous volume of utter guff that streamed out of his mouth. One pisser about Winning System, Darren reflected as he continued to enjoy Simon's initiation into the prevailing insanity of the department, was that a hierarchy of delegation always surrounded him wherever he went. A professor would need something doing and Winning System was the man for the job. There was no way the professor was going to waste his valuable time listening to why Winning System couldn't do it. Delegation level one would therefore arise as the professor passed the instruction down to one of his research staff, who would pass it on to a lower member to create delegation level two, and so on until it inevitably reached some poor bugger who would look down and see nothing below him but his feet, and who would have to spend the afternoon lumbered with Winning System or simply carry out the required task himself to avoid the misery of the great man's company. Darren began to think about rescuing Simon. The ceremony was getting a little out of hand. Winning System didn't seem to have drawn breath for a good ten minutes or so.

'. . . and so it's no use you asking me to help you out with whatever paperwork Dr White thinks you need without first seeing my boss, and telling him that you think I should stop doing what I'm doing, drop all the projects I'm taking care of, throw all my other stuff in the bin, tell Laura from the second floor that I can't help her, and Steve . . .'

'Stop!' Simon yelled, almost desperately. 'Look, are you going to help me or not? Yes or no?'

'It's not that simple, really, because if . . .'

'Yes or no?'

'As I say . . .'

'Yes or no?' Simon was shouting, in command suddenly, his tone rising.

Winning System paused. This in itself was a rarity, but what came next, Darren conceded, was somewhat of a miracle. He cleared his throat, sniffed and eventually, in an unexpectedly meek tone of voice, mumbled, 'I'll see what I can do.'

'Right,' Simon answered, standing up. 'I'll come and find you later when I know what I need sorting.'

Darren finished the last of his coffee and caught up with Simon in the corridor. Simon swore at him and Darren laughed. Simon had passed the initiation test with flying colours. Things were looking up.

Telephone Banking

Darren studied Simon as they chatted in the coffee room the following afternoon. He had enviably hairy forearms which lent his wrists a false impression of breadth. This was the first thing he had noticed about Simon – rolled-up sleeves, patterns of arm hair like iron filings in a magnetic current, a watch lying like a tent in a field of wheat. They were the sort of forearms that might have made Simon a good dentist or surgeon. Away from the wrist area, he was of reasonable height, unreasonable even, if you were, as Darren was, shorter than him. Simon's posture was fair to middling, particularly in the middle, where there was a fairly noticeable absence of anything resembling spare poundage. In common with many men over-endowed in the follicular department, the hair on his head was beating an honourable retreat back to base. There was, in its slash-and-burn absence, the faintest suggestion of a comb-over, where several strands of lighter and more flyaway hair sought to give the false impression of the arrival of reinforce-ments. Over the course of his first two days at the Institute, Simon had occasionally worn glasses, although the nature of the occasion was highly vari-able, and gave Darren no clue to whether he was near- or far-sighted. All in all, Simon looked solid, dependable and not particularly flash, much like the Volvo he had parked in the Institute's car park. Indeed, just as scientists may be accused of growing to resemble the rats, mice or rabbits they work with, they may also, in common with most people, come to mimic the cars they drive. Quite what this said about Darren, who drove an ageing one-litre Polo with an inadequate radiator, other than he didn't have enough money to buy a new Polo with an adequate radiator, was open to question.

'Did you see that thing on the news last night,' Simon continued, 'where they said that Nissan are investing two hundred million in a car plant on Tyneside?'

Darren shook his head. He hadn't watched TV for three or four weeks so this was news to him. Not particularly interesting news, but news all the same. 'A lot of money.'

'Yes, but how many jobs do you think that's going to guarantee?'

Darren shrugged. 'Ten thousand?'

'Two hundred,' Simon announced.

'So what're you saying?'

'That's a million pounds per worker. A million *each*. I mean, how skilled can these workers be for Christ's sake?'

'Yeah,' Darren said, the tone of his voice suggesting half a laugh as the word travelled through his throat. 'I mean, we earn, what . . .' He thought of his own salary and then subtracted two or three thousand in case it was much more than Simon's. 'Twenty or so, and we're supposed to be highly trained. Christ knows what you've got to be able to do if your job's worth a million a year to a company.'

'Fucking rocket science . . .'

'You ever driven a Nissan?'

'No.'

'Socket science would be pushing it.'

'I'd be careful – I've seen your car – it's not exactly going to win any awards itself.'

'Cheeky cunt,' Darren grinned. For a moment, his troubles were forgotten and his brain returned to thinking like normal brains think. Gavin entered the coffee room and sat down next to Simon. Darren performed the introductions. 'Gavin, this is Simon, just started in our lab.' They shook hands. 'Gavin is in Diagnostics, up on the second floor.' Simon nodded and then looked down at the floor. A short silence ensued now that the cosy chat had been interrupted by the advent of a new arrival.

After a few seconds, Simon said, 'There was something else as well, on the news, about accents and banking.'

'What do you mean?' Gavin asked.

'You know everything's heading towards telephone banking?'

'Mmm.'

Darren sat and watched, interested to see how Gavin and Simon would get on.

'All the companies are relocating to Tyneside.'

'The place where jobs cost a million each?'

'Yeah.'

'And?'

'Well, the thing is that it's all to do with accents. Banking centres are relocating to Newcastle and Sunderland because the Geordie accent is acceptable to most people.'

'So?' Gavin asked.

'I suppose the point is that if you're discussing your financial status with someone you've never met, you need to be able to trust them. But you can't see them.

They're just a voice on the end of the phone. It could be anyone. So you have to decide whether they *sound* trustworthy. And Geordies, they've decided, sound trustworthy. The only regional accent that does, they reckon.'

'Hang on, hang on,' Gavin said. Darren had been waiting for this. It was difficult at the best of times getting a point across without Gavin attempting to ruin it, but it was going to be especially troublesome for a new member of staff. 'I knew a Geordie once, and he was a right wanker.'

Simon glanced at Darren. 'A limited sample size though . . .'

'And what do you mean regional accents aren't trustworthy?'

'I didn't—'

'Are you saying that anyone without a BBC voice isn't fit to work in a bank?'

'Hang on, Gav,' Darren interjected, 'you're saying you'd rather be told the bank was pissing itself about the state of your finances by someone who sounds like they used to be in the Wurzles?'

'No, it's just he—'

'Makes a lot of sense to me. I mean, OK, you're talking to a cockney – they'd sound like they were ripping you off, somehow. The Irish would be pissing it up against a wall. East Anglians would be feeding your money to their cows. The Welsh would be setting light to it, Yorkshire folk hoarding it, Scousers spending it and Brummies boring it.' Having run out of regional stereotypes, he added, 'And so on.'

Simon nodded. He looked like he couldn't think of any gags either, so remained silent, which allowed Gavin to start up again.

'So I wouldn't be fit to look after your savings because of my Scouse accent?'

'You haven't got a Scouse accent, Gavin.'

'That's not the point. Anyway, is it any wonder I haven't with attitudes like your friend's here?' Gavin said, nodding at Simon. 'I mean, you try growing up on the Wirral and then speaking with authority about complex genetic syndromes.'

'No thanks,' Darren said, standing up. 'Come on, Si, I'll show you the autoclave room.' Simon followed him out of the coffee room. When they were safely out of earshot, Darren said, 'Failed medic' and mimed the wanker sign.

A Fitting Man

Hunters Bar on a November evening, and I'm heading to a garage for some petrol that I don't need and some fresh air that I do. Not that there is anything particularly breezy about the air which has been sucked into my car, passed over the engine and blown out across a heating filament in the direction of my face, but another minute in the numbing, stultifying, soporific heat of my house and I would have had to cut myself with my scalpel just to stay sane. Stoned as I am, something catches my attention. A man fitting on the pavement, limbs flailing, nearly break-dancing. It is cold. Two or three people are standing around him, their breath decorated momentarily by passing headlights – a short man who seems to be kicking him, or trying to sort his snaking legs out by stamping on them, a taller man in a leather jacket, who is just staring down, watching him like it's some sort of floor show and a passer-by, who is shaking his head and thinking about passing by after all. And me, in my car, slowing to second, rubbernecking, hoping that as it's all playing out in front of a pub it's just a fight and the blue man isn't fitting at all, but knowing that he is, recognizing the signs from my aborted medical training, ticking them off one by one, remembering the mnemonic – All

Girls Love It Up The Gary – but little of its substance, only managing Airway, Infarction and Tachicardia, wondering what the fuck the Gs stood for, and the L come to think of it, and all the time sensing my own paralysis, my own defeat, my own failure, my own panic, looking in the rear-view mirror not to see whether the cars behind are slowing but to look into my eyes, my own fit surely just seconds away, the steering wheel slipping through my clammy fingers, the oncoming headlights interrogating, 'Prognosis? Prognosis? Come *on*, we're not here for our health, you know. Anybody else? Anybody care to tell this chap the obvious? Mr James? MODY, yes, good. And would you care to tell him what that stands for, as I have a feeling he won't know. Yes, Maturity-Onset Diabetes of the Young. Good. And as for you, I shall see you in my office after the rounds.' The cunt. Hounded by the cunt, hounded into oblivion. Separate the weak or the different from the flock, that was medical training. The short-arsed, small-man-syndromed cunt. That's SASMS to you. Third. He is still fitting, but in the rear-view mirror now. Fourth. I am shaking slightly. He is almost out of sight. I try to calm down. A police car pulls out across me. I stop sharply to let it out. The copper waves. He thanks me for letting him go and do what I should have done in the first place. *He* is not paralysed with fear. This is average for him. *He* is calm enough to wave. I am gripping the wheel too tightly to wave back. I get a sudden burst of paranoia that he has recognized me, and has suddenly put two and two together. Those tests, of course. There was something there, something not quite right, so we looked at them again. And there he is, after all this time, still here in Sheffield, slowing down to let me out. I accelerate, along with my dope fear. Doubtless, he is coming back for me. The policeman will let the fitting man die, the man whose two chances of survival were me and the copper, before I passed him by and the copper chased after me. I pull into a bus lay-by and rest my forehead on the steering wheel. If he wants me he can come and take me. It's just not worth it any more. I have an over-whelming urge to give myself up, like lying in bed late for work and just closing your eyes and letting the warmth of the bed seduce you back to sleep. I turn my head and look back through the rear window; there are no blue flashing lights. I plead with my body for some calm and try to take slower, deeper inhalations, but this just makes me short of breath. I grip my thumbs inside my fists and attempt to squeeze myself calm. Suddenly the car is full of light. There is a horn. It is all over. I can see nothing in my mirror but light. Another horn. I am paralysed and feel sure I am about to have a fit. I feel an unexpected surge of adrenalin and manage to force the notchy gearbox into first, slam the handbrake down and spin the wheels out of the bus stop. I try not to check my mirrors but can't help myself. Never look back when you're being chased. This is the first rule. And I should know. I look back. It's a bus, a huge double-decker bus parked up my arse. I look down at the gearstick, unsure of whether I've changed gear at all and realize that I'm doing about thirty-five in first. Relax. It was a bus. No-one is after you. Relax. Clutch, straight into fourth from first. Relax. No more paranoia, I say, mouthing the words to myself in the mirror, staring into my bloodshot eyes. No more paranoia. I get a sudden urge to find out what happened to the fitting man, so I swing the car around and head back. There are more people, now that the police have arrived. The copper is holding the man's arm and speaking into his radio. I speed up and pass by, and don't look back in my mirrors until I know I'm too far away to see anything.

Materials and Methods

Christmas Countdown

The second batch of chemicals arrived with similar ease. As before, doses were the crucial thing. Certainly, the *British National Formulary* Darren had acquired could help a bit, particularly with prescription drugs, but other than that, he was in the dark. It came down to the old animal experiments argument. Reading from the catalogue, the Home Office data sheet suggested that Pentobarbital had an LD 50 of 25 mg per kg of rat body weight, which meant that, on average, 50 per cent of a population of rats weighing 200 g would be killed by ingesting 5 mg of Pentobarbital. By implication, therefore, Darren's 68 kg body would only survive a dose of 1.65 g of pentobarbital on every other occasion he chose to take it. These were not great odds. Darren decided to make it his policy, therefore, to take no more than 5 per cent of the rat LD 50 dose of any drug at one time. This did however beg the question of whether what is benign for rats is also benign for men. A chemical that rats could eat all day, force-fed by the defeating fingers of an animal technician, could be highly cytotoxic were the rats to ram it down the throat of the technician. And vice versa.

On the plus side, Darren was pleased to note that he was getting better at the forgery required to receive his illegally ordered drugs. He signed the authorization with a flourish, bold keystrokes with a generous bottom left to top right slant, and came away with the distinct impression that Neuro Girl was impressed. He felt like some sort of forgery expert faking the president's signature. It was, of course, vital that Neuro Girl didn't find out his full name. But a couple more deliveries should just about do it. And the beauty of the scam was that the Home Office would be busy writing to Dr Rob Jeffries, asking him to explain his recent foray into the purchase of controlled substances, envelopes marked Confidential, so no-one would open them, and as no-one knew his forwarding address, Dr Jeffries, recently of Australia, would be none the wiser.

It would be a pity to never see her again though. There had been what Darren could only describe as an adolescent surge when he had seen her for the first time, somewhere below his stomach and above his genitalia, an almost uncomfortable rush of anticipation. He had tried not to get distracted, but inevitably found himself thinking more about her than the service she was providing. Darren wondered whether he might even consider a calamitous attempt to ask her out. He was no expert, but it was within the bounds of possibility that Neuro Girl found him attractive. Probably married or something though, he sighed. This was the unfortunate, or maybe, considering the general standard of the female scientists he encountered on a daily basis, fortunate, state of affairs in science. Single attractive girls just seemed to end up in other careers, like advertising or marketing or anything else which ended in -ing and didn't involve filling test tubes. He decided against asking her out.

Darren opened one of the small brown cardboard packages and read the label. Tropococaine hydrochloride. Molecular weight, 281.8. Chemical formula,

$C_{15}H_{19}NO_2HCl$. Lethal dose for rats, 2 mg per kg of body weight. A quick reckon up. On that basis, a 10-gram dose would be alternately lethal. He decided to take half a gram. Unsure of the correct method of use, since this wasn't mentioned in the accompanying drug information, Darren weighed out the required quantity of tropococaine hydrochloride, tipped it into a glass of water and swallowed it like some sort of bitter LemSip.

A few hours later, Mormon Dawn entered the lab and fixed Darren with a predatory smile. She was going to reel him in. He could see she was going to say it. He looked helplessly over towards Simon. She always smiled when she was about to say it. Darren felt a sudden heavy tightness in his head which reeked of violence. Please, for your sake, don't say it, he whispered. She was still smiling, and just a few feet away. Darren crushed his teeth together and felt the movement of his jaw press up into his temples. She was opening her mouth. Darren prepared himself.

'Only a hundred and eighty-seven more,' she said, beaming at him.

Darren relaxed a little, puzzled. He had been wrong and felt slightly embarrassed. The drug had long since deserted him, leaving a mess for him to clear up after its departure. 'What?' he asked.

'A hundred and eighty-seven more.'

'Sorry, I don't quite . . .'

'Days till Christmas.' Her grin widened. 'A hundred and eighty-seven more days to Christmas.'

Darren had lowered his guard, just for an instant, and she had pounced. He walked towards the door, fists clenched, fingernails biting. She had started her Christmas Countdown. Already. It was June and she had started her Christmas Countdown. Simon shrugged in bemused solidarity as he passed. There were another 186 days of this to endure. And then, at the end of it, Christmas. A double whammy if ever there was one.

Darren retreated to his office and locked the door. Personnel aside, science had, in many ways, been a letdown for Darren. It wasn't simply that familiarity bred contempt, although this was partially true. When you understand what most people never will and find that it isn't difficult to comprehend, just drowning in impenetrable jargon, your confidence in the unobtainably erudite world of science is bruised slightly. But more saddening than this was the fact that no-one deals with big ideas any more, just small ones. There are no more Newtons or Darwins or Mendels, no big, all-encompassing theories. Granted, small ideas these days *are* big ideas in many ways, given the intricacy of everything, but this is the reverse funnel of modern science. The more you look into a problem, the more underlying and interwoven variables you unearth. A small problem becomes a big problem because the more you discover, the more you find there is to discover. Darren often felt that science, rather than progressing, was just fanning further and further out from a central source of curiosity. You find out, for instance, that variable x affects variable y. All well and good, and thirty, forty, fifty years ago, this would have done, and you could have packed up your rudimentary apparatus, rounded up your thermos flask and Bakelite sandwich box and gone home satisfied. But now, by studying y, you find that y interacts with z, and z with a whole family of other variables a to e. Now, a to e are part of a feedback loop which controls genes f, g, h, i and j. In turn, f, g, h, i and j act so that f, g and h stimulate factors k and l, whereas i and j inhibit m, n and o. All well and good, until someone throws a spanner in the works by working out that j, n and o can interact with another family of related variables, p, q and r, which, in turn, inhibit h and j via the gene product s. s, it turns out, is responsive to the substances m, t and u, which can form a secondarily active compound v, mimicking the action of compound w. Compound w is a promiscuous agent, in that it is able to influence the expression of a whole host of genes and their products, from a to d, g, i, j, k, l, and s. And that is what you have discovered. A lot of genes, their products and various biochemicals interact in divergent ways with one another to achieve disparate aims under different conditions, and all in the absence of one single, clear, overriding aim that you can discern. Rarely, if ever, will your scheme make it back to y, the original point at which you came in. Yes, science is infinitely complex because nature is infinitely complex, but that didn't stop Darren cursing the perpetually disappearing horizon that was pure scientific research.

What the world of science needed, then, was a large kick up its arse, a big thought, an encompassing idea, a unifying theory. No ifs and buts and wherefores, just yeses and nos and therefores. It needed to forget the scrappy details and get on with the wider picture. In short, it needed an ideas man. Darren had decided some months ago that he would put himself forward for the job. While everyone else was peering down their electron microscopes or poring over their sequencing gels, concentrating on the minutiae, he would be looking the other way. He was going to be thinking big. He would be working on one last big theory. Whilst they all focused down on pinhead science, Darren was going to be looking up at the starry universe. And then maybe, just maybe, when he had given the world its one final hypothesis of life, he was going to try and explain the mystery of caravanning.

Fading Features

First Track of the Day: 'Don't Come Around Here No More' *by Tom Petty*

He came again, still on fire. Did my best to ignore him. Been doing my best to ignore everyone who's been coming around here today. Something funny about him this time, something wrong, something broken. Don't know whether I just didn't notice it the first time. I don't know. But he is definitely intriguing. Talks rapidly, never quite looking straight at you, eyes just skimming the surface of contact, as if he's blind and has turned to face the approximate direction he hears your voice coming from.

Tried to picture him in the two days between seeing him again. Couldn't quite sum his features up. All I remembered were the eyes. Tried to mould his fading features into a picture that made sense, but I could never quite get it. The focus would be wrong. I'd try for the nose or the chin or the mouth, and I might get one fairly accurately, but then the others would slip out of focus and I wouldn't be able to see him. Gave up in the end.

As soon as I saw him I realized it would be silly to ignore him. Gave it a go, of course, for the sake of pride, but it was futile. He just kept talking and I got drawn in. Said he was expecting more deliveries and I wondered whether he was saying this to tell me he'd be back. Seemed like he wanted to ask me something. I felt my stomach turn icy, thought he might ask me out or something. I asked him if there was anything he wanted to say to me – just said it out loud – surprised myself. Assertiveness classes are paying off. Said that there was something. I said yes, making it sound like the longest word ever spoken, like yeeeeeeeesssssss. Looked straight at me for the first time and said I'm working on this theory but it's so big I can't fit all of it in my head at the same time. Said he just wanted to tell someone. I didn't know what to say. I felt like a balloon which has been let down then half blown up again. In a way, he made it sound like a compliment, like some sort of trusted confidence.

This time he took Nitrazepam, Pentobarbital and Temazepam with him. I deduced that he must be doing some sort of controlled substance research with Home Office Approval. Has a very half-hearted signature though. Watched him sign the HO waiver. You can tell a lot about a man from his signature. Or so says *Cosmo*. But his was very poor and ill-defined, muddled even. A strong signature makes a strong, bold lover. His would leave him approximately impotent according to my sources, which may or may not be very reliable.

Biological

Biological. The logic of biology. But biology isn't logical. Biology and logic are contradictions, and this is where Darren had started to go wrong. Trying to work logic into biology was like trying to work cheese into football. Sort of. Living systems aren't governed by numbers or equations or statistics. They may be described in such terms, but that's not to say they have the remotest interest in being anything other than just alive. And being alive isn't a logical thing. Being alive is a matter of luck, of random mutation, of the independent segregation of genes, of favourable conditions, of, when it comes down to it, being in the right place at the right time. All life can be accounted for in such terms. Sure, there are principles which must be adhered to. Natural selection – the survival of the fittest, for instance. But the prerequisite for natural selection is mutation. Natural selection must have some variation to act upon in the first place. And mutation is nothing if not inherently random.

For several weeks, Darren had been going to the library and just reading, really reading, with-eyes-open reading, consuming books like they were written in a new language of digestibility, scanning and flicking and scribbling and satiating as if his life depended upon it. He sloped off to the associated university library as often as he could, on the pretext of research for techniques relating to his work, and carried heavily bound volumes back to his office like secret treasures. He opened books on genetics, on physics, on mathematics; on natural selection, on chaos, on statistics; on mutation, on quantum theory, on probability. Although a lot of it was dry and unpalatable, somehow, maybe through osmosis, it seemed to stick somewhere. He could never have written down what he'd learned from book to book, from day to day, from week to week, and yet when he closed his eyes there was something forming, something lurking, something almost tangible. Work was the only thing getting in his way now.

Darren spent his working days just doing things, menial tasks, hand-occupying, brain-freeing chores which allowed him to think. But all the time, Darren felt that as he assembled the pieces of his theory, he was becoming fragmentary. He remembered when his life was an American Waltzer, slow on the outside, rapid through the centre, but all the time safe and strapped in. In short, he appeared outwardly calm, but was always going like the clappers inside. Things had changed, then. He was still going like the clappers inside, but his outer calm had gone. Somewhere along the line he had lost some buffering. He now felt raw and exposed. He realized that people only had to look at him to know what he was thinking. A temper was emerging from somewhere, and now it had nowhere to hide. Darren was impatient, jumpy, anxious, and knew it. He was being chewed up and spat out by something entirely of his own making. He was losing the plot in order to find his way through the maze of thoughts he had begun to construct. Maybe it was the drugs, but either way, something had to give. He was expanding all the time, and the wider he became the more his boundaries disappeared, enticing him wider still, until all that was left in the middle was a vacuum. He was like an elastic band. When you stretch an elastic band further and harder and wider, and look at the ends of the band as they pull into the fleshy bulbs of your thumbs, they seem fine and barely to be taking the strain at all. It's only when you look down at the middle of the elastic band that you see the true force of what you are doing, marked out in vertical striations, the rubber curiously thin and pale in colour and the whole band in imminent danger of tearing itself molecule from molecule.

Darren squeezed out all of life's non-essentials, and many essentials, and continued to absorb everything. He read and scribbled and memorized on the bus (driving was becoming dangerous), while he walked, while he set experiments up, when he drank coffee, while he bolted his lunch, on the phone, while he sat on the toilet, while he did anything which didn't need his full attention. Darren became an expert in ergonomics. He stripped everything down to almost nothing. He stopped shopping and cooking in favour of takeaways, which also took care of washing up. He drove less and less because driving and reading had caused a few close scrapes. Besides, there is nothing else you can do on public transport but read. Darren stopped watching TV, and this saved time both watching and discussing programmes. He stopped talking to people, reasoning that almost everything worth saying has already been said before. He barely listened to music. True, it was possible to read with music on, but the time spent selecting CDs and inserting them into his stereo was time which was lost for ever. And lost time is no good to you when you are labouring on the one last great theory of the twentieth century.

Perhaps most fatally of all though, Darren stopped working. His job was going nowhere. He wasn't in the right place and this had become patently obvious to him recently. He was a square peg in a round hole, and when clichés start making sense and ringing true, you know you're in danger. And he *was* in trouble. He was looking for gaps which might or might not be there, holes which should never be sought, regardless of their actuality. When you start searching for gaps in science, things which are missing, and finding them, feel whole again, then you really are flirting with disaster.

Dates

Simon entered the lab, said hello and sat down at his bench. Darren answered with a cursory grunt and resumed his quest to transfer tap water from the Eppendorf tube on his left to the one on his right. He had started the morning with one millilitre of water – roughly four or five drops – and by transferring ten per cent of the volume at a time, he took the entire measure across in either direction in ten movements, occupying around a minute of his day. So far so good, but Darren was noticing that the tenth transfer of fluid was coming in short. Somehow, he was losing fluid. He stared intently at the pipette tip and at the two bullet-shaped Eppendorf tubes in front of him. There was no evidence of even the smallest leakage of water. As he continued, the volume of the last passage continued to dip alarmingly over the following minutes. Eventually, there was no tenth transfer. Nine movements were sufficient to account for the total volume. Darren had therefore lost ten per cent of his original stock of water. But where was it going? Everything seemed to be watertight. Evaporation couldn't be that rapid, surely. He should have just topped his reservoir up with the missing water, but he couldn't. He had to account for it, had to discover where it was disappearing, had to know where he was losing it. As Darren continued to examine the apparatus he realized that this was like a sort of metaphor for something or other in his life, but couldn't figure out quite what. And then he realized that even metaphors were eluding him.

Simon studied the month-to-a-page calendar in the front of his diary and cleared his throat. Darren looked around. Simon's eyebrows moved closer to each other, forming a small double undulation above the bridge of his nose, which he squeezed between his index finger and thumb as he prepared to speak. Darren waited.

'You know something,' Simon said, looking up from his diary, 'I reckon this summertime wintertime thing is all wrong.'

'What do you mean?' Darren laughed.

'Well look,' Simon glanced at Darren and then turned the pages chronologically from January onwards, 'spring starts on March the twenty-first and ends on June the twentieth, right?'

'Yes.' Darren saw where this was heading and laughed again.

'And summer is June the twenty-first to September the twentieth, autumn's then till . . .' He flicked through the calendar.

'December the twentieth.' Darren speeded the process along, chortling through the twentieth.

'Yeah,' Simon said, with exaggeratedly raised eyebrows, 'and winter is December the twenty-first to March the twentieth.'

Darren was about to respond but stopped for a second. Something was bothering him. He was uncomfortably aware that he had been laughing at the end of his own sentences recently, particularly ones which weren't in the least bit amusing. This was a little disturbing. Maybe he had stumbled across a new side effect for 1-methyl-5-phenyl-3H-1,4-benzo-diazepin. He confined his answer to a single, sober word. 'So?'

'Well, you can't tell me that a freezing day in the middle of December is autumn, or that a roasting day in June is spring, or a cold afternoon in the third week of September is summer. It all just seems out of kilter.'

'Yeah.'

'It doesn't make sense. Summer should be, what, June, July, August. Autumn should be September, October and November. Then you've got winter as December, January, February, and March, I suppose, and spring can be, what, April and May. There, that'd be more like it.'

'Four-month winter?' Darren asked solemnly, trying not to freak Simon out any further.

'Feels like it.'

'Yep. Had the same thought myself.' A small giggle escaped. Darren tried to concentrate. 'Don't know who carved the year up originally, but they did a shite job of it.' He flicked through his diary and its empty pages made him shiver involuntarily.

Simon broke the silence. 'Anyway, where were we?'

'Shit, yeah. The meeting.' Darren opened his diary at the relevant page. 'Any day's good for me. Towards the end of the week would be better.' What he meant was any day was terrible for him, it made no difference. He had nothing to contribute because he'd done no work, so any day was as fine or terrible as any other.

'Shall I leave it with you then?'

Darren looked over at Simon. He wanted to get down on his knees and beg Simon to cover for him. He wanted to tell him everything, to let it all out in one cascade of tearful honesty, to explain his theory, to show him just how big it was going to be when he'd finished building it, to tell him he'd done nothing,

nothing at all at work except mime and think, and fake and calculate, while all the time he was growing and expanding and absorbing, and he had nothing to show Graham, not one speck of work that he hadn't already shown him a dozen times and that he was so terrified at the prospect of having a meeting with his supervisor that he couldn't sleep at night if he so much as considered the idea, so he said yes, leave it with me, I'll arrange a meeting.

There was, of course, no way that he could expose his heart, not just like that. If only Simon would say something. It would be easy that way. But he wasn't likely to say anything and he couldn't bring himself to utter the words, so his work would have to recede in silence as his theory consumed everything in its path. He was aware that Simon wanted to say something. Darren closed his diary, expectantly. Simon kept his open, flicking through the pages and occasionally looking over at him. Simon shut his diary.

'Darren.'

He glanced up from the blankness of the floor. 'Yes?'

'There's something I've been meaning to say . . .'

This was it. Get it out in the open. Face the crisis armed with someone else's courage. 'Yes?'

'Well, I don't know how you're going to take this . . .'

Butterflies emerged and fluttered inside his stomach. 'Yes?'

'I couldn't borrow your pipette, could I?'

Lost in Minutiae

It was no good. Darren couldn't focus. He was trying to get things out of his brimming skull and on to the empty paper on his desk. It should have been simple, like pressure or diffusion. There was clearly a gradient, and one which was largely heading in the right direction. His head was full. The paper was empty. It was not, for once, the other way round. But he couldn't get his thoughts out. There were so many of them, like shoals of shimmering fish, so that when he plunged his eager hands into the water and tried to seize just one of them, the whole shoal darted suddenly away in a new direction and all he could do was to pull his empty hands out and shake them dry. And then as he stared through the page in front of him, Darren spotted an imperfection on the paper, an oasis of dirt on a bleached landscape, and managed to grasp a thought, not a good one, but enough to get the ball rolling. Difference – that was the very point of everything. Without variation there would be nothing. The bleached sameness of the world . . . he needed a pen. He couldn't find one. He lifted pieces of paper up, brusquely and optimistically, not wanting to lose the meagre thought. All he could find was a pen top which has lost its matching pen. As Darren hunted, he came across a scientific paper which he had been on the verge of trying to track down for about six months. He picked the paper up and its Abstract caught his eye. He made a stab at reading it, but couldn't concentrate, so tried the Introduction. That was no good either. The Materials and Methods were similarly impenetrable. Results ditto. The rigid structure of this, as with all scientific papers seemed suddenly alien to him. The Conclusions were unfathomable and the Discussion therefore arbitrary. Finally, he had a stab at the Summary but was still unable to focus, and noticed for the first time that the paper wasn't stapled together. Darren found his stapler, but it chomped into the loosely bound sheets of paper like a mouth with no teeth. Darren examined it and found it didn't have any staples. He searched his drawers but couldn't find any. He left the office and went to the Key Cupboard, where all the Institute's keys were housed in numerical order. Darren removed key number 62, the Stationery Cupboard key, and walked to the promised land of the Stationery Cupboard. He pocketed the required staples and also filled up with Tippex, Post-it Notes, paper clips, drawing pins and anything else which would stand little danger of ever being used constructively. He walked back to his office and swore. He had forgotten to return the Stationery Cupboard key. Darren walked back up the corridor and returned it to Slot 62. On the way back to his desk, he realized that he hadn't managed to get a pen from the Stationery Cupboard. Darren swore again, returned to the office penless and unloaded the accumulated booty. As he took the Tippex out of his pocket and glanced at his desk, Darren recalled that he had been trying to send a letter to his building society for some days, to complain about his ever-increasing mortgage, but hadn't been able to until he had deleted a couple of swear words which had somehow crept in to the final draft. Darren located the letter and Tippexed out a wanker and a couple of cunts. He hunted round for an envelope to put the letter in and found an A4 envelope, which was overdoing it a bit, but he folded the letter up and inserted it anyway. Turning it over with a dry gummy taste in his mouth Darren realized he still didn't have a pen to address the letter with. He was getting irritated. He returned to the Key Cupboard, got Key 62, returned to the Stationery Cupboard, got a pen, returned the key to the Key Cupboard and returned himself to his office. Darren glanced at his watch, sighed, and addressed the envelope. Then he searched through his pockets for a stamp but couldn't find one. He banged his fist on the desk. A small corner shop a couple of hundred yards away sold stamps, so Darren picked up the envelope, left the office and then the building and headed for the shop. Inside, he bought a stamp and returned to work to put it through the external mail. He made his way to the secretaries' office, where he placed the envelope in the Out tray. On his way back to his office, he was trapped by Graham. He had been dreading this. Phone call for you, Darren. Right. My office. Oh right, sorry. The receiver lay on Graham's desk like a fish out of water. He picked it up. Hello? he said, looking out of the window. Hi, is that Dr White? Yes. This is Kelly James from Delta Biochemicals. Darren started to panic. Shit. They were on to him. They had tracked the controlled substance orders back to him. He glanced over his telephone-free shoulder and took a sharp and unsatisfying breath. Yes? he asked, without confidence. Graham was standing behind him, waiting to reuse his desk. Darren felt himself blush slightly. I'm going to be in Sheffield on Thursday and wondered if you'd like to chat about some new product lines we're running? What? Oh yes, fine. His blush receded. Three o'clock OK for you? Fine. Bye. Graham cleared his throat as a way of saying get the fuck out of my office. Darren got the fuck out of his office, relieved, and headed back to his own office, pleased. All loose ends tied. But then as he sat and pondered his last three-quarters of an hour, he wondered what he'd actually managed to do. This was becoming the norm for him. He was headless and chicken. Deleting non-essentials had left Darren with no capacity for structure. He had thoughts but they didn't seem to connect any more. One thought happened, was replaced by another and so on, with no sense of continuity or purpose, each thought immediate and disposable. He wondered whether non-essentials provided a framework, a sort of mesh, to bind everything together and stop it all falling through into the oblivion of the present. For without the mundane for a frame of reference, even important thoughts were becoming trivial, and were disappearing as soon as they arrived, to be replaced with more of the same. Maybe this was true. Darren didn't know. All he did know was that he was running around chasing his tail. He looked at the blank page on his desk with its inky imperfection and tried to remember just what the hell it had reminded him of in the first place.

The Meeting

Darren was bound by an unwritten rule to report his progress, or, recently, lack of it, to Graham on a monthly basis. The protocol was this. Darren did some work, and if it worked, he arranged a meeting with his supervisor to show him that it had worked. If it didn't, he kept quiet and tried something else until that worked, and then showed him that. If something worked in the weeks between meetings, Darren was always careful not to let on. He would create buffers against the pressure. If you always had some data in the bank, you were always ready for barren patches and emergencies. Sometimes the impetus for meetings came from Darren, particularly if he hadn't shown Graham any work for quite a time. Mainly they would meet alone, but occasionally Simon would join them. Graham would never ask directly though. There would be a canine expectancy in his eyes when three weeks had elapsed since their last meeting, and he would find trivial excuses to hang around Darren's bench chatting. He would insert pauses. It was like Morse code. He would leave gaps and wait. And after a while Darren would give him what he wanted and ask him if he had time to get together. This was always the phrasing. They would never just meet, they would have to 'get together', as if they were going to have a few beers and play pool.

Inevitably in such a system, Darren was his own worst enemy. He couldn't have it both ways. The better he did, the more was expected of him. The more he failed, the more he had to promise, and so the greater the anticipation. Either way, there was crushing expectancy. And the best Darren could do was to hope to get ahead, to save a little data up for a rainy day, to lighten the weight of anticipation.

But the situation now was becoming desperate, and his cushion of data had long since burst and shrivelled. Everywhere Darren walked he was surrounded by a vacuum of achievement. He cursed himself for not holding more back, for not tucking an emergency ration of graphs, autorads or sequences away in the depths of his cluttered drawers. Darren knew of course that even if he had, he would have consumed it long ago and he began to dread Graham's appearance. Like working out the possibility of a missed period, Darren tried to count back four weeks to see if they were due a meeting. He couldn't remember exactly. He couldn't remember a lot of things recently. His diary was blank. It might even have been five weeks since they had last got together. He had tried not to be around as much as possible, but one afternoon, sometime in the twilight hours after lunch and before home time, Graham came and hung around Darren's bench, and generally refused to go away. The pauses became longer. He wasn't going until he'd got what he wanted, and without asking. Darren was forced to take the bait. Graham had him and he knew it. Darren suggested Simon join them and he agreed. This was good. Simon would deflect some of the attention away from him. Darren went home and began panicking.

* * *

The following afternoon, Darren and Simon enter Graham's office together. Simon leads the way and takes, as Darren hopes he will, the chair nearer to Graham's desk. This is good. Darren shuffles his chair slightly nearer the door as he sits down, to further distance himself from the proceedings. Graham starts, as he always does.

'So, Dr White and Dr Bird, what have you got for me?' There is no formality intended by announcing titles, just a gentle doctoral pat on the back, combined of course with a reminder of his own professorial status.

Darren looks at the floor and at Graham's wastepaper bin. He suddenly feels the enormous burden of hope closing in around him, squeezing him, making him breathe faster through shrunken lungs. Graham stares from Simon to Darren. It is obvious, Darren panics. Graham is onto him. It is all over Darren's face, his fidgeting hands, his crossed and uncrossed legs, his lacklustre torso and his contact-avoiding eyes – he has done nothing, not one thing, for weeks and weeks. He has sat and stared, and scratched and fidgeted, and thought and reasoned, and daydreamed and meandered, all the time moving his empty arms and idle hands to give the impression of industry. And it has been remarkably successful. This time Darren's results aren't numbers or bands or lines on graphs but the hopefulness in Graham's eyes, which are hunting him down like searchlights, tunnelling through Darren's irises and into his skull.

Graham tries again. 'So, who's going to start us off?'

He is looking at Darren, who is, after all, the principal investigator. Darren begins to sweat, and feels an uncomfortable blush bloom across his face. He opens his lab book. There is page after page of nothingness. Darren has already shown him all previous data in the book. On the emptiness of the pages the feint lines don't appear quite parallel. He makes a mental note to measure them. Simon looks at Darren and clears his throat.

'Well, I've been working on a couple of things,' he says, looking at Graham and then over at Darren, 'that's if you don't mind me butting in.'

Butting in, my arse, Darren says to himself. You can't butt in if you're the only one in the queue. 'No,' he says, out loud.

'Go on then,' encourages Graham.

Simon talks at length about his recent experiments. They have worked well. Darren curses him and stares into the bin, half hoping there might be some discarded data in there he can rescue. Simon has cloned a short coding sequence, which he plans to express. There is an attractive (within the bounds of science) girl in one of the opposite labs. She glances over, momentarily. The sequence hasn't, as far as he is concerned, been published. Jammy bastard. She has short dark hair. Not bad at all. Mediterranean, maybe. There was, however, that big paper three or four months ago which suggests that the product might result from alternative splicing at the TPR locus. Breasts a bit on the large side. Too large, maybe. Neuro Girl's, on the other hand, are magnificent. In fact, the whole lot of her looks fairly magnificent. Bound to be married though, a girl like Neuro Girl. Didn't see a ring, but they always are. And always to scientists. It's like a safety net thing, one life instead of two, work and home blending into one terse, serious, comfortable nightmare.

'Darren?'

'Hmmm?'

'You're OK with that?'

With what exactly? he wonders. Fuck knows. The question doesn't matter, just the tone it's asked in.

Darren guesses he wants to hear yes. 'Yes,' he says, and to compensate for his lack of attention, 'Of course.'

'Good,' Graham smiles. The girl in the opposite lab is no longer visible. 'And presumably you've got your own reasons for wanting to go with that?'

Fuck knows. He tries to sound positive. 'Oh yes.'

'And you've talked to Simon about it?'

Darren glances at Simon, who knows he's on thin ice. 'Yeah.'

'And what are those reasons from your side?'

Shit. Darren wants to confess everything. He can no longer bear the weight of his own deceit. He is dead wood, washed up, dried up, useless and beached. Research is about doing things, trying things, not faking things. He feels plastic and see-through. This is his opportunity to own up. He can go no further. Graham has made it easy for him. He has opened the window and let Darren stand on the ledge. He can see the pinheaded people and matchbox cars scurrying down below. And then, as he stares down at them, fascinated, one by one the people turn their pink little faces up towards him, flushed with expectancy, crowding together, pointing and chattering, and shouting up, 'Do it!', 'Go on!', 'Nobody call the police!', 'We won't catch you!' and placing safety blankets carefully on the pavement over exposed manholes, so Darren will drop through and fall even further into the sewer below. He looks down at them and readies himself. He will try to take out as many of the stupid, ugly, sweaty creatures as he can when he goes. He will aim for one particularly eager group and land with his arms and legs spreadeagled to catch them all with his heavy limbs. They roar him on, oblivious to his plan. They are shouting louder and louder. 'Darren! Darren! Darren!' He looks up at Graham.

'Darren?'

'Yes?'

'Is this true?' he asks.

Again, fuck knows. He listens to the tone. Graham is regarding him quizzically. This doesn't help. It's a close call, but Darren guesses he wants to hear no. 'No,' he says.

'No?' Graham flashes Darren another muddy look. He must be running out of them by now. 'So you *haven't* talked to Simon and *haven't* spent the past four weeks helping him get his transfections going?'

Wrong. Darren hears the *Family Fortunes* 'Ni Na' buzzer. 'Yes. Er, sorry Graham, miles away, I mean yes. I did agree, er, with Simon, to, you know, help him . . .'

'With his transfections?'

'With his transfections. Not much else to report really.' Darren steps in from the window ledge. Safe for another month. He wants to marry Simon. This is going to cost him heavily in beer.

Genetics is Luck

Darren couldn't face returning to the squeezing confines of his house, and so treated himself to a couple of pints in the hospital bar before driving home. He had spent the rest of the afternoon doing anything he could to avoid thinking about his theory, which was in danger of imploding and sucking him into oblivion with it. He needed a break from thinking. It was strangling him and he knew it. A little alcohol and a modicum of reasonable company and his brain might wander into lighter, clearer pastures. He wondered whether Neuro Girl would be there, and whether, armed with a pint or two of Danish courage, he might actually be able to talk to her without making an idiot of himself. Or failing that, whether Simon might be around to collect his due reward.

He walked over to the bar via a complex series of windowless subterranean hospital corridors which were haunted by lingering smells of unappetizing food and clinging antiseptic. Darren was increasingly aware that one of his shoes was squeaking. It had been dogging him intermittently for a couple of weeks and seemed louder now, amplified by the echo-chamber corridors. The other shoe was almost silent against the dull, tiled floor. He stopped and had a good look at the sole, which seemed fine. Everything felt OK from the inside as well, so where the squeaking was coming from was a mystery.

When the squeaking of his shoe had first become apparent, Darren had tried to fix it. He smeared Vaseline into every crack and crease of the sole, in the hope that a bit of lubrication might do the trick. This proved dangerous though. A squeak was one thing, but a broken neck was quite another. He had even tried walking differently, heel first on his squeaky foot, which didn't work; toe first, ditto; and even foot tilted outwards or inwards, both of which made him look somewhat crippled and generally defeated the object. As he turned into the penultimate corridor before the bar, in one brief unexpected moment of salvation, Darren managed to get his footstep completely in synch with a fellow-sufferer of shoddy footwear, and for a few glorious seconds his companion's suffering became Darren's suffering, his alternate squeaking Darren's alternate squeaking, his misery Darren's misery. Darren wanted to follow the man around all day, hidden in his squeak, blameless, silent and complete, but presently the man stopped to wait for a lift, and Darren was forced to hobble on alone, like a ghost of his companion.

Sitting down with his drink in the low-ceilinged bar, Darren had a quick scan around him. Neuro Girl wasn't there, and neither was Simon. Gavin, however, was and Darren caught his eye, just long enough to make it obvious that he had seen him and had no interest in pursuing the matter further. But just as cats are attracted to people who don't like cats because these are the very people who don't make eye contact with them, Gavin failed to take the hint and lumbered over. By the look of things, he was already several pints to the good, and, Darren noticed unhappily,

Gavin's shoes appeared to be free from the squeaking which haunted his own scruffy footwear.

'Gavin.'

'Darren.'

They started talking. Gavin asked him what he'd been up to. Darren told him about his theory. Gavin demanded specifics. Darren was unable to furnish many. Gavin didn't appear particularly impressed. After a minute or two of silence, Gavin said, 'You know, for all your thinking and reading, it doesn't sound like you've discovered the real truth about genetics.'

'What do you mean?'

'The real truth about genetics. That genetics is sheer luck.'

Darren took a long mournful look at the condensation forming on the side of his glass. 'And how do you figure that?'

'Sheer fucking luck,' Gavin repeated, 'when you think about it.'

'I have thought about it.'

'Listen. It's obvious. What you've got is what you've been given. And what you've been given has been given to you by your parents. And what they've been given has been given them by their parents.' Gavin leaned forward, as if he was about to share some treasured secret. 'But the real problem with genetics is that you think you've got some God-given right to have what you have, just because some distant father of a father of a father happened to give it you on a plate. But you got it by luck. Luck is something that you had no hand in. And that's what genetics is. You had no hand in who your great-, great-, or not so great-grandfather fucked, did you? And you think you're a good footballer or top rocket scientist or irresistible to women because you deserve to be, because you've worked hard at it, because you just tried harder than some poor sod who can't kick straight or is stupid or who is extremely resistible to women. Bollocks. It's all because some distant relative fucked some other distant relative and you happened to get a lucky deal out of the arrangement.'

'But you've got a say in what you pass on of course.'

'I suppose,' he said, withdrawing slightly and allowing Darren to breathe, 'you do get to choose whose DNA you fuck. But what's making the choice? It's your fucking genes, that's what. The genes that you got by chance. What sort of a choice is that?' Gavin took a deep swig of beer. 'No, you don't really have much of a say when it comes down to it.'

Darren nodded, just to keep the peace. Maybe Gavin did have reason to curse genetics. After all, one way or another, his genes didn't seem to have done him many favours.

Darren had one final forlorn scan of the bar for Neuro Girl, finished his drink and left.

Paper Cuts

On the way there, I tried to imagine what his house would look like. It was in Dore, a flat village eight rural miles from Sheffield. Dore was unusual. It sprawled, in a way that English villages traditionally don't do. Instead of huddled stone cottages and shrunken terraces crouching together in friendly conspiracy, Dore looked as if it had stretched taut at some time during its history so that no one house impinged on any other. A long narrow park ran alongside almost the entire length of the village, allowing you to see it in cross-section as you passed by on the Chesterfield to Sheffield train. As I left the local Sprinter service I felt a sudden surge of anger, realizing that it would take some time to find his house. Undoubtedly the old cunt had money. It would be a nice house, a tidy house, a well-tended and edged and trimmed sort of house. It would be made of sandstone, several shades lighter than the equivalent city stone ravaged by the industrial revolution. It would be imposing and solid and Yorkshire proud, standing firm against the elements, confident in its belief that it was impenetrable and here for eternity.

When I found it, I was disappointed. It was larger than I had imagined, but also substantially tattier. Whatever the cunt did with his spare time, it wasn't

DIY. In fact, the house was a mess, and looked as if it had been added to at various points in its history, and not always with any sort of consistency or fluency in mind. It certainly didn't look too difficult to break into, and there didn't appear to be an alarm. From the edge of the garden I could see two lights, one in a downstairs room and one on what looked like the landing stairs. No-one was visible, so I crouched down by the garden's thick hedge and wallowed dog-like in the misery of waiting. Time passed with inevitable reluctance and I grew cold. I needed to piss, and relieved myself into his hedge. There was a degree of disbelief in my mind as I crouched down again. I had made myself come this far, had convinced myself that I, the persecuted, was going to become the persecutor. I had even written a mantra down in deeply etched biro, like some sort of paper tattoo – Get The Bastard, Get The Bastard, Get The Bastard – said over and over with stomach clenched Gs, and yet, I still felt as if I might just walk back to the train station, go home and forget this madness. It seemed almost farcical to be lurking in his garden. I found myself lacking conviction. But as I folded my arms across my chest to conserve heat, I felt the slim delicate blade of my scalpel push into its protective sheath and nudge me in the ribs. And with that slight discomfort my memory was also nudged, and my bruised pride kicked back into life, and the loathing and poison began to flow again with renewed vengeance. Get The Bastard, Get The Bastard, Get The Bastard. I had come this far, and I wasn't going home until I had dealt with him for good. I opened a packet of gum and chewed maniacally, quickly grinding all flavour out of the dry stick. The sugary gum made my teeth hollow and itchy after a while, so I spat it out, and continued to mesh my jaws together regardless, waiting for the right moment.

Rules to Live By

Today had been a day of rules for Darren.

Rule One was never ask someone you don't know and have no interest in knowing for advice, particularly at work. Darren decided that a bout of photocopying would allow him to appear busy without perceptibly taxing his brain. The Safety Form he decided to duplicate meant photocopying on *both* sides of a piece of paper. Darren didn't know how to do this – only the privileged or the autistic do – and there was no way he was going to risk reading the photocopier manual. There were two other people in the photocopier room, both of them of similarly little use to him. Winning System was busy telling Tea Break Terminator at great length why he couldn't help him carry something back to the labs, on the grounds of being too busy. Tea Break Terminator, on the other hand, was engaged in telling Winning System that the zinc coating on the inside of used bullet casings could be retrieved by scraping their interiors with a braddle wrapped in emery paper, should you need zinc filings at all for anything.

'Look, really, I would help you,' Winning System continued, oblivious, 'only a technician has asked me to sort a couple of problems out for their professor, not that I've really got the chance to do that, as some paper-shuffler from the Home Office keeps insisting on coming over to visit Dr Jeffries, who has left, but he still wants to visit anyway, and I'm telling him that he's wasting his time, and my time, which is precious enough, as I've only got one pair of hands . . .'

'So US marines scratched out the zinc, apparently, with tent pegs, the ones with hooks, straightened obviously, used the filings in coatings, melted it all down over their gas stoves, which is interesting because butane only burns at . . .'

'And there's no way I can run about doing this for this guy, the other for someone else, I mean it's not as if I can go up to Johnson and ask him to cover my paperwork while I'm busy running around trying to explain why loads of deliveries have gone missing, all with Home Office licences in tow, and which are now going to be revoked . . .'

Darren swallowed hard and tried not to look guilty. To focus his mind, he scrutinized the complex series of hieroglyphic instructions stencilled on the side of the machine, which suggested how, if he could only break the code, he might actually go about performing the neurosurgery which is photocopying. While he tried vainly to match the machine's series of impossibly futuristic symbols to anything even vaguely relating to duplicating pieces of paper he glanced back at Winning System and Tea Break Terminator. One of them would know how to do it, without a shadow of a doubt.

'Works on the same basic principle as the Zip drive,' TBT droned on over the top of Winning System's rundown of work he was not about to do. This was becoming a battle of wills. One of them surely was going to have to collapse or slip into a coma or something. 'CD technology, really. Thirty-two bit, though sixty-four apparently suffers from large conflicts, obviously, if you're running it through an LPT1 port in parallel, digital was never designed that way . . .'

He wondered whether he might ask one of them to help him, but quickly chickened out. Mercifully a technician from another department, who Darren had generally avoided up to now because he looked more than a bit dull, entered the photocopying room. Here then was a dilemma. WS and TBT were out, for obvious reasons. It would probably take the technician less than thirty seconds to impart his God-given wisdom. Thirty seconds. But that was the very problem. Darren had to weigh up the transient happiness that knowing how to photocopy on both sides of a piece of paper would bring him, against the misery of having to say hello to the technician every time he walked past him or was in the same room as him for the rest of his working days. Even now, after rigorously applying Rule One for most of his adult life, there were still people with whom Darren's entire shared dialogue consisted of 'All right,' without even a question mark of curiosity, just because once, on a dismal afternoon maybe three years ago, he happened to be stupid enough to ask for their advice.

Darren removed the Safety Form from the warm glass of the photocopier. As he left the room, he heard the technician commit verbal suicide by butting into the conversation and asking whether either WS or TBT might be able to help him with a computer problem he was having. Darren smiled to himself as he wandered back to his office. WS would launch into another lengthy airing of his existing work commitments, and when finally beaten into submission, TBT would doubtless inform the poor technician over a couple of hours where he was going wrong, without once telling him what to do about it.

Darren was about to begin work at his desk, when he

noticed a general absence of disarray and looking up realized he had wandered into the wrong office. He had been enjoying the thought of TBT and Winning System pushing someone who was already barely alive over the edge and into a coma of boredom so much that he had wandered into the wrong room. The office was empty and so no-one had spotted his fuck-up, which meant that it only needed to be classified as an act of minor stupidity, and not as one of gross stupidity, which technically required a witness. In the absence of any onlookers, Darren swore and put it down as the result of a hangover he didn't have, muggy weather which the country wasn't suffering and overwork which he wasn't doing. For when it comes to making fuck-ups, even idiots are smart enough to give themselves the benefit of the doubt. Darren made a dignified retreat. Back in the familiar confusion of his own office, he sat and thought about the nature of fallibility. On the whole, Darren believed himself to be more than a little incompetent. OK, so he had various pieces of paper which to some extent proved he wasn't, but when he compared the paper of his certificates with the reality of the breathtakingly stupid acts he perpetrated on an almost hourly basis, their ink seemed to fade somewhat. Discounting moments of idiocy involving the opposite sex, which can afflict all men regardless of aptitude, when Darren counted up the mistakes he made even just counting the mistakes he made, it was enough to make him swear. And as Darren sat at his desk, quietly cursing, he wondered whether he ought to just do the decent thing and hand his qualifications over to the police and demand to be tried for fraud. But this was Rule Two. No matter how incompetent you believe yourself to be, never ever own up to it, unless by owning up to it you can get your way out of another scrape.

After lunch, having spectacularly failed in the photocopying department, Darren set off on the often perilous journey to the Safety Unit, to get to the very source of the problem, and pick up some new Safety Forms. It wasn't as if there was actually anything to be gained from filling in a Safety Form – the life-shortening consequence of spilling phenol over yourself was hardly going to be neutralized by having at some stage completed a form advising you not to spill phenol over yourself – it was just that he had started the day with the mission of accruing a few spare forms, and had been remarkably unsuccessful up to now. There was no way he was going home until he had at least managed to tie up this solitary loose end. In the cheerfully dangerous Safety Unit, Rule Three of the day sprang into action. Rule Three was never answer any general questions on genetics.

Darren found himself cornered by one of the secretaries. Medical Genetics, isn't it? she asked. Darren confirmed that it was. You know, I've been meaning to ask someone who knows about those things, genes and that, because my husband's sister is, you know, a bit on the *large* side, and we're thinking, you know, about starting a family and that, and I saw this documentary, and it's all in the genes, isn't it? And I was just wondering what the chances are if we have a daughter that she will, you know . . .

Obviously, never answering general questions on genetics isn't a prevailing rule that everybody can live by. It's unlikely, for instance, that many postmen are going to be asked on a regular basis defeating and pointless genetics questions based on common misconceptions. And the most common misconception is that anybody who works in genetics fully understands genetics. Obviously, if you work in genetics, you probably understand quite a bit about it, but frustratingly, on the grand scale of the subject, probably not enough to explain a lot of the things you see in the world around you. So when someone says, 'You work with genes? I wear Levis myself,' and laughs, and seeing little mirth and a fair amount of irritation in your eyes continues, 'but, seriously, my cat's a tabby and I think she's been mated by a white tom from down the road, so what colour will the kittens be – will they be a mix or will some be white and some tabby?' the best thing to do is to express your opinion with a swift punch to the face. This will save a great deal of time in the long run.

Rule Four, and a rule Darren seldom broke, was never ask a girl out if you can possibly help it. Life is already stacked with sufficient disappointment not to go looking for it deliberately.

Hard to Get

First Track of the Day: 'Watching the Detectives' *by Elvis Costello*

One hour to home time and I was struggling. Looked at my watch on the minute, every minute. Deliveries dried up ages ago, so another afternoon spent filing papers and nails. Will have no nails left soon. Paperwork is endless though. Lunch was a disaster, hanging around outside the police station down the road for half an hour. Pointless, really. Sometimes this system just doesn't work. Looked back at my watch. Time had sneaked fifteen minutes past me when I wasn't looking and I panicked. Quickly started scanning the *What's On* cinema listings for suitable films. And there he was, the door closing behind him. Deliveries finished for today, I told him, putting down my magazine. Thought so, he said. He stood and stared almost at me, his eyes duller this time, focused on the wall behind me. Not as wild as before. Subdued, nearly. I stared back, unexpectedly nervous, trembling slightly. This time I was the one on fire. Dragged it out. Paused, sighed, then said, Do you want to do something one night? When did you have in mind? I asked. Scratched his forehead and frowned. This seemed to have thrown him slightly. Probably not even expecting to get this far. Tonight perhaps. Can't tonight – watching a film, I said. Which film? he asked. I don't know, a police one, probably. What, you don't know what film you're going to see but you know it's going to be a police one? Yes. Do you have a thing about the police, or something? No, I told him. It isn't the police. What then? Said it wasn't easy to explain. Try. Another time I said. When? he asked, for the second time. Direct, I will say that for him. Not the wild shambles of our previous encounters. Hard to get, I whispered to myself. Treat them keen, keep them mean. Or was it the other way round? Next week, I said, possibly Tuesday or Wednesday. Sounded disappointed. Not sooner? he asked. I liked that. Made me feel desired. Before, the desirer, now the desired. OK, how about Monday, I relented. He said yes, flushed slightly, scratched his head again. The door opened and some-one entered, passing between us. A distance, suddenly, an awkward silence. A small fire seemed to ignite in him, his eyes back to darting around the room. Any more of those misdirected deliveries due soon? he asked. So much for romance. I checked my book. Tomorrow, I told him. Good, he said. Tomorrow, then. He left and I opened my magazine. *Lethal Weapon 4* was a distinct possibility.

Fear of Science

There are many phobias in this world. In fact, seen from most angles, the world is nothing more and nothing less than one big, sweaty-palmed, gut-seizing house of phobias. You name it and someone's phobic about it. And the more benign it is, the more common, the more mundane and the less likely to harm anything, then the more phobics there will be lining up in silent misery to worship it. And Darren was no exception. He was firmly in line, shaking cold, damp hands with hydrophobes, looking into the many eyes of arachnophobes, hugging claustrophobes, social climbing with altophobes, offering escargots to Francophobes and patting the backs of homophobes. But Darren's phobia wasn't mundane or common or ordinary. It was a recent phobia in terms of human experience and consequently no-one had got around to naming it, to giving it a prefix to call its own. That or he was the only fucker suffering from it. This was doubtful. Either way, he thought that maybe he should be first to name it. Scienceophobia might do the trick. Or cursedbytheenormousweightofitallophobia. Because that's how it was. He was torn to shreds at the size of it all. He would wake up at five fifteen, three and a half hours after drinking himself to sleep, and the dread would already be climbing into bed with him, wrapping the blankets tightly around his chest and helping him breathe quickly and inefficiently, and his first conscious thought in the early hours of every morning was that science was slowly, analytically and methodically fucking him over.

Darren's fear of science was very much like his fear of heights. Often, a fear of heights doesn't have very much to do with the height itself. A large drop from a high cliff, for example, wasn't something which particularly filled Darren with panic. If he climbed a hill he didn't worry that the hill might collapse under him or that he would lose his footing and tumble down its rocky face. No, heights themselves are generally fairly stable things. The real issue of fear, therefore, came down not to the height itself but to the person. It came down to a matter of trust. The height was there whatever and was unlikely to do anything in itself to harm him. Often, when Darren looked down from a precipitous building at the pavement below, part of him would tremble, and for a moment, he would get the disturbing impression that he wasn't quite in control of the situation. He would wonder, if it came down to a vote, whether that little part of him which was always saying go on, see what it feels like, might overwhelm the rest of him and throw him off. In short, a fear of heights was a fear of the self. And likewise for Darren, a fear of science was a fear of himself. It was a problem not with the shortcomings of science, but with the shortcomings of Darren.

Sometimes in the slow, silent darkness while the rest of the population dozed in warm contentment, Darren closed his eyes. Behind his eyelids he saw images of science, a 600-foot wall made up of single rocks, each one placed there by the labour of a different scientist, and linked to all the other rocks by the cement of honest endeavour. Darren would stand at the top of this wall with his own rock, which, as he looked closely at it, seemed crumbly, fragile, small and inconsequential, as if it would scarcely increase the height of the wall if he pasted it in. And he would look down, all the way down, and wonder whether he shouldn't just throw his rock over the edge and onto the indifferent ground below and, seeing it collapse into a million grains of sand, throw himself after it.

Staffing Services

Graham was sitting uncomfortably, shifting between buttocks as if he was suffering from piles and couldn't risk both cheeks coming into simultaneous contact with the chair. On his left was a senior member of the Trust personnel. She was smiling at Darren, a kind of mouth-only smile which hadn't asked her eyes to join in the fun. Graham had cleared his throat approximately ten times already. Whatever was in there was going to take some shifting. He looked at Darren and then back at the personnel woman, cleared his throat one more time for luck and took the plunge.

'Darren, this is, er, Joanne King from Staffing Services, who is going—'

'Hello,' Darren said, cutting Graham off. He could see where this was heading, so he might as well enjoy himself while he could. Graham hated being interrupted, which was unfortunate given that he rarely made any meaningful progress with any of his sentences.

Graham glowered at Darren, and then attempted a smile. 'Joanne, and I, of course, which is not to say that we didn't both agree to this . . . this meeting together, as one, as it were,' he rambled, 'have asked you here today, this morning, at tenish, to, er, to . . .' Graham looked helplessly over at Joanne.

'Er, yes.' Joanne picked up the thread and tried to disentangle it. 'Darren, I'm here because Professor Barnes has had some discussions with myself and other members of Staffing Services with regard to your current employment within the Trust.' Darren nodded while Graham traced his fingers along the edge of his desk, following wooden veins as they parted around knots in its surface like water flowing around rocks. 'I think I can speak for Professor Barnes,' Graham nodded vigorously, 'when I say that your time here hasn't been without its troubles and that progress hasn't been particularly forthcoming.'

Progress. What did either of them know about progress? Darren wondered. Minutiae were all that they knew. Progress on a tiny scale. 'Mmm,' he replied, non-committally. He would take his verbal warning gracefully. And then he would show them progress.

'Now, the situation is that you still have nearly a year to run on your contract, and as you will be aware if you have read the contract document thoroughly, each successive year is dependent on, and I quote,' Joanne moved her pen down to a passage Darren could see highlighted amongst many other uninviting chunks of text, '"sufficient progress brackets intellectual and/or with regard to the accrual of data of scientific interest close brackets as agreed, in cases of arbitration, between the senior scientific investigator and the Trust staffing services . . ."'

The bastards! They were going to fire him! No verbal or written warning, they were going to simply tell him to fuck off. 'But,' Darren blurted, 'I'm entitled to warnings, surely, a verbal or written warning – you can't just sack me.'

Joanne glanced at Graham, who looked away. 'You *have* received a written warning, have you not, Darren?'

'No,' he replied.

'Well, we sent you one,' she said.

This was entirely possible. Darren hadn't been opening his mail for a good eight weeks now, just to save time. But he certainly hadn't had a verbal warning. Not one he was aware of anyway. 'Look, maybe I've been sent a written warning, but I certainly haven't had a verbal one.'

'Professor Barnes assures me that you have.' Darren watched him fidget. 'Graham?'

'Well, Darren and I did have a word or two, a few actually, to be more specific, when was it now, it would have been at the beginning or thereabouts of last month, I think, or maybe the end of the month previous to that . . .' Once again, Graham felt he had done a sentence justice and left it just hanging there with nowhere to go.

Darren racked what was left of his brain but couldn't recall any such occasion. 'I don't remember.'

After a lengthy pause, Joanne prompted Graham. 'Professor Barnes?'

'Er . . . well, you know, we had a chat, more of a discussion really, here, in my office, or in the lab . . .'

'And what exactly did you say to me?'

'I, er, told you, informed you, well, made you aware, shall we say, in one sense at least . . . I hoped I was quite clear . . .'

Darren glanced at Joanne, who momentarily raised her eyebrows in solidarity, before quickly resuming her permasmile. 'So, it would appear that you have in fact had your two statutory warnings . . .'

'A matter of opinion . . .'

'And therefore the Trust is within its employment remit in giving you one month's notice of the termination of your contract. Do you have anything you wish to say?'

Darren just sat and stared at Graham's fingers as they played along the worn surface of his desk. Sacked. Just like that. Ten minutes ago, a job. Now, nothing. Wankers. Bastards. 'Fuckers,' he said out loud, surprising himself slightly as he did so. Graham and Joanne also looked a little taken aback. It wasn't a conscious act, it was just a symptom of the difficulty he was having these days in keeping his thoughts and words from mingling. Joanne got up to leave but Darren couldn't move. She walked past him and smiled again. Graham sat and fiddled and cleared his throat from time to time. Darren sensed he was going to say something so got up and left the building, refusing to see out his month's notice on the grounds that he could fake his work just as easily at home, and without the misery of having to turn up at the Institute every day.

A Better Life

First Track of the Day: 'Unfinished Sympathy' *by Massive Attack*

My bell doesn't work. Hopefully, my bell doesn't work. This is the irony for me. I sit around all day in Neuro waiting for deliveries to come, and when they come, I don't want them. Except his deliveries, of course. But generally they just mean more drudgery, hassle, people to phone, delivery notes to process. And here I am at home, actually wanting the door to open, wanting a man to come through, wanting . . .

Spent the day trying to feel sorry, but never quite completing. A large offensive of incomplete empathy. The first boy I kissed who got run over and I never saw again. The troublesome young dog I had as a child which Dad sent off to a better life on a farm somewhere. Aunt Susan who had to have a breast removed and then stopped visiting. A long day, but satisfying somehow in a pleasurable suffering sort of way. Concluded for the first time in adulthood that there is genuine joy to be had from making yourself feel upset over things which don't really upset you. That or my period is due sooner than I had calculated.

Felt drained by the time I got home. Sat down for a

bit and then started to get ready. Seven thirty he said. Worked my way through the machines of preparation. The shower. The hairdryer. The clock. The iron. The stereo. The clock. The hairdryer again. The clock again. The television. More television. One more bout under the hairdryer. The clock almost permanently. Finally, picked up the telephone. Seemed to be connected OK. Put the receiver down carefully, making sure I replaced it correctly. Looked from several angles, just to make sure. Nothing. No knock at the door, no phone call. Poured myself a drink and tried to relax. No pleasurable suffering any more, just suffering. Bastard, I said out loud. No-one is an hour late, not even me. Kicked my shoes off and began to feel sorry for myself. And he had seemed so keen. This is probably typical of my powers of observation. Started to run myself down as I poured another measure. A long sorry day. And who would have thought it would be me I ended up feeling sorry for? Messed my hair up, lit a cigarette and thought about that boisterous dog of mine. Mum told me a few months ago that it had never been anywhere near a farm. Dad had taken it straight to the vet's. Bastard, I said, again. The days I passed as a kid imagining my dog frolicking through field after field of open space, tail wagging, barking at live-stock . . .

Clinical

It is nearly raining, and my leather jacket feels slippery. I try to see my watch but it is much too dark. The downstairs light goes out. I reach in between two buttons of my glistening jacket and stroke the slim metal scalpel in my inside pocket. That such a delicate implement can do so much harm, and, under different circumstances, so much good. It doesn't feel dangerous though – it feels ridiculously like a toothbrush, given its enlarged, protected head and slender body. I retract my hand and ready myself, trying to catch my breath, waiting for the landing light to go off like a visual starting pistol. The light stays on. I need to piss again, and once more treat the hedge to a generous watering. Still the landing light remains on. What is the old cunt doing? Then the plumbing provides the answer, as water sluices through pipes from somewhere at the top right of the house. There is too much water for a toilet flush. He has been taking a bath. What the hell is wrong with showers, I feel like shouting. They are economical, refreshing and, most importantly, should you ever find yourself standing uneasily in the half-darkness in a cold, damp garden, they are quick.

Although I am ready, I realize I mustn't rush. Everything must be planned and clinical. I smile as I think of the word. Clinical. Pertaining to medicine. Clinical. Analytical, Business-like, Cold, Detached. This is what The Cunt instilled in his students. His ABCD of medicine. Analytical, Businesslike, Cold, Detached. It had a rhythm all of its own. You could rap it if you really wanted. Analytical, Businesslike, Cold, Detached. It summed up all that was wrong with medicine and The Cunt. It was medicine without care, patients without patience, cardiology without heart.

I count out five minutes under my breath, as slowly as I can, which probably takes around sixty seconds, and then count another similarly abridged period to be on the safe side. This is still not enough. I decide to count breaths instead, which will take longer, and manage sixty empty inhalations, each one through cold, anxious lungs, with sixty accompanying exhalations, individually terse and unsatisfying, as if I'm trying to blow up a burst balloon.

I am willing to bet the fucker sleeps soundly and deeply, his conscience clear, his mind peaceful and empty. But even if he tosses and turns all night and takes an eternity to fidget himself into unconsciousness, I have to act quickly. My nerve won't hold for ever. The longer I stand on his lawn breathing myself to death, the easier it will be to turn away and meander back to the station to catch the last train, scalpel safely sheathed, respiration turning from shallow whispers of retribution to deep sighing breaths of defeat, the lunacy ebbing, the bitterness softening. I count out another minute and step out from the shadow of the towering hedge, taking the scalpel and a pair of surgical gloves out of my pocket. I struggle my sweaty hands into the dry powdered latex gloves and unsheathe the scalpel. I plant it handle first into the grass beneath one of the side windows of the house. It is important to keep the blade clean. I hold the sheath, which is composed of several thick layers of wide brown parcel tape, in my hand. I unwind the tape from the outside of the sheath and, as each length emerges, stick it onto the glass of the waist-high window. After a couple of minutes, during which the tape seems more interested in adhering to my gloves than to the glass, I manage to fill a portion of the window with horizontal brown strips of tape. I hunt around for a small stone, and finding one, position it in front of the newly covered area of window. I give the glass a swift tap and then wait for ten or so jittery seconds. Nothing. No-one stirs. The lights remain off. I examine my handiwork. The stone made a surprisingly subdued, blunt sort of noise as it smashed the window, and the glass, unable to escape from the adhesion of the tape, held firm. I begin to carefully peel the tape away from the window, to reveal a small but perfectly formed hole through which I can reach my arm and undo the latch. I stop again to listen and then pluck the scalpel from the lawn. The window proves easy to enter and as I clamber through I find myself on top of a work surface strewn with a plethora of unclean plates, mugs, cutlery, pans, glasses and saucers. This is good. His wife must be away. And the lazy bastard, for all his airs and graces, has been living like a fucking student. I step around the clutter and jump quietly down onto the ceramic floor. Inside the kitchen, I flick my Maglight on and follow its thin beam around the room until I find the doorknob. The door opens quietly and I make my way to the foot of the stairs, clutching the metallic handle of the scalpel hard enough to be able to feel the indentations on its surface with my palm.

Results

Something Ticking

October 1998

In bed, with the duvet wrapped around and under him,
as if he's the meat in a sausage roll, Darren tries to clear
his head. He orders a shutdown of all conscious
thought, but it only comes reluctantly. He closes his
eyes and imagines he is in a cave. It is howling with
rain outside, but he has a warm cosy bed where the
cold can't touch him. He is safe and bulletproof and
the womb of the cave lulls Darren into semi-
consciousness. But through the calm a sound starts to
chip away at the rock of the cave. It is a regular and
constant chipping. He tries to ignore it, but the hammering continues. The cave wall becomes eggshell thin
and he no longer feels safe. Darren opens his eyes and
looks in the direction of the noise. He sees the luminous dial of his alarm clock and realizes that its ticking
is disrupting his calm. He listens to it and hears
patterns in its disquiet. There is ticking within the ticking and, as Darren focuses in, he even hears ticking in
the cracks between ticks. He can also hear the second
hand move its stuttering way around the luminous
face, and its movement seems somehow out of phase
with the symphony of clicking, tapping and beating

which drives it. Darren tries to ignore the clock, but he realizes that you can't *try* to ignore something – you either ignore it or you don't. Trying doesn't come in to it. It is like trying not to care about something. If you are trying, then, by definition, you are caring. The ticking continues, relentless and unfeeling. He untucks himself, picks the alarm clock up and shakes it. It continues to mock him. He shakes it harder. It ticks louder. Darren can think of no way of stopping it, as it has no batteries, so he wraps it in a jumper and takes it into the kitchen. He gets back into bed and begs his ears not to go searching for the sound, but they don't listen to him. They quickly track it down – a barely audible ticking which says fuck-you, fuck-you, fuck-you, fuck-you. He is losing his patience. He gets out of bed and goes to the kitchen, where the noise reverberates around the unfriendly surfaces. He takes the clock out of its swaddling towel. It is Hammer Time. He gets his claw hammer from the cupboard and smashes it into the face at an acute angle, claw end first. After three or four blows Darren hits springs, and knows he has it on the ropes. It limps on, just ticking now, the tocking having ceased for ever, slowly counting out its demise with its own broken hands. Two more attacks and its heart stops beating. Darren leaves the broken clock, goes into the bathroom and opens the cabinet. There are several bottles of various sizes, shapes and colours, and with variously cluttered labels. Some are open, others are still packaged in Delta plastic bubble wrap. He surveys them, thinking, but then changes his mind and returns to bed. He takes the hammer with him, just in case the clock is playing dead.

Back in bed, Darren wraps himself up again and tries to return to the cave. But something is very wrong. He can still hear ticking. Again, his ears have gone hunting and have found what they were looking for. He wonders whether there's something in his room, and realizes suddenly that it must be his watch. He picks it up and places it against his ear. It is digital, but it is certainly ticking. This doesn't seem entirely logical. He puts it in a pair of socks and puts the socks in a drawer. Darren closes his eyes but the noise is still there saying fuck-you, fuck-you, fuck-you. Understandably, he has had enough of being mocked by a digital watch. He takes the pair of socks out of the drawer and, without asking any questions, smashes it repeatedly with the hammer. It is not as satisfying an experience as smashing the clock, as the socks soak up most of the hammer impact, but he still enjoys it. After all, he reasons, he can buy another digital watch from a garage for £1.99, and one which probably won't tick. Darren climbs into bed, but as soon as he puts his head on the pillow, he hears the noise again. It is still there. It is everywhere. Darren tries to pin it down, but wherever he walks around the bedroom, it follows him. The ticking is omnipresent. He can stand it no longer. He puts his fingers into his ears to block the noise which is chipping away at him, but it just gets louder. Darren removes his fingers from his ears and it subsides. He tries again – the same thing. He reaches a startling conclusion. This is really bad, worse than he could have imagined. The ticking is coming from inside his head. He returns to the bathroom cabinet and pours a small quantity of powder from a random bottle into a glass of water and drinks it.

Waiting Room

Darren made an appointment the next morning. He had to, he could have gone off at any moment. Your head doesn't just tick for no reason. He had figured it out during the night. He knew he was taking a risk with the lives of the other patients in the surgery, but he didn't want to add to their worries by telling them the truth. They looked nervous enough as it was, worrying that their symptoms might disappear before they had a chance to show them, or that their illnesses might overwhelm them so they would expire before even getting a chance to see a doctor. Darren understood such things, having been in waiting rooms before, and he knew that it was no fun. You sit there, fingering the token that says you are Blue eleven, trying to guess what everyone else is in for, wondering why doctors aren't perpetually ill, flicking halfheartedly through *Woman's Own* and getting mildly embarrassed by a two-page special on thrush, watching the officious receptionists filing cards and insisting on the phone that no, Dr Jameson can't see you till Wednesday, while the warm moist air infused with disinfectant slowly closes in around you.

Darren sat as far away from other people, particularly women and children, as he could, just in case he went off. On the way there, he had been cautious not to move his head around any more than necessary. The ticking was as plain as day, which was good, because he realized that the doctor might have a bit of difficulty hearing it through his skull. Darren certainly didn't want the doctor thinking he was a nutter or anything.

Buzzer number eleven sounded, briefly and impatiently, and Darren headed carefully down the corridor to a door with a blue light illuminated above it. He knocked and entered without waiting for a 'Come in'. By now the ticking was so loud that he was having difficulty hearing anything else.

'Ah, Mr White,' the doctor said, looking up from a folder in front of him.

'Dr White,' Darren corrected him as he sat down, quickly wishing he had kept his mouth shut.

'*Doctor?*' He looked at Darren, not entirely convinced. 'Are you clinical?'

'No, Ph.D., I'm afrai—'

'Thought not,' the doctor muttered, opening the medical record on his desk. He was squat and broad and for a second Darren pictured him playing scrumhalf for his medical school. He was relatively young, or maybe Darren was just relatively old, and had a brusque, no-nonsense manner which might have made him a good bus driver. 'What can I do for you then?' he asked.

'Look, I know what you're going to think of me, and that's fair enough,' the doctor looked up from Darren's notes, suddenly interested, 'but I think, that is, I know . . .'

'Yes?'

'It's driving me mad, and maybe you shouldn't get too close, maybe you should call the police or the bomb squad or something . . .'

'Bomb squad?' the doctor asked, raising his eyebrows. 'Look, what *is* the matter?'

'I've got a bomb in my head!'

'A what?'

'A bomb.'

'Oh.' The doctor regarded Darren with momentarily raised eyebrows, then started looking through his record in more detail. Having failed to find anything which might explain this pronouncement he sighed and rested his chin on his right thumb with his fist obscuring his mouth. 'A bomb, eh? And what makes you think you've got a bomb inside your head?' he asked, uninterested.

Darren sensed where this was heading and knew he had to convince him. 'I can hear it ticking, as loud as anything.'

The doctor fiddled with a biro on his desk. Somewhere along the line he had obviously taught himself how to twist a pen through a horizontal 360 degrees around the tip of his thumb. It was quite a good trick and Darren watched him for a few seconds, wishing that he could do it. 'Hmmm,' he said between revolutions, 'loud, you say?'

'Yes. Like I'm talking to you now, that loud.'

He stopped fiddling. 'And wouldn't you think that if it's as loud in your head as our voices, that I would be able to hear it?'

'You mean you can't?' Darren asked, exasperated. This really wasn't going well at all.

'Not from here,' the doctor replied, twiddling again. This time he switched to a new trick. Holding the end of the pen loosely between his thumb and finger by its blunt end, and letting the nib end hang down, he flipped the pen through 360 vertical degrees, caught it in its original position, and then proceeded to repeat the manoeuvre. This wouldn't have been the least bit diverting, were it not for the rapidity with which he could flick the pen through a full circle and catch it ready for the next revolution. The first trick was skilful, but this one was a feat of exquisite timing. Darren was sick with jealousy, and made a note to buy a pen on the way home and practise on the bus.

'Maybe if you came a bit closer,' Darren suggested, trying to swallow his envy, 'and used your stethoscope.'

'I'm not sure that would . . .'

'Look, you're treating me like some sort of care in the community case.' The doctor's indifference, coupled with his pen prowess, was really pissing Darren off. 'I mean, you're putting people's lives at risk here – I could go off at any minute!'

The doctor looked up from his pen, his eyebrows again giving the game away. 'OK. I think I just might have the thing for you,' he said, guiding his pen into writing mode and pulling a pad out of his drawers.

'A fucking prescription? What the hell's that going to do for me?' Darren shouted. 'I need defusing! And soon!'

Wheel of Fortune

Darren sat and stared through the fourteen-inch black-and-white portable, as if it was some sort of gateway to a fuzzy land of contentment and opportunity. It was an old and jaded set which had seen too much mediocrity in its twenty or so years and had decided to liven things up by haunting every figure appearing on its dusty screen with a shadowy ghost. The television and Darren had reached an agreement during their formative weeks together. Darren wouldn't fiddle with its aerial and the TV wouldn't drift between frames or flick through channels of its own accord. This arrangement seemed to work fairly well, especially when Darren didn't want to watch anything, which was most of the time. For sitting and staring purposes though, it was ideal.

Wheel of Fortune. A miserable game on the best of days. Darren tried not to watch by looking through the façade and into the promise of the unfocused world beyond, but there it was all the same, mocking his existence. Turns of the game read like months of his life. Two hundred pounds. Miss a turn. A hundred pounds. Bad luck. Just missed the £1000. Lose a turn. Three hundred. That's more like it, mate. Go on, gamble, have another spin. Go on. What've you got to lose, eh? Bust.

What a shame, old son. Game over, I'm afraid. Still, you've won a free *Wheel of Fortune* umbrella to keep the rain from falling on you. Hang on, I don't understand. What do you mean it's always raining *upwards* in your life?

There was a tentative knock on the hollow door. This was most unwelcome. Darren looked at the video display: 12:00, as always. His neck hurt. He must have slept. He ignored the knock and thought about climbing into bed. Maybe he would sleep on the sofa instead. It seemed a perilously long journey to the bedroom. Another knock, bolder this time. Couldn't they tell that he was busy? Darren thought about answering. Bed or company? Bed was looking the best bet. Not that he would sleep, but at least it meant he didn't have to face anybody. A big crash. He looked up. The door was open, the frame gaping and splintered. Four youths of variously poor posture stood in the doorway, surprise and curiosity freezing their faces. One by one, they straightened slightly. They were fifteen, at most, but looked as if they had lived a good deal more years than they had on the clock. They stood and stared at Darren. Their uncertainty began to evaporate as he sat and stared back at them. The shortest and nastiest-looking youth took a couple of tentative steps forwards, pulling his shoulders back and puffing his chest for all its worth through his ghetto jacket.

'Deaf are ya, cock?' he asked, grinning back at his gang, who feigned confidence and took a couple of steps forwards to join him.

'No,' Darren replied, distantly. 'I didn't want to be disturbed.'

'I don't think it's polite not to answer the door,' the youth persevered. He was trembling slightly.

'Don't you? And just what—'

'No, I don',' the youth interrupted.

'No, me neither.' A similarly attired and younger-looking accomplice joined in the fun. The two other youths surveyed the mess that was Darren's room. He was aware that they were looking at his TV.

Short, quick words to hide the tremor in his voice. 'D'you think it's polite to kick my door in then?' Darren wanted it to sound authoritative, but instead it came out like a mild question of ethics.

'Dunno.'

'I'm sure you don't.' Flight. Fright. Fight. Darren's endogenous adrenalin was kicking in. He looked towards the bathroom, wishing he had time to get some of the liquid stuff inside his veins as well. He clenched his fists on the arm rests of the chair, feeling his fingers slide across sweaty palms, and his biceps engorge and pulse. The two more confident youths conferred, terse, quick, whispered words. Clearly they couldn't just withdraw, and maybe they could see that Darren was scared. One of the quieter duo, who had the outfit of an athlete and the body of an invalid, slouched over to the TV, traced its lead back to the wall, and pulled the plug out.

Darren used to imagine as a child, youth and maybe sometimes as an adult that he had ten secret vials of power, vials that only lasted a minute, but a minute in which he was invincible. Ten vials equalled a life's supply, so he had to choose carefully when to use them. This was part of the excitement – deciding when things were serious enough to merit consuming a vial of invincibility, and then having just sixty seconds to finish everyone off and to escape. And here he was, with several unopened vials of adrenalin in his bathroom cabinet. The literature he had read suggested that consuming adrenalin neat was not a particularly safe thing to do, and should in any case only be performed by intramuscular injection. Despite this, Darren couldn't help thinking that the answer to the present circumstances might lie in his bathroom cabinet.

'Right, Sad Bloke,' the confident one said, smirking at his friends and bringing Darren back to the reality of the situation, 'sit y'sen there, and you'll be as right as rain.' Darren surmised that Sad Bloke must be his nickname in the flats. The confident one gestured over to the barely upright one. 'Jonno,' Jonno looked at him with horror, 'get the fucking telly.'

'But . . .' Jonno protested.

'Shite,' said the confident one, realizing his mistake. They weren't going to make career criminals by announcing their names at the scenes of their crimes. 'Just get the fuckin' box,' he snapped. 'Now,' he said, turning back to Darren, 'any shite from you and we'll be back. Right?'

Darren stared at him, continuing to mine his fingernails into his palms. He could take him, easily. And the other fuckers. Kids. Fucking kids. Just take care of the confident one and the rest would scatter. Humiliate the ringleader and the ring would collapse in on itself. Darren was still trembling, but trembling through ready muscles. One good square punch in the face and he would run home to his mother, salty tears running down his bum-fluff cheeks. Cheeky cunts. And the state of the fucking door frame. The ringleader took another couple of paces towards Darren, who could see fear in his eyes. He too was trembling, but barely perceptibly, under the baggy clothes which did much to disguise his physique. Probably a skinny runt under his arseless jeans. Darren could see his fear wasn't much to do with him though. It was the fear of not confronting him, the fear of losing the respect of his group, of backing down from the situation he found himself in. This made him more dangerous. But for Darren, the fear was also a fear of judgement. He was being judged by society, specifically, by male society. He was letting a small group of acned pale skinny fucking children intimidate him. Darren was a man. He was being bullied not by some weightlifting thick-neck but by kids. A primal, hierarchical, territorial surge of dominance snapped Darren's jaws together. He bored into the ringleader's eyes, ready.

'Right?' the youth demanded again.

Right, Darren thought. He sprang up from his chair . . . and then stopped. Something was wrong. He rocked back into the seat. He was numb and unfocused. He must have hit his head on something. Darren felt his face. It was cold, wet and dead, as if he was dribbling in the dentist's chair after an injection. He focused. The youth was standing over him, fist coiled back under his shoulder, ready.

'Right?' This time there was urgency.

Darren touched his nose and looked at his fingers. They were red with something. Blood, it must be blood. He felt his face again. He had been hit. The fucking kid had hit him. Darren tried to stand up and instantly felt his head rock back again. There was an uncomfortable scraping feeling in his mouth as his teeth jarred against each other in a way they weren't meant to.

'Right?' the youth screamed. 'Right, Sad Bloke?'

Darren's jaw didn't quite move like it used to and his teeth felt numb – as if they were normally highly sensory, but had suddenly been stripped of all their nerve endings. He moved his mouth, which seemed to have lost some of its control. 'Rie,' he muttered.

'Right,' the ringleader said, withdrawing his fist. He gave Darren a curiously pitying look. That it had come to this – to be pitied by a fucking teenager. Darren shut his eyes and listened to the shuffling trainers and the sound of the plug of his TV dragging along the floor. Kids. Fucking kids. This was the ultimate paranoia of society – when society is afraid of its own children. He opened his eyes and the door stood open, the flat empty, the cunts having slouched off, probably to throw his TV off the top floor, using some unsuspecting sod below as target practice.

Darren just sat and sat and stared and stared at the space previously occupied by his fuzzy TV. He tried to align his upper and lower rows of teeth as they used to be, lower incisors sitting snugly up behind upper incisors, canines much the same and molars and pre-molars intermeshing, peaks into troughs and troughs into peaks. But the geography had been changed. Certainly, no teeth were broken or chipped even, so it couldn't be the teeth themselves. It was probably the ligaments of his jaw. He tried talking out loud and had some difficulty, so stopped, which was just as well because he felt a bit of a twat, sitting and watching an empty space, swearing unclearly, bleeding and shivering, with the door of his flat flapping around on one hinge. Numbness had given way to an all-defeating depression. Darren decided he should shut the door, but the black hole sucking the light out of his skull was so intense that he could only sit and stare at it in pathetic discomfort. After twenty minutes he summoned sufficient enthusiasm to stand up, and then to slouch over to the door and wedge it shut with a screwdriver jammed into the side opposite the broken hinge. There wasn't much else to be had from the flat, but now that they'd been introduced to each other, Darren's visitors might feel inclined to call back some time, so he dragged his empty bookcase across the room and placed it flat against the base of the door. It was by no means impenetrable, and would mean stepping between the empty vertical shelves if he wanted to cross the room, but it would at least slow them down should they choose to drop by again.

Darren went to the bathroom and had a look at himself from several different angles. His nose was swollen and bloody from the front, but OK from the sides, he was disfigured in one direction only, which wasn't as bad as it could have been. The bridge held firm when he tried to waggle it between thumb and forefinger, so he guessed that it wasn't broken. This was slightly disappointing, as there is little point enduring eye-watering pain if you have nothing to show for it. A broken nose would certainly carry some credibility. 'Yeah, six of the fuckers, massive fuckers, broke my nose when I told the cunts there was no way they were having my telly.' Intact as Darren was though, there was little to salvage from the situation. He tried to figure out just why his jaw wouldn't do what he told it, but could get no further than a vague stab at some sort of muscle problem. He felt like a footballer whose leg hurts and who invariably receives the touchline diagnosis of having 'ligament problems', even if the leg has quite clearly been broken off at the knee. Darren moved his lower jaw from side to side and felt an uncomfortable clicking just below his right ear. It wasn't much fun waggling his jaw but he continued to do it, watching himself in the mirror, making himself angry, ridiculing his own gormless slack-jawed countenance, chanting 'Sad' as he moved his jaw right and 'Bloke' as he moved it left, trying to provoke himself into anger rather than defeat. He wanted revenge rather than acceptance. He wanted prejudice rather than understanding. Suddenly there was banging at the door. This was it. The fuckers were back. Darren walked into the kitchen. Every film he had ever seen told him that he should open the cutlery drawer. The banging was louder this time. Darren entered the lounge and stood with his legs apart, feet between adjacent shelves of his bookcase. The knife had a heavy balance about it which felt good in his hand. This time the knocking was close. Hollow bangs echoed around the cold surfaces of the flat. Darren watched the broken door handle turn. He fingered the notches on the handle of his knife. This was it. He hoped he would have time to maim them before he was overpowered. The door was being forced open. He stood firm and the shelves of the bookcase pressed against his legs.

'Oi! Sad Bloke.' A voice breached the door.

Darren didn't answer. He looked down at the knife. The longest one he could find. A black plastic handle housing an eight-inch blade, serrated on its lower surface.

'Sad Bloke! For fuck's sake, let us in.'

He was in charge. He had the weapon. It was time to let them know. 'Fuck off. Just fuck off,' he shouted back. The knife had changed the balance of power. 'Fuck off, you pathetic little cunts. Or I'm going to come outside and fuck you over.'

The door was pushed more violently. Darren held firm. 'Sad Bloke, come on, open up for Christ's sake, I've got your telly.'

Of course the fuckers had his TV – they'd stolen it from him less than an hour ago. 'Look, just piss off and leave me alone,' Darren shouted back through the six-inch opening in the door. The tremor in his voice was still there, in command though he was, and try as he might he couldn't stop it rattling his vocal cords slightly. 'Or there'll be trouble,' he added, as menacingly as the panic which was slowly consuming his voice would allow. I have a weapon, he told himself, and I am in control.

'Look, Jesus,' there was an exasperated pause, 'not only are you sad, you're thick as shit as well. Just let me in, for fuck's sake, 'cos it's cold out here and I've got your telly.' And then, after another pause, 'It's Sam.'

Sam? Sam? Oh fuck. Sam. As if things could get any worse than they already were. Jesus, Sam. Darren thought he'd better check, just to be on the safe side. After all, with a bit of luck, it might just be the violent bastards from earlier, playing some sort of nightmarish trick on him. 'Sam who?' he asked, crossing the fingers of his knife-free left hand.

'Sam. You know, Sam. Sam Hendry. Sam from uni. Come on, Daz, I'm frozen.'

Bugger, it was him. Darren shut his eyes and exhaled slowly. He cursed and stepped out of the bookshelf. 'Push,' he shouted, and the bookcase slid harmlessly across the carpet as the door was eased open. Sam was standing in the doorway, big and crazy, curly dark hair, glasses, Darren's portable under one arm, a rolled-up sleeping bag under the other and a rucksack on his back. Another bugger. He was coming to stay.

'About fucking time,' he complained, dumping his luggage on the floor and giving the flat a cursory inspection. 'Jesus, what a mess,' he said, turning to face Darren.

'Well, obviously I would have tidied up if—'

'No, you. You're a mess. A right mess. And what the fuck were you hoping to do with that thing?'

Darren looked down at the knife that was going to level the score, and let the handle droop impotently between his index finger and thumb. He replied quietly and a little self-consciously, 'Oh, teach a few kids a lesson.'

Sam continued to stare at the knife. 'What, with a fucking *bread* knife?'

Darren realized it must look a bit daft, swinging there between his fingers, and felt a little foolish. 'Yeah, but . . .'

'And what lesson might that be exactly? How to slice

bread? The lost art of sandwich-making? What, were you hoping to *bore* them to death? Jesus, it looks like I've saved you making a right twat of yourself.'

'Look, it was the biggest one I could find.'

'I think you're missing the point. Which is exactly what that thing,' Sam said, nodding in the direction of the knife, 'is missing – a fucking point. You can't stab anyone with a bread knife, any more than you can slice bread with a hunting knife.'

Darren turned around and put the knife back in the kitchen drawer. Holding on to it would just maintain Sam's momentum, for he would never let a squabble die if he could help it. Often, by prolonging the debate well past its natural conclusion, he would end up losing, but for Sam, it wasn't so much winning a dispute as sustaining it that mattered. Consequently, arguing with him, particularly when you were on the defensive, was somewhat of a pisser. Darren returned to the lounge. 'So how come you've got my telly?'

'Offered it for a tenner by a bunch of scallies on my way up.'

Darren's jaw was hurting and his words sounded as if someone else was saying them, but he persevered. 'Bow dew no in twos my?'

'What?'

He concentrated on the movement of his lacklustre jaw. 'But how d'you know it was mine?'

'I asked them where they'd got it and they said the Sad Bloke in number twenty-nine. Seemed a bit chuffed with themselves.'

'And?'

'Well, I grabbed it off 'em and gave one of the skinny runts a clout. Ran off almost in tears. Surprised you didn't do the same.'

Darren changed the subject. 'So how come you're here?'

Paper

'Got a call from Owen, said you've gone a bit loopy, told him I'd come over and look after you.'

Darren's heart sank. To be looked after by Sam was like being invited round to the Hitlers' for a lampshade-making evening. Or something. But it wasn't very good.

Flat

Sam began to quiz Darren about his current status, or apparent lack of. It was painful for Darren because it meant telling the truth. It's usually OK justifying things to yourself, but justifying them to someone else and doing so out loud, listening as your own unconvincing words struggle over the sentences which harbour the harsh realities of your life, is another matter altogether. But he had to tell Sam everything, just to hear it for himself. As Darren talked, he tried to listen as an impartial observer might listen to his story, letting words spray uncensored out of his mouth and into the damp air of the flat. Darren told him about his gentle academic firing after months of neglect, about his ideas (he glossed over these to spare Sam's short attention span), of how he had been ineligible for mortgage relief for thirteen weeks following his departure from work, about how he'd spent his slim life savings during his first few weeks of unemployment, about how forty pounds a week isn't enough to live on, about the heavy mortgage sapping his funds, about the only reasonable course of action Darren had if he was going to keep his house which was to rent it out and live somewhere shit until he sorted himself out, about how he couldn't sort himself out until he had worked through his ideas,

133

which were becoming less and less sortable every day, about how his whole life was in danger of slipping through his fingers while he was powerless to close them . . . Darren told Sam everything, and a sorry tale it proved to be. After he had finished, Sam was quiet for a few moments, which generally would have been a blessing, but now just gave Darren's words time to envelop him with their blackness. What about your furniture and stuff, Sam asked eventually. Rented the house as furnished, Darren told him. But this place is shit, he said. I know, Darren replied. So how much is it saving you? Eighty pounds a week. Almost worth it, he said. What about your parents, won't they help you? he asked. Skint themselves. Suggested I move back with them. Sam inhaled. Bit of a mess really, he sighed. Mmm, Darren agreed, adding it's amazing how quickly you can fall through everything. Especially if you've lost it, Sam interjected. But Sam, I haven't lost it, Darren said. I'm on the verge of finding it. Something big, something important. Bollocks, Sam said getting up and nosing around the flat, occasionally tutting as he did so.

Darren sat and drank. Sam unpacked his things as he swigged from a can. An inky depression leaked into Darren's thinking. He drank quickly and deeply, and the depression edged towards anger. Eventually, he stood up and became quite animated. 'Look, Sam,' he said, 'I wanted to suffer, I wanted to fall. Can't you see the torture of just hanging by a thread all the time? Afraid of the next day and the day after that? Wishing days away until your wages come, always paid at the end of the month, the carrot always held just out of reach, forcing you to rush days like meals before play-time? I wanted to burn out, to have a glorious flight to the sun, to be alive, to be on fire, nerves blazing, muscles pulsing, eyes wide and staring, fists clenched, head buzzing, heart thumping . . . I wanted to explode. I wanted to come up with the theory to end all theories, and I still will. And then, when I've done my job, death. I want to die, to live gloriously and then die. I want to be a fly emerging from my pupal bed on a sunny day, feeling the warmth of the sun on my back, hot air rushing through my spiracles, blood thinning, wings drying and opening, colours alight . . . I mean, what do we know about being alive? About being truly alive? We're tepid, diluted, half-hearted, stagnant, idle. I mean, we're so fucking sluggish that we can't even *imagine* how it might feel to be truly alive, like a housefly with a nervous system ten times quicker than our own, or a leopard in the chase, or a humming bird feeding on the wing or . . . or anything that is actually alive, truly alive. I want to feel like that, to give everything, and then, well, OK, I'll live with the consequences.'

Sam sat in silence. Darren returned the TV to its rightful place, switched it on and resumed the diversion of staring through it.

'Bit dramatic, that,' Sam said eventually, before unrolling his sleeping bag and lying down in front of the TV. After a while he stood up again and walked over to his rucksack. 'Anyway, I brought you a present. It's not exactly free, but it may be the very thing you need right now. Have a play, see what you think.'

Undeleted

Darren prised the grubby laptop open and ran his fingers over its well-worn keys. 'What's the catch?' he asked.

'Two hundred quid,' Sam said. 'Otherwise I'm taking it back tomorrow.'

'Where did you get it?'

'Mate of mine is getting a more powerful one – just wants rid of it. But someone else is interested – said he'd give you first shout.'

A couple of hours later Darren offered Sam a hundred and seventy pounds for the computer, and began to see what it could do. A computer, he realized, could virtually write his theory for him. He could get back on track, start to make sense of everything again. Computer memories, after all, rarely disappear up their own arses.

Owning someone else's computer is a bit like moving into their house after they have left. Remnants of their occupancy live on – pale squares highlighted by dusty borders where pictures once hung, and stains on the carpet which you couldn't see under strategically placed chests of drawers. But unlike moving house, it is possible to summons back the previous occupant's furniture long after they have departed.

Computers rarely delete anything, even if you ask them to. It might *tell* you it's been deleted, but under cross-examination you will find that it has done nothing of the sort and has merely swept your dusty junk under the nearest carpet it could find. In this way, the ghosts of pictures and chests of drawers long since removed and dumped can be brought back to life.

And this is just what Darren did the following morning with his newly acquired laptop. He went looking for recently deleted files and simply selected them to be undeleted. Whatever that meant. To his surprise, there were hundreds and hundreds of files, all in one directory called Paper, all roughly the same size, and occupying a grand total of 800 megs of disk space. Darren highlighted the files, said, 'Fuck it' and undeleted them. The light of his hard drive flashed like a particularly frenetic and inconsistent firefly. He stood up and went to the window, and realizing there was nothing to be gained from the exercise, went and sat down again. File names appeared, were undeleted and then stacked up alphabetically. This took a little time and so Darren walked over to Sam's cocooned form and kicked him somewhere, he hoped, around the midriff.

'So what does this mate of yours do?' he asked.

Sam coughed and generally ignored the question. He hadn't scheduled to be awake for at least another couple of hours, and when he did so, it would be without the aid of a kick in the shoulder. What mate, anyway?

'What mate?' he grumbled from the inside of his sleeping bag.

Darren sighed. 'Your mate that sold me this PC.'

He stole computers, obviously, you twat. Maybe that wouldn't be the best response. Sam feigned sleep. Darren kicked him again.

'That's my head, you cunt!'

'Look, what does your mate do?' Darren asked once again.

Sam decided that a good, solid, vague-but-satisfying lie should do the trick. 'He works with the police,' he said, and then cursed himself silently, wishing he hadn't.

'He's a copper? How do you know a copper?'

Another pause shortened by a swift kick. 'No. He's like a civilian who works closely with the police from time to time.' Another pause. 'Sometimes more closely than others,' he added, trying to work some truth into the lie, in order to have less to be caught out by during any future cross-examination.

'Oh.' The hard drive finished flashing and Darren ended the interrogation. Sam moaned, stretched, farted and, satisfied with his performance, got up. Darren returned to the seat in front of his recent purchase. The message '377 files successfully undeleted' appeared at the bottom of the screen. Darren selected one file, highlighted it and pressed return. The hard drive buzzed again and Darren was mildly surprised to see the DNA sequence analysis program he had installed on his computer boot into life. He sat and stared at the screen and poked a finger deep into his ear. On a black background, fluorescent blue, green, yellow and red bands of various intensities lined up in a series of single-file formations from the top towards the bottom of the screen. Darren closed the file and opened up another random one. The same story. And another and another. Each screen was filled with a sea of bright bands of subtly different pattern. He had seen similar bands before. Most molecular geneticists had and he quickly guessed what they were. They were profiles of different-sized fragments of DNA. They were DNA profiles. Darren spun round and heard the front door close as he did so.

Everything is Related

Having puzzled over the computer's unexpected treasure for ten minutes and come up with nothing very constructive, Darren resolved instead to set about rescuing the shreds of his theory. He pasted formulae and scribbled thoughts from written page to word-processed image, generating a miscellany of seemingly random words and numbers. After an hour or so, he stopped and stared at the mess illuminated before his eyes. He needed a fresh start. He opened a new file and gazed into the whiteness of the page the laptop presented to him. The cursor flashed impatiently, like a child stamping its feet and waiting for something to happen. It was funny, but the word processing page on the screen made him feel even more helpless than a real, empty piece of paper would have done. Its blankness was just as frightening, but there was something remote and untouchable about it. Darren couldn't take the image and throw it in the bin. He couldn't run his fingers over its featureless geography, and wonder how his words might form an inky landscape. It was almost mocking. He tried to touch the image, but was repelled by a sharp crack of static which lingered on the surface, waiting for just such an attack. This was useless. An illuminated projection of his brain on a cold plastic screen. Darren stood up and rubbed his eyes. How does it start? What is it that overcomes the crushing inertia gripping every half-conceived idea to the sticky tarmac? He needed a spark, a shaft of light, an escape velocity. In short, he needed to get pissed.

Three hours later, Darren tried to focus once more on the screen. He was four pints and five chasers to the good. Somehow chasers had caught up with and overtaken their pints. Maybe he had had two in a row, maybe he had finished on a double, he didn't know. All he did know was that he was now moderately pissed and his computer was staring back at him with the harsh whiteness of an interrogating spotlight. At the top of the page was a heading, in bold capitals. **EVERYTHING IS RELATED**. Beneath it, a mess of as many equations as he had been able to plunder from the university library's textbooks. Darren blinked in the laptop's glare, slow, gradual blinks, the sort of difficult, lazy blinking you do when you've been drinking, his head lolling forward with each loitering sweep of his eyelids. The idea was forming again. If a letter or a constant appeared in one formula, it might also appear in another. And if it was there in both, then the two equations were linked. Darren began to blink more quickly, and sat upright. The trick was to try and link equations via common variables. He started with the obvious ones. If everything is related, then the theory of relativity seemed like a good beginning. $E = mc^2$, where E is energy, m is mass and c is the speed of light. He scanned through his list of three or four hundred equations. Mass was also important in several others. In one of them, which described kinetic energy, mass equalled $2E_k/v^2$. So he substituted it into $E = mc^2$, and came up with $E = 2E_k/v^2.c^2$. Next, he looked for v^2 in other formulae. In terms of motion, $v^2 = u^2 + (at)^2$. So substituting v^2 for $u^2 + (at)^2$ then gave him

$E = 2E_k c^2/u^2 + (at)^2$. A little less catchy than Einstein's version, admittedly, but this was progress. Then Darren really began to have fun. The speed of light (c) cropped up in a number of equations, which he similarly introduced to the party. Passing strangers of formulae were also invited to join in. In fact, anything which even remotely overlapped was entered, along with a good deal of things which didn't. He inserted expressions describing pendular motion, quantum energy, isothermal change, centripetal force, genetic drift, atomic separation, thermodynamic change, mutation rates, Doppler effects, gas expansion, biological behavious, hydrogen bonding, internal resistance, gravitational pull, mate attraction, electromagnetic fields, surface tension and even the movement of the planets, whether they liked it or not. His momentum built and patterns started to appear. He worked feverishly until he could work no more, before collapsing in a heap. But he was excited, too excited to lie on the sofa. If the theory was making progress, what about the Paper directory? This was a rare burst of energy and Darren decided to exploit it to the full. He returned to the laptop and opened his Windows Explorer, examining the list of 377 files. Each was sequentially numbered with an eight-digit description. He clicked on a random file and renamed it with a document suffix. Darren used to do this sometimes to DNA sequence files when he worked at the Institute, just to see the wealth of nonsense that spewed onto the screen as the computer struggled to convert filetypes. He opened the file in his word processor. The file was huge, as he'd imagined, and a fairly random nightmare of meaningless characters at that. Out of feverish curiosity, Darren scrolled down through the hieroglyphic code. At the very bottom, several pages in, he found four lines of something vaguely intelligible. He stared at it:

```
Colfer, SJ
DOB 19:10:67 Cauc M 12:04:93
Case: Paper/ Thorn
Tech: Dr J Sammons Sheff Inst Pol For
```

Darren screwed his eyes up. If this was a DNA profile, and it certainly looked like one, it might well be a
profile of one Colfer, SJ. Whoever he was. Presumably
a Caucasian male born in October 1967, at a rough
guess. Darren closed the file, and similarly changed the
filetype of another random folder entry. This time, the
file ended with:

```
Jones, CA
DOB 21:06:66 Cauc F 11:04:93
Case: Paper/ Thorn
Tech: Dr J Sammons Sheff Inst Pol For
```

The next read:

```
Abnett, PT
DOB 09:04:67 Cauc M 12:04:93
Case: Paper/ Thorn
Tech: Dr J Sammons Sheff Inst Pol For
```

Sheff Inst Pol For? Sheffield Institute of . . . ? Pol
For? Sounded like a French beer. Pol. Politics. Police.
Pollution. Police maybe. Police Force. Seemed to make
sense. He drummed the table, thinking. DNA profiles.
Forensics maybe. Police Forensics. That was more like
it. Paper/ Thorn didn't make much sense though. Sam
had some explaining to do. A mate selling his laptop.
Bollocks. This baby was stolen, and by the looks of it
from the police, which seemed to make the crime
worse, somehow, like two sins for the price of one. He
wondered whether he ought to try to return it. His life

was shit now, really shit, but it could be a fuck of a lot worse if he was caught in possession of stolen police equipment. And there was no danger that someone of Sam's non-stick disposition would bear the brunt of the law's wrath. Darren closed the open file and sat and thought. It wasn't every day you got your hands on a police database of suspects or known villains. He glanced up from his computer and over to the phone. He was thinking something. It was in the pipeline but had yet to make its purpose clear. Darren continued to stare at the phone. It was sitting on top of a phone directory. He at last caught hold of the idea and walked over and retrieved the phone book. Colfer, S.J. and Jones, C.A. were both listed. Abnett, P.T. wasn't though. Admittedly there were a few Jones, C.A.s, but Colfer, S.J. was certainly residing in the Sheffield area. He wondered what Colfer, Abnett and Jones might have done. Jones was female, which was interesting. Three hundred and seventy-seven names. They could of course just be part of one of the wide genetic screens you occasionally heard about, when all the people from a given village are tested in a sweep designed to flush out a rapist or murderer or sheep shagger. Clearly, then, the crime had to have been a serious one. You don't do genetic testing on hundreds of people just to flush a shoplifter out into the open. Encouraged, Darren selected all 377 files, changed their filetypes and began, from the top, to open each one successively and note the name of the potential miscreant. Periodically, Darren checked a group of names against the phone directory. About a third of the names seemed to be Sheffield residents. But he started to notice a trend in the Paper names. At least half of the entries in the phone book were doctors.

This was interesting. It was late, three or four probably, but Darren was still on fire. Another obvious trend in the database was that the numerical list had been constructed around an alphabetical list of the people, so that the first twenty or so records he had opened were all As, and he was now working his way through the Bs. All records had `Case: Paper/ Thorn and Tech: Dr J Sammons Sheff Inst Pol For`, and varied only with respect to their identifying name and date of birth. About twenty-five names in, Darren looked up the name `Bird, S. (Cauc M, DOB: 5:5:68)` and saw that there were fifteen entries in the phone book. He was about to proceed to the next file when he stopped and stared at the screen. Nineteen sixty-eight. That would be roughly thirty, which was in the right ballpark. Same age, same surname, same initial. Jesus. This could be Simon. He checked again. Darren didn't know Simon's date of birth, but he did know his telephone number. He ran his finger down the list of Bird, S. entries. Simon's number wasn't there. He checked again. Bugger. So Simon wasn't in the phone book – ex-directory, maybe. This was annoying. Statistically though, the odds were still on Simon's side. Fifteen to one, give or take. But, as he sat and thought about it, suddenly enlivened, he realized that some of the fifteen Bird, S's must be older than thirty and some younger. Darren stared back into the screen. Next to the DOB entry was a date, presumably: 12:04:93. All the records he had checked thus far had a similar date – the 12th or thereabouts of April 1993. Maybe the date the files were created. He closed the current record and looked at the date of creation of a number of the files, and finding that they were all roughly the same, wondered what Simon might have been doing in April 1993.

Jammin'

Sam was a disaster, a blissfully unaware, smiling-through-it-all disaster. He came to stay and wouldn't go home. Sam didn't do hints or nudges or suggestions or leave me alone you are a nightmare happening around me, or threats even. Sam just did whatever the first thing he thought of was. Usually, thought was too strong a word. There was no sense of propriety, of reason, of purpose. There was just an impulse, pure and unadulterated by thought, an impulse that had to be satisfied. Sporadically, Sam collected jumpers. Darren had no idea what he did with them, but he certainly didn't wear them. He made the mistake of asking him once.

'What d'you mean what do I *do* with them?' Sam pronounced 'do' with enough disdain to imply that Darren had suggested something unnatural. 'I collect them, don't I?'

'I just meant, you know, if you don't wear them, then what's the point—'

'Hang on. Does a stamp collector post his stamps? Does a beer-mat collector mop drinks up with his beer mats? Does a coin collector spend his coins?'

'No, but jumpers, they're hardly collectables, they're items of clothing to be worn.'

'What do you mean, not collectables?' Sam was shivering slightly, wearing just a T-shirt. '*I* collect them, don't I? Therefore they're fucking collectable.' Darren let it rest. Sam hugged himself to keep warm. He must have had fifty snug, thick, woolly jumpers just lying around at home doing nothing. The problem was that Sam had gone in one seamless movement from being dressed by his mother to being dressed by his girlfriend, until his girlfriend had at last left him. Unable to move backwards and have his mother buy his clothes, and unable to find a woman prematurely senile enough to go out with him, Sam's record had got stuck somewhere, so that jumpers were all he could now focus on. And at this very moment, Sam had gone out on another impulsive jumper hunt.

Darren surveyed the mess around him. The flat was awful, and looked like some sort of adventure playground for garbage. It was strewn with cold cups of tea, empty biscuit packets, gravy-stained plates, Sam's sleeping bag, which seemed to perform a dual function as a sort of bed-cum-very-squashed-settee, screwed-up clothes, horizontal cans of beer and variously folded and half-destroyed newspapers. Impulsive though he was, and repulsive much of the time also, one urge which never occurred to Sam was the urge to tidy up. Darren was no housewife, but he did require a certain order to things. Dusting, polishing and vacuuming, for instance, had no relevance in his life, but sorting did. Papers should be stacked, records in their sleeves, clothes on the bed or in the wardrobe, rubbish in the bin and fucking sleeping bags rolled up. He had tried to reason with Sam but he wasn't interested. 'What mess?' he had asked, lobbing another fag packet across the room and missing the bin by a considerable margin. There was no joke intended, but Darren had laughed anyway in a kind of involuntary spasm.

But this is the very point about Sam, Darren thought to himself. He is funny in an involuntary sort of way. He is funniest when he sits there shivering and talking about jumpers, as if the two are separate issues. He is funniest when he rings up the flat and asks what he went out for in the first place because he can't remember. He is funniest when he gets lost on the way back from the shops and staggers around for a full hour before he randomly happens upon the flats. He is funniest when he lights up a fag, swigs on a can of cider and announces that he's going on a health binge. In short, he is funny whenever he tries not to be, and not particularly funny when he tries to be, and is especially unamusing when he habitually fucks the flat over and refuses to move out until, as he puts it, his work in Sheffield is done.

In the early hours one morning, when the television had given up even the pretence of being entertaining, Darren began to talk. 'Yeah, those were the days when I had a life.' Sam had dozed off, or was pretending to have, so Darren judged it to be a good time to open his heart to him. 'Cruising through the Rockies, you know, really cruising, cruise-control cruising, just the two of us, big fat American car, big fat stereo with big fat speakers. Mountains like walls, everywhere, but we still felt free. You know, free from time and hopes and expectations.' He stared at the vacant 12:00 flashing on the display of the video recorder. It had become a battle of wits, which Darren was edging. The numbers flashed continuously and timelessly all day and night, pleading to be set to the correct hour, at which point they would cease flashing. Darren sometimes caught himself watching the display, wallowing miserably in the victory. He took another swig from his can. Sam stirred a little. 'So we're cruising right, and on the stereo we're listening to Bob Marley's greatest hits, and it's great—'

'It's shit,' Sam interjected, turning over in his sleeping bag and pretending to sleep again.

Darren tried to believe that Sam actually was asleep because he didn't want him to hear the rest of what he was going to say. But he had rediscovered a memory which suddenly made sense, and he wanted to get it out before it faded into insignificance. 'Anyway, Bob Marley, and on comes "Don't Rock My Boat" and she says this is my favourite one. And I think, well, it's a bit shit really. I mean, if I had to pick the shittest song on that album it would be that one or "I Shot the Sheriff", I don't know, or maybe . . .'

'Get on with it.'

'I didn't think you were listening.'

'I'm not,' Sam sighed. 'I'm asleep.'

'Right. Anyway, as she says this I listen to the lyrics, and they go something like "Don't rock the boat because I don't like the boat to be rocky . . ."'

'Wow . . .'

'. . . and "I like this, and you make me feel like I've just won the lottery and you don't know what you do to me."'

'So?'

'Look, stop listening, will you.'

'OK, OK, I'm asleep.'

'So I say, it's all right, but it's nothing flash, I prefer "No Woman No Cry", and she says that's typical, men seeing the bachelor perspective, and I say no, it doesn't mean if you don't have a woman you won't be crying and she says what does it mean then, and I explain but we still have a massive row and I can't figure out why.' Darren took another hefty swig. 'I couldn't figure out why she should be so upset that I liked "No Woman No Cry". It always bothered me every time I heard the song after. Still does. But I could never understand why she just cried and cried.'

'Well, she's a bird, isn't she,' Sam offered helpfully.

'No, you're missing the point, and so was I until I heard the song this morning. She wasn't saying I like this song,' Darren said, pausing to scratch his head. 'She was saying I like this sentiment and this is the only way I can tell you. She was telling me that, despite rocky patches and all the shit, she was happy, really truly happy. It was fucking oblique, granted, and I missed it by a mile. But it was the only way she could tell me. And after that, things never quite seemed . . .' Darren tailed off. Sam yawned. Darren sat there and contemplated. How different things could have been. Had he just . . . had he only . . . if he just could have . . .

'So what are you trying to say?'

'I suppose I'm trying to say . . . oh I don't know, nothing, really,' Darren said quietly, cradling his head in his hands. And then he mumbled, 'I thought you were asleep.'

'I'm doing my best.'

Half a can later Darren said, 'There was this girl at the Institute. Used to bump into her now and then.'

'Yeah? Did you shag her?'

'No. No, it wasn't like that.'

'You mean she wouldn't let you.'

'She was just . . . I don't know really. Not gorgeous exactly, just . . .' Darren sat and stared at the flashing video display. 'Even agreed to take her out once, the same week I was fired. Not good timing, really. Another in a long line of disasters.' After a few minutes Sam dozed off, properly this time. Darren tipped the warm frothy remnants of the can into his mouth and crawled off to a similarly empty bed.

* * *

Days passed and Sam wouldn't go home. Darren drank and tried to collect his thoughts. The theory continued to grow and multiply, and assumed an existence of its own. He rarely went out, except for more beer. Sam, on the other hand, often went out and disappeared for long stretches of time. Indeed, Darren began to believe that Sam was nurturing some sort of secret life outside the flat.

Filtering Through

First Track of the Day: 'I Still Haven't Found What
I'm Looking For' *by U2*

Checking through my order notes for the morning and
I noticed one for Dr Jeffries. Rang a bell, then I realized.
Darren. Sharp breath in, slow smile spreading. Didn't
know where he'd been for the last two or three months,
but he was back in the Institute at last. Blushed slightly
with the memory of The Big Let-down, got annoyed,
then waited for him to turn up and collect his lone
bottle of God knows what. Excited also. Nervous over
lunch and back early in case I missed him. Read the
paper during quiet spells, half watching the door. A
million false starts and the afternoon was almost over.
Decided that enough was enough. Couldn't be waiting
all day for him to deign to collect his delivery. Got
the number listed for Dr Jeffries' lab through the
switchboard and rang it, palpitating, my voice un-
certain. Is Darren there? I asked. No, came the reply. So
he wasn't in. When you see him could you ask him to
pop over to Neuro Deliveries because he's got a parcel
to collect? I'm afraid I can't, the man said. And then
the kick in the ovaries. He doesn't work here any more.
He must do, I half pleaded. Sorry, he left a few

months ago. Oh, I whispered, I thought maybe he had come back. No he hasn't, I'm afraid, but I could come and get the package if you want. Just tell me where you are.

Watched the door distractedly while leafing back through the paperwork. After a few minutes I sussed out what had happened. The order had been out of stock, by the looks of things. Rare chemical as well – wouldn't have thought the company got many requests for chlordiazepoxide hydrochloride. Added to that, appears that it was held up at the request of the Home Office. Just been a while filtering through, that's all. The door opened slowly. He was late twenties, maybe older, balding a bit, tallish, glasses, affable. Said he'd come for Darren's order. Asked him what happened to Darren, said I was a friend and wanted to get in touch with him, told him the home phone number that Staffing Services had given me wasn't right. He said Darren had moved, and that he was Simon, by the way. Where does he live now? I asked. He shrugged. Might have it written down somewhere. I handed over the small white parcel in quiet hope. Tell you what, I'll ring you from the lab if I can find it. Straight away? I asked. He grinned and took the parcel.

I counted. Couldn't be further than three minutes' walk back to Medical Genetics. Watched the clock as though each tick was a footstep. Two minutes to find the address if he had it. I looked from the clock to the phone and back again. Nothing. Useless. Seven minutes, bad news surely. Eight and I was suicidal. Eight and a half came and went, and then it rang. Picked it up casually, let it ring three times first, even though I was practically sitting on top of it. This is Simon from— Do you have it? I interrupted. Simon came up with the goods.

Results

And that was it. Left work there and then. It had started out as a day to track down what I wanted, and was about to end that way. Got a tram down West Street and headed for Darren's new abode.

Debris

Sam ambled through the centre of Sheffield, looking, as he watched his moving image in the windows of the shops he passed, pretty fucking sexy. The female mannequins adored him and passing reflections of girls wanted him. His posture straightened slightly as he imagined he was able to enter his own reflection, the shallow reflection which inhabited the shiny world of shop windows, with their dynamic, strutting, fearless dummies. He followed his progress through the shop-front world of Debenhams, where he mingled with the mannequins, through HMV where he became famous and joined several bands, through a sports shop where he scored goals and dunked baskets in fancy trainers, through bankrupt clothing where he donned jackets and jumpers and looked detachedly into the middle distance, through Waterstones, where he appeared pensive and erudite, and lastly through the shopfront of Mark One, where he felt cheap and cheerful. The thrill of being watched by a million passing eyes soon wore off as Sam became bored of living in a world full of dummies. Fame certainly had its price. Then, in the next window along, he spotted a jumper. It looked a bit itchy – a wool mix maybe – but as he wouldn't actually be wearing it, that would be OK. Reduced to forty-eight quid. Sam fingered the wad of notes in his pocket from the sale of the laptop. Maybe he'd buy the jumper later. For now though, there was the chance of another computer. He mined his pockets for the piece of paper he'd been given and headed for the Hare and Hounds pub. Not that Sheffield city centre was likely to see a lot of hunting, or for that matter had much of a rabbit problem, but Sam had decided long ago never to let a name come between him and a venue for drinking. As he headed down Fargate, he examined the paper debris that had been littering his pockets for some weeks now. Surely he couldn't have lost the bloke's number already. And what the hell was his name? He tried to think, but that didn't help much. He turned right into Norfolk Street, then swore and retraced his steps, alternately cursing his sense of direction and his pocket filing system. What was the fucker's name? A quiet pint might loosen it out.

The pub was a modern pub, which wasn't necessarily a good thing. Technology manages to improve most of life, but leaves pubs distinctly worse off from the deal. Generally with drinking establishments, the older and more knackered they are, then the better they feel. Sam opened his account at the newly installed bar. 'Pint of Löwenbräu. And a Southern Comfort.' He did after all have some serious thinking to do. 'Better make it a double,' he instructed the barman. He took his pocket debris out once again and rummaged through it. He had a system when it came to scraps of paper. Any remotely important piece of paper he came across was carefully folded up and filed away in a rear pocket of his jeans. After a number of weeks, when the pocket bulged enough to annoy him when he sat down, he removed the bundle of scraps and threw them in the bin. In this way, Sam kept on top of his paperwork. The assemblage in front of him was approaching disposal size and would soon have to be jettisoned. Natural wastage often helped him out at this stage, when he would invariably take the wad of paper, tickets, receipts and telephone numbers out of his pocket to find something he needed and then forget to replace it when he got up to leave. Important scraps of paper had a very limited timespan in Sam's trousers, and this was how he had come to lose the number he was now in need of. There was an anonymous number on a torn-off portion of a cigarette packet, but he was sure he had written a name alongside the dodgy geezer's mobile number, and these digits, as he looked at them, appeared to be in someone else's handwriting. He decided to use them anyway, and shuffled his drinks along the bar to the phone and pressed the appropriate buttons. The phone was answered promptly.

'Hi?' It was a female voice, which was promising.

'Hi.'

There was a pause before the girl repeated the greeting. This time the word was longer and less confident, and rose in tone slightly towards the end. 'Hi.'

'Hi.' Sam had no idea who it was, and hoped to flush her out into the open without giving away the nature of his predicament.

'Look, I'm really sorry, um, who is this exactly?'

'Oh, yeah, sorry, my fault, it's Sam.'

'Sam?' Another pause. 'Sam who?'

'Sam Hendry,' Sam replied. 'And who might you be?'

'This is Karen, Karen Fullwood. Not that it's any of your business. Do I know you?'

Karen. Karen. Kar— The penny dropped. Bollocks. Sam tried to change his voice and hoped she wouldn't remember him from the day before. 'Er, no, no. I think,' he tried to sound a little Scottish, 'mibae ah've goat a wrong—'

'Hang on. Sam, right? Sam that lives with Darren?'

Bugger. He never had been very good with accents. 'Er, yes.' He wished the money would run out but he'd optimistically put a twenty-pence piece in the phone and at local rates that might last all day.

'So Sam, what can I do for you?'

'Oh, nothing really, you know, I just . . .' Quick, think of something.

'You *did* give Darren my message yesterday, didn't you?'

Of course not. 'Yes. Yes, I gave him your message. Straight away.'

'So what did he say?'

This wasn't going particularly well. Sam took a hefty swig from his pint, and a fairly healthy one from his Southern Comfort, and answered, 'Well, that's what I wanted to say to you. I mean, that's really why I rang.'

'Well?'

This would take some quick thinking. Out there in the smoky haze of words which swirled around the bar were exactly the right ones to explain why he was ringing her. Also out there were the words to convince Karen that he *had* told Darren that she'd called around to the flat while he was out, leaving her phone number on the back of a fag packet, and saying, 'Ask him to call me.' Sam took a deep breath of the smoky air and answered, 'Yeah, he . . .' Come on, brain. Just this once. 'I mean I told him, obviously, that you had got his address from his friend Simon at work and that you'd been round,' come on, brain, please, I'll buy you another drink, please, 'and he said, well, he said . . .' go on, I'll even read a book or something – you'd like that, wouldn't you? 'He said, yes, he'd like to meet you, next week some time, if that's OK.' Sam sighed. Not bad. Only kidding about the book though.

'Why couldn't he ring me himself?'

Come on, for fuck's sake run out of money. 'He would have, only he's been busy.'

'Doing what?'

'Oh, you know . . .'

'No, I don't.'

'Well, just . . .' Beep beep beep. 'Oh, I've run out of money.' Beep. At last.

Beep beep. 'Yes, but what day next week?' Beep beep.

Beep. 'Sorry, I seem to have . . .' Come on, come on, run out of money. Beep beep. Come on. How many fucking beeps do you get these days? Beep beep. 'I'll tell you what, how about next—' Beeeeeeeeeep.

Sam put the receiver down and drank the rest of his pint, vowing that if he ever came across an anonymous phone number among his effects he would leave well alone. He ordered another drink and had one final sort through his scrap heap of pocket paper for the phone number he needed, finding it eventually scribbled in faint pencil on the back of a jumper receipt. He ordered another pint and picked up the phone.

Do the Right Thing

So, what do you live by? Do you trust the judgement you make when you are in the thick of a situation's bitter realities, or the judgement you make now that the situation is a sweet and ever-thinning memory? Obviously, you have to live for the now, and decide for the future. But what if you feel there is no right thing to do and that both choices leave you similarly broken?

Did I do the right thing? A thousand times a day, I ask myself this question. I list all the fors and all the againsts. Often, it comes out fairly even. There was a time, though, when even wasn't good enough. Now, it sometimes comes out worse than even. I know it's the benefit of time and a selective memory, but it's there all the same, and every time I respond to each one of my daily thousand questions, the answer is therefore no — I didn't do the right thing. This is not to say that at the time I left her I didn't ask myself two thousand times a day whether I was doing the right thing. But then anger and frustration were doing the answering, and coming up with marginally more yeses than nos. Now though pain and defeat are giving me a borderline no.

I saw her today. Our cars passed in a street near my house. For a moment I wondered whether she was on her way to visit me. She didn't see me. She looked happy and there was somebody I didn't recognize in her passenger seat. I felt a kick in the stomach as we passed, and, as I edged forward at a roundabout a couple of minutes later, still vainly checking my rear-view mirror, I noted that my clutch leg was trembling as I struggled to find biting point. I wanted to swing around the roundabout and follow her, to find out where she was going and what she was doing, and why she looked so happy, and who the fuck was sitting next to her. Instead, I had another quick reckon-up, probably the sixtieth or seventieth of the morning, and convinced myself that I had done the right thing. But as I crawled along in the stop-start traffic, it struck me that I had left her and that she was happy and I was miserable and overall it didn't seem particularly fair. Surely I was the one who had done the damage and inflicted the pain. OK, maybe she was just smiling at something on the radio, a tepid smile painted on the cold surface of her life, but I couldn't help thinking that I seldom smiled these days, even if I did hear something funny on the radio, which wasn't often anyway.

As I finally pulled into the Institute's car park and sat there listening to the cooling fan kick in over the flustered engine of my Fiat, I decided once and for all that the issue was settled, rightly or wrongly. And besides, things weren't too disastrous now. Sarah made me more than happy, so I should be grateful for that. Not many women would put up with me, at least not these days. But as I walked around the quadrangle towards my laboratory, the omnipresent shadow of the hospital darkening one side of the building, Fiona again haunted me with a memory, as I recalled an incident I often thought about, but had recently tried to bury somewhere under my unhappiness, an incident that was both the cause and effect of my misery, an incident that nearly stopped me smiling ever again.

Born-again Virgin

Darren swung the front door of the flat open with an exuberance that unsettled the sole surviving hinge. Sam greeted him with similar enthusiasm. 'For fuck's sake, mind the door.'

'Guess who's chuffed with himself then?' Darren said, sitting down next to Sam, who was desperately trying to focus through the snowy reception of the TV.

Sam got up and fiddled with the circular and fairly pointless aerial, which only served to antagonize it. 'Dunno.'

Darren tried again. He didn't want to just come out and say it. He wanted it teased out of him, detail by successful detail. 'So, who do you think I just bumped into?'

Sam continued to show no interest. 'You're ruining the reception,' he said, getting up once more to swear at the TV. 'And why don't you get a decent telly, instead of this shite?'

'You'll never guess.'

'I mean, what's the point, for fuck's sake? I may well have just spent the last half hour watching international ice dance for all I know.'

'Anyway, I did it!'

'What?'

'I asked Neuro Girl out. Again.'

'Neuro girl?'

'That girl I was talking about from work. From Neurogenetics.'

'Oh.' Sam got up and thought about kicking the TV. 'I thought you meant she was neurotic.'

'She might be. She's called Karen though, she said yes, and that's the important fact here.' Darren had a cursory and fairly pointless flick through the TV guide. 'Still haven't lost the old magic,' he said, putting the guide down and interlocking his fingers behind his head.

'You never had it.'

'Bollocks. What about when I was at university?'

'What about it?'

Darren realized the evidence wasn't on his side. 'Anyway, I'm going to meet her in a pub in town.'

Sam wondered whether he might have got away with it, and tried to change the subject just in case he hadn't. 'And then what?' he asked.

'What do you mean?'

'Well, you're going to have to have a bit more of a game plan than that.'

'Yeah?'

Sam raised his eyebrows. 'Jesus, you're out of practice.' Darren nodded, sullenly. 'In fact you've become a bit of a Born-again Virgin since what's her name.' Sam could never remember her name. 'I mean, there are Mother Superiors with virginities in more danger than yours.'

'Yes, yes, OK, stud features, like I haven't seen you exactly beating them off recently.' Sam grunted, but otherwise tried to put a brave face on his lack of success. 'And all right, maybe I have hit a bit of a dry patch . . .'

'A *bit*?'

'But the fact of the matter is that I've got a date, and whether it has or hasn't been a barren spell . . .'

'It has.'

'Then it's about to end. And, for the record, your long, hot, hymen-healing desert of success might just be in its protracted infancy.' Darren turned to face him. 'Anyway, while we're on the subject, I've got a bone to pick with you.'

'Yeah?'

'Yes. Something Karen said.' Sam continued to stare at the TV. He knew what was coming. 'She asked me,' Darren continued, 'why I hadn't bothered to ring her after she'd been round here last week and left her phone number.'

'Oh.'

'And she said that you'd rung her from a pub and told her that I'd meet her this week some time.'

'Hmm.'

'Well?'

'Well what?'

Darren glared at Sam. '*Did* you ring her up?'

Sam tried to avoid eye contact. 'Yeah.'

'So why didn't you pass her number on to me?'

'Lost it.'

'But you had it to ring her up.'

'No, after that.'

'You useless bastard! Useless! You're a disaster, Sam, a fucking disaster. Jesus!'

Sam looked as if he was about to say something. Darren waited. This ought to be good. After a pause of ten or so seconds, Sam replied, 'You can't make an omelette without breaking a few eggs.'

Darren stared at him. 'What do you mean by that?'

Sam shrugged and picked up a newspaper. Darren walked over to his computer to avoid the possibility of bloodshed, and soon became engrossed once more in his theory. He had been making good progress over the last few days. Things were coming together. He had even been taking his laptop to bed with him, folding it up in the early hours when he was too tired to concentrate, feeling its warmth like some sort of high-tech hot-water bottle, surrounding his theory like a sleeping baby.

Preoccupied

First Track of the Day: 'West End Girls' *by The Pet Shop Boys*

Bumped into Genetics Boy today. Shopping in town, vaguely in the west end, looking for a pet shop, and there he was. Looked a little lost, forlorn, scruffy even. Said he had been sacked. I said I knew. Said he was working on something new. I asked where? At home, he said. So you're working from home? I asked. Not really, he said. So why didn't you show up? He just looked at me and shrugged, helplessly. Stared down at his tatty shoes. Said a quiet sorry and mumbled something about bad timing. And why did your friend Sam ring me? I demanded. Seemed confused and said he didn't know. You did get the message I left when I called round to your flat last week? Again, he seemed confused. Generally seems a bit addled though, as if he's been working too hard or thinking too much. Then he started babbling on about everything being linked. Still doesn't make much sense. But he has something. He definitely has something. And despite everything he still seems interested. Wouldn't go away, just hung around looking awkward. Restless, but not on-fire restless, just fidgety, preoccupied, nervous even. I liked that. Thought to myself, look, Genetics Boy, I have no idea why you didn't ring me, and I have no real idea why the hell I'm hanging around, but I know why *you're* hanging around, not really saying anything, so why don't you just spit it out and be done with it. But he ummed, tapped his foot, scratched his nose, sniffed then finally blew his nose, maybe for luck, and then made a big show of making sure he hadn't left anything hanging out of it, checking and rechecking by casually running his index finger under his nostrils and examining it out of the corner of his eye when he thought I wasn't looking. Pitiful, all in all. Tried to tell me again some nonsense about how science is shaky, and a whole gamut of other nervous and unfocused conversation. I pretended to listen and then began to lose patience. I tried to send him brain messages. Like in *Cosmo*. Get to the point, just get to the fucking point, I transmitted. Didn't work though. 'How to Make a Man do Whatever You Want.' Another *Cosmo* flop. The 'Whatever' had even been in italics, as if anything, *anything*, that you desired would be fulfilled just by concentrating your brain energy in his direction. Decided I'd had enough of him concentrating his rambling brain energy in my direction. Just came out with it. Made it easy for him. Look, is there anything you want to say to me? An open goal. Come on, come *on*. No, he said. Useless! Hung around, though, looking at his feet, at passing shoppers, at my tits when he thought it was safe. Had to take the plunge myself. This was going nowhere, and not very quickly. I wanted him to burn me with his fire. Would you like to meet me for a drink some time? Please say yes. You're the only vaguely interesting man I've met in months and months. Useless with it, but you can't have everything. What do you say?

He said maybe he would.

Hope Springs Infernal

Childhood is anticipation of ecstasy, adulthood is anticipation of calamity. Hope as a child is as natural as breathing. Hope as an adult almost always ends up suffocating you. Maybe that's why adolescence is such a miserable transition. It represents a journey from optimism to pessimism.

Child:	I hope I get a bike for Christmas
Adult:	I hope I don't get a bike for Christmas
Child:	I hope it snows
Adult:	I hope it doesn't snow
Child:	I hope it's fish fingers for tea
Adult:	I hope we have run out of fish fingers
Child:	I hope my school burns down
Adult Parent:	I hope the school doesn't burn down
Adult Teacher:	I hope the school burns down

It's just so rare as an adult to hope for anything *positive*, and Darren was no exception. It was always, I hope x doesn't ruin my hair/ set off late/ get woodworm/ realize I'm useless at my job/ come out of my account until after pay day/ lose the game/ smell my breath/ close before I get there/ spot me in this outfit/ have an enormous tailback/ plough into a mountain etc., etc. At the moment, Darren's hope was that Simon had nothing to do with the Paper database. This was typical of Darren's life. Hope had become hope not, somewhere along the line. This might have been entirely natural. The older he had become the more often he had been let down, the more he therefore expected to be let down, and the more miserable he was. But being miserable had a lot going for it. He knew that things weren't going to get much worse than they already were, and might get a whole lot better, although if they did, he probably wasn't going to be able to enjoy them, miserable bastard that he was. But he had drawn a line, a line he wasn't unhappy with, a line of tolerance, which said that his expectations were this high (knee height, say) and his hopes were this high (groin height, say) and his dreams were this high (chest height, say) and his wildest dreams were this high (about mouth height, say). Generally though, they were about knee height, and that was fairly tolerable. After all, he felt, if he perpetually held his hopes at chest height, someone was inevitably going to come along and kick him in the bollocks sooner or later.

Darren also reasoned that if the majority of the population were adult, at least in terms of age, it must be a fairly bleak outlook for the species, given that most people devote an unreasonably large proportion of their thoughts to hoping that some disaster or other isn't just about to happen. There are positive hopes, of course – real hopes, not hope nots – although many of these often turn out to be less than charitable. But hopes are terribly shallow affairs anyway. How many people, Darren wondered, have honestly ever woken up and sincerely hoped for world peace? Compared to waking up and hoping the car will start or the train won't be late or that slightly damp patch you can feel under you all of a sudden is just sweat?

The problem was that if ever things started to go particularly well for Darren, he would begin to suspect that they were going a little too well, and that something shite must also be in the post, to even things out a bit. This was, as he saw it, entirely the fault of the phrase 'Pride comes before a fall'. Although quite clearly nonsense, it was ruthlessly efficient in preventing Darren from enjoying any meagre good times that transpired as thoroughly as he felt he should. This was despite knowing that falls came whenever they wanted, which was usually fairly regularly and that pride came fairly irregularly, arriving as it did only on the back of a tide of good events, a tide which was almost constantly being interrupted by unseen falls. Seemingly ensconced over recent months within an interminable fall, Darren found himself uncharacteristically optimistic. If pride did come before a fall, it stood to reason that it had to come some time after it as well. After all, pride didn't come before pride any more than fall before fall, unless you were desperately lucky and unlucky, respectively. So Darren began to look forward for once. He had bottomed out, surely, and could sit back and wait for things to get better. In fact, as he thought about it, things were already improving. The theory was growing and expanding, and he now had a police database to play with. And, as a final bonus, there was even the remote chance of a shag on the horizon.

Random Entry

Darren decided to leave his theory alone for the morning and concentrate instead on discovering whether Simon was on a police database. And, if so, why. He picked up the phone, dialled one four one for reasons of anonymity, and then dialled the number he had in front of him on a page torn from the phone directory.

'Hello?' A female voice.

'Hi. Um, is Simon there?'

'No, he's out at the minute. Can I take a message?'

'No, it's fine, thanks. No problem. I'll ring later.'

'Who shall I say—'

Darren hung up. He put an asterisk next to one of the numbers on his list and then dialled the next one down.

'Hello?' A male voice.

'Hi, is Simon there?'

'Simon who?'

'Simon Bird.'

'Think you've got the wrong number, pal.'

'Oh right. Sorry. Bye.'

Darren put a cross through the number and picked the phone up again, opening up the Paper directory and continuing to work through its list of names.

Results

An hour later, Darren leaned back, stretched, and then rubbed his eyes. They felt dry, as if the dusty screen had been sucking the moisture out of them, or perhaps his eyes had just been gathering a layer of dust of their own. This was tedious work. He wondered what else had been deleted from the computer on its journey to him and once again listed the undeleted files. Whoever cleaned it up had made a lazy job of it. Really, they should have formatted the hard drive, although this meant that the drivers would have needed to be re-installed to get the thing up and running again. The advantage, however, was that the next owner wasn't left with lingering ghosts of files that should have been deleted for ever.

DNA sequence files aside, all sorts of junk had been hastily thrown out. Darren clicked on a few random folders and undeleted them, but they were either inaccessible or uninteresting. He examined the dates of the files, which were spread from 1996 to 1998. Clearly, the Paper directory had been copied from another machine at some point in the last two years, given that the profiles had been carried out around 1993. A small number of files had been created before 1996. Darren listed all files in reverse order of creation and undeleted the folders from 1993. There were a handful of files of various classifications – some word processing, some apparently image-based, some spreadsheets. The word processing files were filled with technical and barely decipherable information. The images were gel pictures. The spreadsheets were strings of numbers and accompanying words, like uncert, low, N/A, yes, med, unlikely, no, high, poss. Darren rubbed his eyes again with his fists. They were starting to itch. He walked into the bathroom and stared into the mirror at the blood-heavy capillaries which had come out to play in the milky whites of his eyes. He gripped the straggle of his upper eyelashes and pulled, so that the top lid peeled away from his eye, and . . . he let the lid snap back against his inflamed eyeball and dashed over to the computer. Names, numbers and words. Shit. He opened the spread-sheet and scribbled down the first three numbers of the first column. Then he opened the list of names he had already plundered from the Paper database. After about twenty seconds, he had located all three numbers. This was good. Very good. He cross-referenced the numbers with his existing list of names, and then wrote beside each one the text from the second and third columns of the database. Darren scrutinized the piece of paper in front of him. Just to be sure, he repeated the procedure for an additional random entry. He looked at his list. It read:

```
Mole, D/ Yes/ Med
Davis, S/ Yes/ Uncert
Fort, R/ No/ N/A
Pearson, B/ Yes/ Low
```

Encouraged, Darren tracked Bird, S.'s number through his original list, and then hunted the relevant database description down. This was something.

```
Bird, S/ Yes/ High
```

So, Bird, S. was High, whatever that meant. Darren had an idea what it might mean, but tried to reason it through first. This was the hangover of a failed scientific career. Never ever believe the first thing that your eyes, dusty or otherwise, show you. Take your time, distrust, think, be sceptical, try to disprove, then, begrudgingly, accept. This way you won't constantly be building your ideas on the thin ice of first impressions. In fact, Darren had carried this so far that he almost ceased to believe anything. And so, he took his time and tried not to get too excited too soon. He similarly assessed other database entries against his own lists. Eventually, however, he was forced to concede the likelihood that his first notion had probably been correct, which eroded his confidence somewhat, given his propensity for being wrong. What he might have was a file of risk, a correlation, an indication of the importance of each individual profile, an appraisal of probability for each of the punters examined, an estimate of their chances of culpability. Fort, R., for instance, was one of only two or three files that Darren had been unable to open. N/A – surely this indicated that, for whatever reason, no sample had been obtained, or, if it had, that it hadn't been possible to profile it. As Darren continued to cross-reference, he began to notice that female entries were almost exclusively associated with the description Low. The police must have suspected a male. And Bird, S., who was, more than likely, Simon, a male, was defined as High. A quick scan down the risk column of the spreadsheet pulled out only two other Highs. That was three out of nearly four hundred. Darren puffed his cheeks out, walked over to the sofa and swigged from an open bottle. Simon, his one sane friend, might well be a chief suspect in an unknown crime.

Gs and Threes

The small keyboard of the laptop was grimy in a way which suggested that the majority of its use had been confined to a subset of its keys. Most of the right-hand side was bordering on the spotless, while the left side, from T to Q down to C to Z, looked and felt as if it had been incessantly hammered by a filthy tramp with lead fingers. Apart from a small coffee stain on the right side, you could have been forgiven for believing that two keyboards, one a low-mileage, careful lady owner example, the other a high-mileage road-rage model, had been welded together as some sort of insurance write-off.

Having discovered that Simon might well have been a suspect in a serious crime, but unable to think of what to do next, Darren decided to return to his theory, hoping that some of his new-found excitement would carry over into the realms of this more erudite work. After a couple of minutes of frantic typing, he stopped and stared hard at the left-hand keys. It was official. He now had a keyboard that wouldn't do Gs. Threes were becoming a little awkward as well, and could only be coaxed onto the screen by a vigorous hammering of the keyboard, that either yielded no threes at all, or about twelve, which then needed to have eleven removed using the backspace key, which did, at least for the moment, backspace. So, threes were do-able, but Gs were hopeless. How the fuck, he wondered, was he supposed to type gene or genetics? He tried substituting Hs for Gs, on the grounds of typographical proximity, but it didn't really improve the situation and at times looked a bit random. Gardening became hardening, for instance, and gate hate. Not that he particularly wanted to type either word, it just showed that meanings could become confused. After a bit of debate, Darren found J to be an adequate stunt double for G. Of course it meant that he would have to deal mainly in jenes and jenetics, which wasn't much of an improvement on henes and henetics, but would at least be tolerable. But like an embarrassed non-roller of Rs, Darren found that as he continued to write he was consciously avoiding the letter G wherever possible. He was fast-forwarding through oncoming sentences and equations, editing out the guilty letter. Gs were often difficult to replace without any outside assistance, and so he roped his thesaurus in to do the donkey, or ass, work for him. Which showed the danger of thesauri – donkey may be a synonym of ass, but donkey work is seldom likely to be confused with ass work, whatever that might be, except perhaps in Turkish brothels. Some words, however, didn't appear in his thesaurus, often words of great importance as far as inheritance theories are concerned. One such word was daughter. Daughter was unavoidable, and there was no way of just replacing it with a G-less synonym. So, for daughter, Darren resolved henceforth that he would insert son. It might not have been entirely faithful, but it was thereabouts. And there was no way he was going to type daujhter It looked Dutch for a start. But even slight inaccuracies failed to derail his enthusiasm. Through the tangle of equations on the screen, patterns were emerging. A feeling of roundness was pervading the work. The edges might have been fuzzy, but the message was becoming clearer. While Sam came and went under dubious circumstances, Darren sat and hammered away at the keys of his computer, which did nothing to improve their condition. But the more he typed, the less clutter appeared before him. This was, after all, an exercise in rescuing a single, clear message from among all the chaos, a message which daily was becoming more lucid.

Scarface

My face is numb. Something has happened. She is just staring, shocked, pale, the blood draining from her cheeks. I am not sure what's going on. I touch my face and look at my hand. I am fairly drunk, admittedly. I try to focus on my fingers. There is blood. I stand up. She runs out of the room. She is saying no, no, no. I walk to the bathroom, slowly. I am calm. Something is wrong but I am calm. I am someone else. I am not sure who, but some poor sod anyway. I look slowly up from the bathroom floor to meet my face in the mirror. There is someone else facing me. Blood is streaming down his cheek, drip, drip, drip on the lino. She is sobbing in the background. I touch the mirror and then touch my own face. I realize that it is me in the mirror. My cheek is sliced open. I am calm. I take some tissue and wet it, wash the blood from the wound. The cut seals momentarily and then floods again. I do this again and again, squeezing watery blood into the sink. My face feels numb and I want to piss. There is a lot of blood. I look like a Saturday night casualty case. I tremble at the sight of the blood. Not because it's mine, just because it's blood. Still can't stand the sight of the stuff. She enters the bathroom. Looks me in the face. Says shit, once, twice, three times. I turn away from the mirror, confused. I don't know exactly how this has happened. Blood drips on the floor, running off my chin. She is still holding the broken glass. There will be stitches. Ten or fifteen, maybe. She cowers back. I am not angry. She is sobbing, saying shit over and over again. Something else has happened to me. It is not shock either. I am saying I love you. I have the proof in my bloody hands. You have just broken a glass into my face and I love you. I have realized something for the first time. I don't care what you put me through I will still love you. I am half bleeding to death and all I can say is that I love you.

And Fiona says maybe we should just go to casualty.

The Meaning of Life

That was it! The final calculation. Everything which could have been substituted had been substituted. All available equations had been equated. The sum total of assimilations had been assimilated. Terms, constants, integers, digits and multipliers had all been thrown together. A huge, dense, cloudy liquid had been distilled into a single drop of knowledge. Darren examined his handiwork one final time, before standing up and punching the air. An answer. At last, an answer. The dizzy flutterings of success. Someone had eventually had the foresight to join the chemistry, physics and biology of existence to come up with the numbers of life. And here he was, Darren White, humble Darren White, some would say incompetent Darren White, clutching the piece of paper in his hand.

He brings the page up to his chest and holds it proudly aloft. Before him are two hundred of the world's most eminent scientists, gazing with jealous anticipation at a scrawny researcher who has performed the impossible. He clears his throat and a giddy silence follows. 'Fellow scientists, colleagues, comrades, I give you the solution to life.' Wild applause. 'Months of toil have brought me here, to stand before you.' More clapping. 'Hour after hour of looking for the big picture and eschewing the trivial.' They are on their feet, the anticipation too great to be seated. 'And here it is. The Universality of Life.' A hush. People fidgeting. A few cleared throats. 'The Solution, brothers and sisters, is this:

$$\left\|\ln\frac{y}{\eta}\right\|\sum nm_0 = \frac{\sqrt[\alpha^2]{R_0 E^{\frac{(E_0)}{Ai}}}}{\omega^{3.94} r} \cdot \int_{2aT\text{-}logi} Ne^\upsilon \, pq + 1\,,$$

A lull, an uncomfortable lull. Increased fidgeting. A voice from the back. 'Dr White?'

'Yes?'

'You're saying that $\left\|\ln\frac{y}{\eta}\right\|\sum nm_0 = \frac{\sqrt[\alpha^2]{R_0 E^{\frac{(E_0)}{Ai}}}}{\omega^{3.94} r} \cdot \int_{2aT\text{-}logi} Ne^\upsilon \, pq + 1$?'

'Yes.'

'And what does that mean, exactly?'

'Well, in its purest form, that $\left\|\ln\frac{y}{\eta}\right\|\sum nm_0 = \frac{\sqrt[\alpha^2]{R_0 E^{\frac{(E_0)}{Ai}}}}{\omega^{3.94} r} \cdot \int_{2aT\text{-}logi} Ne^\upsilon \, pq + 1$,'

'And in its impure form?'

'What are you getting at?'

'That it's too complicated to mean anything.'

Darren is a little taken aback. 'But this is life, pure life, as far as we can describe it. It is bound to be complicated.'

'But what use is life if we don't understand it?'

'Well, maybe I could make it simpler.' Darren slumped back in his chair and examined the formula. To be fair, it did look a little confusing to the uninitiated. In fact, even to the thoroughly initiated, it was far from clear. What he ought to do, he quickly decided, was simplify, and by this he meant estimate. Besides, this was always meant to be an approximate theory. Darren started to cross out and take similar values from each side of the equation, until it had lost a lot of detail. Then he really got stuck in. Fractions were dealt with by multiplication, square roots were removed by squaring terms on the opposite side of the equation and orders of magnitude were cancelled through. After a feverish hour of red-pen activity, Darren cleared his throat and stood up. Hush once again descends on Flat twenty-nine, Cherry Towers. 'After much deliberation,' he says, 'I have been able to trim the equation to an approximate form. By the resubstitution of constants and rough cancelling out, I am once again ready to give you the Solution to Life.' A chair scrapes. Delegates rub their faces. Sam appears freshly shaven from the bathroom. 'This, then is the result. The Universality of Existence equals . . .' A dramatic pause, the air heady with excitement. Bathroom's free, Sam announces. 'Equals . . . y!'

'Y?'

'Yes. Y.'

'And what *is* y, exactly?'

'Y is life.'

'So y is a constant?'

'Life is never constant.'

'Are you saying life is a variable then, Dr White?'

'Yes. An infinite variable called y.'

'But what is the value of y?'

Delegates appear uneasy. A couple slope out of the room. Restlessness abounds.

'Dr White? The value of y?'

Sam leaves, saying something about a business meeting. Darren sits by himself, staring at the large letter y on the page before him. 'Fuck knows,' he mumbles, summing up as fully as he can his newly acquired expertise on the matter.

He wondered what he had managed to achieve over the long months he had spent trying to explain life in terms of numbers. A mild nervous breakdown. The loss of moderately gainful employment. A bathroom cabinet full of rare drugs. And a friend who wouldn't go home. He had successfully distilled nearly four hundred of life's most important equations into a single letter of the alphabet which meant nothing at all. A partial success, at best. And even the letter was taking the piss. Y the hell had he bothered, he asked himself, cradling his head in his hands. It was, he conceded, time to seek distraction elsewhere.

The Periodic Fable

This was the worst stage of all. Nothing in a relationship quite matches the uncertainty and fear inherent in determining whether someone you really don't know very well is willing to have intercourse with you. It's a wonder that the species hasn't died out yet considering the appalling difficulties involved in getting someone into bed, even if it's someone you have a signed affidavit from telling you that they are basically gagging for it. From you. And are wearing a T-shirt demanding that you both get down to it as quickly as possible. With your name and address and photo on the back. And a big neon sign attached to their head saying 'GET IT HERE'. Surely we could have come up with some sort of a secret ballot system by now, a sort of I'm going to leave the room, the front door is to your right, the bedroom to the left, I'll be back in five minutes to see how you got on. But no, even obvious mutual salivation cannot detract from the misery and bladder difficulties encountered in trying to sleep with someone for the first time.

The previous date had been fine, if a little fraught, and Darren had had a minor crisis of faith on his way by bus to meet her. It had been a long time, a mighty long time, but he would be OK, he told himself. Surely you can't forget how to shag. Just like riding a bike, he mused, then wished he hadn't, because it didn't seem a particularly considerate image to saddle Karen with. Still, he'd be OK. Two pints maximum, sipped in halves, no breath-mutating crisps, polite but mildly flirtatious conversation, staying well clear of contentious moral issues or politics, witty but politically correct, straight down the line, anecdotes designed to reinforce his honesty and sexual prowess, and absolutely no mention of the letter y. But as the bus left the estate and plunged downhill into the darkness, guided by occasional street lamps, Darren panicked suddenly that these rules of certain success would leave him with approximately nothing to say. Wit and political correctness seldom encounter one another in the same sentence, and his theory had so consumed the heart of his life that he had difficulty stringing a conversation together without defining terms and breaking into discussions of the importance of sample size. He took Sam's crude map out of his jacket and unfolded it to reveal all of its biroed glory. He had no idea where the pub was and might have to ask when he got to Leopold Street, which seemed to be, on Sam's map, virtually perpendicular to the direction Darren remembered it being. This was not unusual for one of Sam's maps. He just hoped that Karen had a more accurate idea of exactly where the Hare and Hounds pub was. She had seemed fairly confident on the phone, if not entirely enthused about the venue. Still, with only Sam's recommendation to go by, Darren had decided to be decisive and stick with the plan.

And the whole evening had been an unexpected success. After the first half-pint, he ditched his strategy and decided to just be himself, whoever or whatever that might be. He drank quickly, talked with rare lucidity, told half-true anecdotes about a lively, gregarious, half-true version of himself ('Never looked at another woman while I was living with Michele. Shagged a few, but kept my eyes closed'), even made up a joke or two along the way. And Karen lapped it up. They had parted half pissed and swaying, suddenly finding themselves on firm ground as they embraced and kissed, as if they had trouble standing separately, but together formed a unit of reciprocal coordination. Darren rang her as soon as he got home, but could think of nothing to say. Before hanging up he asked whether she would meet him again the next night, and she agreed.

And here they were, in Karen's rented room, having spent a second evening drinking, laughing and being casual with each other, the alcohol now slowly evaporating through sour breath. Darren had taken the plunge during some heated kissing and was now struggling with the zip of her trousers. It seemed to be caught somewhere from the inside, maybe in her knickers, or maybe even worse, and had ground to a halt, refusing to move either up or down. Darren cursed. He tried sideways, which seemed to be a lost cause as well.

'What *are* you doing?' she asked eventually.

'It's this fucking zip,' he explained. 'It's not going anywhere.'

'Well, what have you done to it?'

'Nothing.' Darren continued to tug, almost desperately. 'Jesus. Talk about the Zipless Fuck – this is more like the Fuckless Zip.'

Karen giggled and Darren stopped wrestling with her jeans. The moment was in danger of slipping away. Had they been long-term lovers, they could have laughed it off and found another way of undoing her trousers. As it was, both protagonists felt an overpowering need not to appear desperate. Darren was happy to encourage the impression that he was a semi-regular Lothario and that it was no skin off his back whether they had sex or not. Karen was burdened with the popular misconception that it is wrong for a woman to appear needy. So they both laughed and Darren let go of Karen's fly. So much for humour getting you laid, Darren sighed to himself.

'Cheap pair of jeans, I suppose,' Karen said, breaking a silence that was rapidly settling in around the awkwardness they were both feeling.

Darren was aware that the onus was on him to break the deadlock. 'No, they're nice. Apart from the zip, that is.'

'I've never had any problems with it before . . . I mean, not like this . . . not that it's your fault, or anything . . .'

And that was it. The F-word had been mentioned. Fault. A damaging word at any time and under any circumstance, but in the sphere of sexual encounter, no matter how remote it now seemed, it was crushing. If clothes removal could be counted as a preliminary to foreplay – a kind of warm-up for the tricky techniques of stimulation which pre-empted the difficulties of sex – then Darren had quite clearly failed at the first hurdle, and Karen was in danger of brokering a refusal. And suggesting fault during sex is a painfully direct accusation that can't be dodged or blamed on anybody else in the way that normal accusations can. Darren could hardly say, No, it wasn't me, it was Jenkins from accounts who filled the wrong form in so that I got the wrong chemical and that's why the technique didn't work. Or, It would have all been fine if the equipment, which was bought in by Davies from Neurogenetics, hadn't been useless in the first place, so really it's Davies you ought to be blaming and not me. No, a rapid scan of the room revealed that Darren was the

only protagonist, and that if any procedure was unsuccessful, or any equipment below standard, then the
blame lay firmly and depressingly with him.

'Look,' Karen said after a pause in which Darren
fidgeted and basically wished he could make a run for
it, 'maybe it's best if we don't, you know, well, do anything.'

'No?'

'No. I'm, well, I'm in the middle of my cycle, you
know, and I don't have any contraception.'

'Right,' Darren answered. This presented a dilemma.
Darren did have some contraception, but worried that
this was Karen's way of saying that she didn't want to
shag him. 'Yes, of course,' he added, to appear sup-
portive. That was that, then. He couldn't just leave,
now that the offer of sex had been withdrawn. To stay
would be similarly unrewarding. Maybe he'd stay for
another coffee and then make a run for it.

'Unless, of course, you do?'

Darren fished subtly around for his keys. 'What?'

'Unless you've got some contraception?'

'Er, yes, I do actually, not that I thought, you
know . . .'

Karen stood up and gently slid her jeans off in one
graceful movement. So that was how it was done. She
stood in front of him as he sat on the sofa, and he found
himself gazing at her white knickers. Female under-
wear comes in many clandestine forms, and you never
know what you're going to get until it is there staring
you in the face. He looked up at her and saw a glint of
hunger in her eyes. She stepped closer to him. He
knew what she was asking. He took his fingers and ran
them around the outside of her knickers, across her
slightly swollen belly, diagonally down the top of one
thigh and up the other, describing a triangle of intent.
Karen leaned closer. Darren repeated the movement of

his fingertips, but placed a finger just inside the elastic of the underwear as he described another journey around her pubis. Karen's legs were trembling slightly as he slid his finger further inside the material. This time he felt her hair as he slowly moved his fingers, and as he drew them gradually across the cotton which separated his fingers from her vagina, he noted that the material felt hot and damp at the same time. Please, she urged him. Darren pulled her knickers down and she pressed herself against his face. He took his index finger and ran it slowly from the mouth of her cunt up between her lips and over her clitoris. Please, she repeated, through a heavy breath. Darren eased her labia apart and kissed her swollen clitoris. Karen breathed in sharply and swayed a little on her feet. Darren started to lick her and penetrated her with one of his fingers. Karen pressed herself harder against him. Then, after he pushed another finger inside her, Karen's breathing assumed a rhythm of its own, and Darren knew he would make her come. He moved his tongue harder and faster, and eased his fingers deeper inside her. She was moving of her own accord now, making a noise somewhere between a moan of contentment and a sigh of reluctance. And then she stopped breathing, for five, ten, maybe even fifteen long seconds, and finally let out a long gasp, a sigh, another gasp and a couple of quick sighs, before collapsing on the sofa next to Darren.

After some thirty seconds or so, she said, 'Look, Christ knows what you must think of me, it's just, well, when I'm ovulating, then you'd better watch out.'

Darren smiled, hoping he'd be around to witness the next ovulation.

Trouble-spotter

The next day, Karen went to work and Darren headed back to his computer. He cleared his desk of everything pertaining to the failed theory and returned his attention to the Paper database. The keyboard, however, was really starting to annoy him. The absence of Gs and threes he was living with, and actually enjoying to a certain degree. They were spokes in his existence, but ones he could fairly easily get around. This made a welcome change from the rest of his life with its wholly insurmountable problems. It was as if by solving a small, insignificant dilemma, Darren could convince himself that he was making progress against all the bigger, wider and heavier problems he simply wasn't dealing with. He worked his way fervently and alphabetically through the Paper database, typing names, dates, addresses and telephone numbers into a mini-spreadsheet of his own. As he did so, Darren began to notice that as well as Gs and threes, he was sporadically losing Cs, and, on occasion, Ts. This was irritating. Watch any edition of *Wheel of Fortune* and you'll see just how invaluable the consonants C and T are. Lose them and you're hardly going to be able to insult John Leslie properly.

Darren extracted himself from his seat and stumbled

into the bathroom. Sam hadn't been around for a day or so and this was confirmed by the marked absence of huge puddles of water over the floor and damp, screwed-up towels in the bath. Quite what Sam did in the bathroom was a mystery to Darren, but whatever it was inevitably ended up as some sort of aquatic catastrophe. Darren stared long and hard at his reflection in the bathroom mirror. He frowned, and as he did so, wrinkles he could have sworn he didn't go to bed with the previous night spread slowly out across his forehead. For approximately the three thousandth time in succession in his adult life he was amazed that he could go to sleep so rakishly handsome and wake up so dog ugly. He headed miserably back towards his chair, continuing to ponder the Paper database. Darren began to pace around the room. He knew, because he had measured it, that his room was 12 foot 3 inches by 14 foot 1. He still thought in those terms at home. At work, his room would be 3.72 by 4.25 metres, but at home, the imperial system struggled on, like some sort of secret language which had been stamped out by science and maintained by a hard core of resistance (Darren). So, the living room, he calculated, comprised 19.95 square yards, or 15.82 square metres, or 0.0016 hectares, or, taking the world's circumference to be 24,000 miles, or 38,400 kilometres, and remembering that circumference equals $2\pi r$, and π equals 3.1415927, and that the surface of a sphere is given by $4\pi r^2$ ... then the earth's radius is 6112 kilometres and its surface area therefore 4.69×10^8 km^2 or 4.69×10^{14} m^2, and thus Darren's 15.82 m^2 gave him approximately one thirty millionth millionth of the earth's surface to pace about on, excluding furniture.

Darren told himself that he really ought to stop thinking like this.

* * *

At first, he had been puzzled by the choice of truant letters. Surely, he reasoned, S or E or I were going to see more action on a keyboard than C, G, T or three. And then he realized that it was a code, of sorts. It was, of course, the genetic code. C, G and T were three of the four bases of DNA, and this tied in nicely with what had become increasingly obvious as the original home of the PC – a DNA forensics lab. Although the three didn't make much sense, he had been pleased with his deduction, so pleased in fact that he had rewarded himself with a can of beer.

But the keyboard continued to deteriorate. Sentences were becoming ridden with bullets of space where consonants should have been. Phone numbers were becoming approximations, at best, and having just taken possession of a high-tech computer, there was no way Darren was going to simply write the information down on a piece of paper with a distinctly low-tech biro. As he sat and stared into the gaps between the characters of the keyboard, he heard Sam struggling with the door lock. He was, as ever, trying each one of his keys in a fairly random order until he hit upon one that would turn the bolt. Darren sat upright and tried not to get annoyed, at least not too soon. A couple of minutes later, Sam opened the door, triumphant. Darren greeted him.

'Why the hell don't you sort your keys out?'

'Why? What's wrong with them?'

'You still have no idea which is the front-door key, have you?'

Sam took his key out of the lock and held it up for Darren to see. 'It's this one, isn't it?' Darren swore under his breath. 'Guess who's got a job, then?'

'Dunno,' Darren replied.

'Me!'

Sam was full of himself, which was fairly

unbearable, but nonetheless better than Darren being full of him. A job. This was unusual. Sam normally tried to steer well clear of jobs. The surface of Darren's curiosity was skimmed. 'Yeah? Doing what?'

'Trouble-spotter,' he announced, as if Darren should know what a trouble-spotter was.

Trouble-*starter* would be more accurate. 'And just what the fuck is a trouble-spotter?' he asked.

'You don't know?'

'I wouldn't be asking.' Sam would never just give you what you wanted to know.

'It's someone who works in nightclubs spotting trouble,' he explained.

'And that's it?'

'No, there's loads more to it than that. You sit up on the balcony with one of these,' Sam pulled what looked like a pen out of his jacket, 'and you point it onto the head of anyone who looks like they might be kicking off.' He pointed it at the wall, at Darren's legs, then at his face and finally at his eyes. It was a laser pointer.

'Then what?' Darren asked, shielding his eyes. 'That's hardly going to scare them off, is it?'

'No, the bloke I'm working for, he's a club promoter, and he says that you get a walkie-talkie as well, and you tell the chief bouncer that you've spotted someone who's acting up a bit, and you point them out from above with the pen, so the punter doesn't know that anything's going on, then the bouncers go up and discreetly take him outside for a kicking.'

'And what makes them think, apart from continually attracting trouble, that you have a propensity for spotting it?'

'Oh, you know, I bullshitted this bloke a bit, said I'd done some bouncing once . . .'

'Yeah?'

'Yeah. You gonna come then? This Saturday.'

'What makes you think I'm having anything to do with this shambles?'

'You've got to,' Sam implored. 'Bring some of your friends.' He looked over at Darren and realizing he didn't have any friends, suggested, 'Or Karen.'

'I'll ask her.'

'And what about that bloke from work?'

'Simon.'

'Simon. Bet he'd be up for it.'

'I don't know. Maybe. But it's been so long since I've been to a club I'd just think everyone was going to laugh at me. I don't have the right clothes for a start. I probably wouldn't get in past the bouncers.'

'Listen, I'll make it a condition that they put you, Karen and Simon on the guest list. What do you say?'

'I don't know.'

'Great. You'll love it.'

Darren was about to get back to the point and ask him just where the fuck his recently acquired laptop had come from but, keyboard difficulties aside, the computer was keeping him entertained, and a night out might not be the worst scenario he could think of at the moment. He decided to let it drop.

Virtually

The inescapable facts were these then. The police said they had a DNA sample. They might be right. Simply saying they had a sample wouldn't force me to panic though, so that particular danger had been evaded by common sense. If the police did have a DNA sample, the chances were that it was mine. This was not an absolute, however. I hadn't left blood or any other fluid at the scene, apart from some watery piss in the hedge, and nor had I left any fingerprints. No, what they may have had, as I thought about it, were hair follicles. Presumably they had excluded all other potential droppers of hair in the house from their investigations. In that case, they would have already extracted the DNA. This was bad – there would be virtually no chance of stealing the hair sample. It would now be a number, a coded Eppendorf tube in a faceless freezer in a blank corridor somewhere. So things weren't looking particularly good. If they had some DNA, it was virtually certain to be mine. They were going to test us all, running away was tantamount to guilt and DNA tests were virtually infallible. I was, therefore, not to put too fine a point on it, fucked. But there had to be a way out, there always is, and of all the people who have ever found themselves in the predicament I was now in, I had to have a better idea than most of them where to look for it.

The word virtually kept cropping up, though. What does virtually mean? Granted, it's a bit stronger than 'nearly', but it's also not as damning as 'definitely'. At the very least it's the sliver under a door or the gap in a fence. Virtually would have to be the hole I squeezed myself through. But science doesn't like virtually. Science prefers definitely. So you might hear that genetic fingerprinting is unconditionally, utterly, entirely, absolutely, unquestionably correct and accurate, but what you never hear is that people are unconditionally, utterly, entirely, absolutely and unquestionably correct and accurate, and with good reason, because people are by definition inaccurate. And when it comes down to it, science is nothing more or less than people.

Head Bouncer

Sam signified his return in the early hours of Sunday morning with another generous jiggling of his keys. Darren glanced across at the clock on the computer. Two thirty. He had nearly finished a second bottle of red but still felt reasonably clear-headed, if less than happy. Despite the gleeful progress he was making with the Paper database, shreds of the anger which had consumed him earlier in the evening had returned with a vengeance, growing and multiplying in the thick of the bitter wine. After a couple of minutes, Sam entered. He was very pissed.

'Fuckers!' he said as he slumped down on the nearest chair.

'Who?' Darren asked.

'Those fuckers at the club,' he repeated. And then asked, 'And where did you get to?'

'Didn't Simon tell you?' Darren's tongue was struggling over the dry, acrid residue of the wine.

'Yeah,' Sam replied, cheering slightly. 'Yeah, he did.'

Darren didn't feel like reliving his own evening. He was still too angry. 'So what happened?'

Sam opened a can and spewed his evening out. 'So everything's going well. It's all fine. I'm sat up there on my perch and I've got my walkie-talkie. I can't see any trouble and I'm thinking about having a quick nap, so I turn my walkie-talkie off and start making myself comfortable. Being paid to sleep – this is more like it. Then all of a sudden, all hell breaks loose. Pandemonium. Everywhere. I'm not really deeply asleep, just a bit, you know, slow and groggy. I look down over the balcony and there's bouncers running left, right and centre, punters being picked up and bundled out all over the place. Looks like we've been invaded or something.'

'Yeah?' Darren asked, perking up.

'So I turn my walkie-talkie back on to find out what the panic's about, and there's a hundred fucking bouncers swearing and shouting my name like it's my fault. So I turn it back off. Well, a couple of minutes later and I'm watching what's going on and trying to puzzle out how I might be involved in it, and whether I can slip out the back way, when the Head Bouncer, an unfortunate term at the best of times, comes shinning up the balcony ladder, swearing at me like there's no tomorrow. What's up? I say. What the fuck do you mean, what the fuck's up? Why don't you fucking tell me, four eyes? I don't know what you're talking about, I say. Haven't you been listening to your walkie-talkie? I tell him it doesn't seem to be working. He grabs it and turns the cunt on. It's bursting with panic. Seems OK now, he says, looking like he's going to kill me. Then a message comes through for him. We've got the bastard, it says, and the Head Bouncer tells me to come with him. This ought to be good, he says. I can't see it myself. I decide I should leave if I get the chance and forget about my wages. Well, we go down the ladder and the main lights of the club are on, the music is off, punters are streaming out, the police are everywhere, there are arguments between bouncers, punters and the police . . .'

'Yeah?'

'Yeah, blokes saying ". . . and he just grabbed me, twisted my arm, threw me against this wall and bust my nose, just for dancing with my girlfriend . . ." and the club promoter's looking very nasty and is staring in my direction. Just then, right, one of the coppers stops the Head Bouncer to ask him not to let any of the other bouncers leave the club without talking to *him* first, so I spot my chance and nip through the bar, duck out of the fire escape and leg it.'

'So what was all the fuss about?'

'On the way home I run into one of the bar staff at the taxi rank and he fills me in. Around the time I fell asleep and turned my walkie-talkie off, a punter entered the club and maybe he knew the system or was just pissing around, but the thing is that he had a laser pointer of his own. So he starts pointing the thing around the dance floor just for a laugh, and the bouncers suddenly see what they think are all these punters that are about to kick off, so they radio me to confirm, but of course I can't hear them. Better out than in they think, and they tear through, lifting punters out, most of whom are none too happy about this, and put up a bit of a struggle. Well, you don't have to put up much of a struggle to encourage bouncers to join in the fun, so all shit breaks loose. And the cunt who's flashing his laser about is suddenly having a real laugh, when he works out he can have anyone he likes removed from the club simply by shining his pen on them. He sets about trying to virtually empty the club of blokes in the general cause of giving himself a better chance with the remaining totty. Fair play, in my book. So he continues to wave this thing around like there's no tomorrow, and anyone he doesn't like the look of gets dragged out. Pretty soon, there are scuffles, the cops come, the music gets turned off and the place is emptied.'

'And all because some poor misguided sod put you in charge of trouble-spotting.'

'Tell you what,' Sam says, not the least bit remorseful, 'glad I kept hold of this laser pen. I'm taking it with me to the next club I go to. Weed out some of the riff-raff.' Sam disappeared into the kitchen and returned with a couple of cans. 'But where did you end up?'

Keeping up with Withnail

Simon was late and Darren was edgy. Darren looked at the vacant space on his wrist where the recently smashed watch used to live in tight proximity to his skin. It was hard to tell now that a watch had ever been there. The hairs had grown back lending the pale area some degree of camouflage. Nightclubs. Darren hated nightclubs. He always felt conned, somehow. Watered-down beer, watered-down music, watered-down fun. Dress policies. That was the worst thing. Wear these shoes and this shirt and you're OK. In you come. We won't be seeing any trouble as long as we let the right footwear in. Darren regarded his own shoes with some apprehension. They were his best, in fact, his only, pair, and they would have to do. True, one of them squeaked, but other than that they weren't too bad.

'Sorry.'

It was Simon, who was suddenly standing beside Darren whilst he squinted at his shoes in an effort to make them smarter.

'Hi,' Darren said. 'You all right?'

Simon said he was and they set off. 'Where's the girl from Neuro?' he asked.

'Meeting us in the club. She had to go and see a film at short notice. Don't ask. It's a long story.'

Simon talked about work as they walked and Darren realized that Simon was trying to tell him, without actually using the words, that he missed having him around. Darren was preoccupied, not only with misgivings about the night but also with the question that had been eating him up for days. As he looked across at Simon, and absorbed his chalky complexion, shallow chest and slightly retreating hairline, Darren saw not just his physical profile but the superimposed pattern of fluorescent peaks and troughs of his DNA profile.

'Quick pint first?' Simon suggested.

Darren tried to snap out of it. Simon was grinning and they were standing outside a pub on Division Street. 'I dunno. Karen said she'd be there by eleven. Maybe we shouldn't dawdle.' Once again, Darren glanced at the newly returned hairs on his wrist.

Simon did the same but with more success. 'Quarter to. Plenty of time.'

They entered the noisy atmosphere and jostled their way to the bar. Simon leaned on the bar and dangled a tenner optimistically in the direction of the harassed bar staff. His candour was rewarded relatively quickly and a couple of carpet-regarding minutes later Darren held a pint of Tetley's and a double Southern Comfort in his damp hands. He put his nose deep into the spirit glass and inhaled.

'Did you ever play "Keeping up with Withnail"?' Simon asked.

'What?'

'Keeping up with Withnail.' Darren looked suitably bemused and Simon expanded. 'When I was at . . . when I was a student, we had this game. You know the film *Withnail and I*?' Darren nodded. 'Well, obviously they do a fair amount of drinking in that film . . .'

'And the rest.'

'Yeah.' Simon stared into the hazy atmosphere as if he was rewinding to some previous and happy time. 'Anyway,' he said, returning to the conversation, 'the point is they put it away like nobody's business, and there's a sort of beauty to it. It's like an art. They have, say, twenty minutes to do the damage, so they get pints and quadruples and take it from there. Now, the thing about Keeping up with Withnail is that you get a stack of booze in and get the film on video and whatever they drink, you've got to drink.'

'Sounds dangerous.'

'It's lethal. The only rules are that it's alcohol only. Otherwise, well, it would be an A and E job. So when they go into a pub and down two pints and four shorts, then you all do as well, and you pause the film till everyone's caught up, then off you go again.' Simon took a sip of his chaser. 'I tell you, I don't think I've ever seen the end of that film.'

Darren's mood lightened, despite the fact that Simon was, more than likely, on the Paper database. Simon continued to chatter away and even retold his favourite joke, which still made Darren roar. It was one of those rare jokes that makes you happy just to hear it. It's not as if the punchline makes much difference when you've already heard the joke. It's just the situation, the language, the inevitability. In short, it's like making love to your wife as opposed to shagging someone new for the first time. It is comforting and enveloping, like a journey in a warm car to a favourite place. Darren forgot his problems and went to the bar, deciding not to ask any questions about Paper. His fishing wasn't as successful as Simon's, but five or so minutes later they were drinking their pints and chasers and laughing about Sam's inability to navigate his way down a straight road.

Leaving the pub and getting slapped in the face by

the raw November air, Darren stopped Simon as they were about to turn onto Leopold Street. 'Simon, have you ever been in trouble with the police?'

Simon looked blankly at him. 'What?'

'The police. I mean, does "Paper" mean anything to you? Or "Thorn"?'

'Not apart from the obvious. What are you on about?'

It had just slipped out. Darren had said it, had just asked outright. It had been swilling around inside his head and had spilled out of his open mouth. Darren called himself an idiot under his breath. 'Nothing,' he said, and they continued on their merry way. Certainly if Simon had been guilty of something, he hadn't been in the least perturbed by the question. Darren felt a small wave of relief flow through his veins pursued by the warm chaser he had just knocked back.

Smart but Casual

'Not with those shoes,' he says. He is standing in Darren's way, blocking his progress.

Darren is slow to catch on. 'What?' he asks.

'Your shoes,' he points, 'too casual.'

Darren glances sideways at Simon, who has passed the shoe test. He looks uncomfortable, unsure of whether to go in or not. Simon's shoes, presumably, are not as relaxed as Darren's.

'"Too casual"? What do you mean "too casual"?' Darren demands. Casual. They'd be buggered without casual. It would have to be insouciant. Your shoes are too insouciant. Or too relaxed. Or too easygoing. Or not uptight enough. Or not likely to start a fight enough.

The bouncer fails to elaborate. 'Step away from the door.' He is short and wide and stupid – two of the three bouncer prerequisites.

'Look, these can't be the worst shoes you've ever seen.'

There is no reasoning with him. 'Get out of the way,' he says.

'I mean, who's going to notice my fucking footwear?' Darren shouts.

'Out.' The bouncer is pushing.

Darren tries a new tack. 'Look, my friend works here.'

'Yeah yeah. Now, out.'

'But I'm on the guest list, and I'm supposed to be meeting . . .' Darren blurts out, as if he's a member of the royal family who has been momentarily mistaken for an ordinary punter. It works though.

'Why the fuck didn't you say? What's your name, cock?'

'Darren,' he says. 'Darren White.' The bouncer removes his hand from Darren's shoulder. Darren smiles at Simon, who is standing in the doorway shifting his weight alternately between his enviably smart shoes. The bouncer consults another inside the door and then returns and stands uncomfortably close.

'You're not on the list, so sling your hook.'

'But Sam . . .' Darren tails off as he wonders exactly what the chances might be of Sam remembering to write his name down on a piece of paper. The bouncer is poking two stubby fingers into his chest. Darren looks down at the fat fingers. They seem to be trying to swallow the rings which constrict them, and are rounded off with nails which have been fanatically chewed by impatient teeth.

'*Out*,' the bouncer demands, increasing the pressure on Darren's chest.

'Just let me in,' he pleads, 'no-one'll be looking at my shoes, I'll find my friend and we'll sort this out.'

'I'll not tell you again.'

Darren knows the bouncer isn't going to change his mind. There is only black and white in the world of bouncers. Black tuxedo. White shirt. Black punters. White punters. Black opinions. White opinions. No grey, just yes or no. But Darren can't let it drop. This is his life. A wall of rejection stands in front of him, holding him away from Karen. A friend just out of reach and doing nothing to help. Trying to move forward but being pushed back. One clear direction and one even clearer obstacle. The bouncer is the world stabbing Darren in the chest with stubby fingers. He feels months of frustration and loathing boiling up and brimming over. Darren is going to enter the club. The bouncer pushes harder and Darren grips his wrist. Two youths walk around the stalemate and enter the club.

'Look at *those* shoes!' Darren is screaming. 'You let those fuckers in.'

Through quickly vanishing patience the bouncer says, 'They're not casual and yours are. Now let go my arm and fuck off.' And then adds one more time, 'I'll not tell you again.'

'Darren,' Simon says.

Darren ignores him. 'What about some of the other lowlifes you've let in?' he demands, his self-preservation gene switching itself off. 'Look, I'm coming in, and if any cunt complains about my shoes then I'll have myself beaten up.'

'One more word an' I'll save you the bother.'

'But . . .' In one practised and paralysing movement, the bouncer tears Darren's grip away from his arm and twists it behind his back. Two other Security appear, hoping to witness a fight. Darren is mute with pain. The bouncer turns Darren around and shoves him while he's off balance. He is on the pavement and his shoulder hurts. Darren looks along the kerb at his shoes, which have been scuffed in the struggle. There seems little remaining chance of getting into the club. If his shoes weren't fucked before, they certainly are now.

'Now get the fuck out of my sight,' the bouncer shouts.

Darren gets to his feet with something approaching dignity. The bouncer stands rooted to the spot, sneering at him. Simon enters the club. Darren's legs are trembling but he is still angry. 'As if I want to come into this shit hole,' he starts to rant, continuing to vent his fury and calling the bouncer a few choice names, among which he is most proud of goat-fucking mother-fucker, dickless fuck-face and bully boy bum-bandit.

Impressive swearing though it undoubtedly is, Darren saves the majority of his name-calling until he is safely out of earshot.

Sam laughed. 'Yeah,' he said, after the enjoyment of hearing Darren describe his ejection from the club had subsided. 'I did bump into Karen.'

'Yeah. She told me. Rang her when I got back. Apparently she hung around till about half eleven when Simon found her and let her know what had happened. She came out but I'd long since gone.' Sam smiled again, no doubt drawing enough consolation from Darren's mishaps to paper over the cracks of his own near-disastrous night. Darren let it drop. Although it had quite clearly been Sam's fault that he wasn't on the guest list and therefore didn't get into the club, he wasn't going to get much sympathy. Soon after, Darren crawled off to bed and tried to sleep. But as he closed his eyes, his overworked brain meandered its heavy way through a series of alternately unpleasant and irrelevant scenarios involving Simon and bouncers, while his body seemed to journey alongside with its own parallel language of twists and turns. Eventually, he conceded defeat. He got dressed, stepped over Sam and went down to his car. Fifteen minutes of empty roads later, he was knocking on Karen's door.

Deaf, Dumb and Blind

Karen returned from the bar carrying a pint for herself and one for Darren, and sat down next to him. It was three o'clock in the afternoon and having eaten Sunday lunch and drunk Sunday beer, they were both mildly intoxicated with a heady, afternoon sort of inebriation. Karen continued where she had left off. 'It's like, if I'm not wearing my contacts I can't hear as well.'

'What?'

'You know,' she repeated, 'if I can't see, then I can't always tell what people are saying.'

'Hang on, this isn't making any sense.' He would explain it to her. 'The optic nerve is here, right,' he traced a lazy line in cross-section with his finger, running it from the corner of her eye to just behind her temple, 'and your auditory nerve is, let's have a think,' he moved his finger just above her skin, down and under her ear, and traced another imaginary and not particularly accurate finger line diagonally up towards the crown of her head, 'around here somewhere . . .'

She turned to face him. 'You're missing the point.'

'Well, maybe a bit higher, then,' he said, moving back slightly, so that he could once again see the profile of her head, and trace a parallel but higher trajectory.

'And again. Jesus, you're on a roll.'

'What do you mean?'

'Look, when I say you're missing the point, I mean that the point is, look,' she turned her head away and muttered, 'Dead hum n bly hid so maid a me pin beau.'

Darren was getting a little irritated. He was still tired from the night before and the beer wasn't helping. Karen had the upper hand and this was a little alarming. Let her have the initiative early on and it was downhill from here. And she had virtually accused him of being thick. And had failed to be impressed by his rudimentary, if somewhat cavalier, lesson in anatomy. 'I can't hear you,' he said, his consonants biting slightly.

'Dee dum an bligh keyed shore blazer mean bimbo,' she mumbled.

'What the hell's that supposed to mean?'

'It means that I am proving a point. Let's try again.' She turned back to face him, and uttered the words again, this time with her mouth visible. 'Deaf, dumb and blind kid sure plays a mean pinball.'

'So?'

'So, you hear by looking as well as listening. Everyone lip-reads a bit without realizing they're doing it. And when I don't have my lenses in, it makes it harder to tell what people are saying, because I can't see their mouths very clearly.'

She had a point, but Darren felt he ought to do the decent thing and oppose it. 'You just said it louder the third time. And you were facing me – the words were bound to be clearer.'

'OK, shut your eyes, and I'll say a phrase facing you, then open them and I'll say it again, and you see the difference.'

Darren sat and thought for a moment. Clearly, this

was nonsense. All he had to do was to prove it. He had an idea. 'OK, what about beards?'

'What about them?'

'Are you telling me you find it difficult to understand what bearded people are saying to you? I mean, you can't see bearded lips very well, can you? So by implication it must be more difficult to hear bearded conversation.'

'That's right. Just think of all the deaf people you know – how many of them have beards? Not many I'd guess. Because if you want other deaf people to lip-read you then you'll know that beards are going to get in the way.'

It had a whiff of bullshit, but Karen had him in a corner because he didn't know any deaf people, and, outside science, knew precious few bearded ones either. Darren wasn't happy about being argued into a corner. He decided to admit defeat, but as sardonically as possible, to take the glory out of it. 'No, it's OK. You win,' he said, annoyed with himself.

'It isn't a competition, you know, I was just saying . . .'

'Yeah, and I was just being scientific, debating the point.'

'Scientific my arse!'

'No, you know, that's what science is all about, it's not just accepting . . .' Darren ground to a halt. He really didn't know what the hell science *was* all about any more.

Karen stood up. 'Look, I've had just about enough of this science nonsense and all your silly theories that go nowhere and achieve nothing. It's not science – it's you. Take a good look at yourself instead. And if you so much as mention your theories or any such nonsense when I get back, I'm off, OK, and you can spend the afternoon in your own sorry company.'

Results

With that, she stamped, a little dramatically, Darren thought, into the ladies. He smiled after her. She had only known him a matter of days and had already seen through him. Then, as he sat and thought about what she had said, Darren had an idea. There was, it occurred to him, a cast-iron way of determining whether Simon was indeed on the Paper database. It was time to let science decide.

Security

This wasn't a very sane thing to do, by anybody's standards. Even Sam might have had doubts about the wisdom of such a course of action. It was Friday night and by rights Darren should be in a pub, trying to swallow his frustrations in frothy pints of Tetley. But no, here he was, skulking self-consciously in the semi-darkness along the path which marked the periphery of the main building of the Institute. There were two or three lights on, but other than that the dark windows bore testimony to the fact that another working week had petered out in vain. Darren felt a pang of regret that he would be spending the weekend living in dread and hanging around the darkened corridors of the building ahead of him. He turned a corner and saw the main entrance some twenty yards in the distance. Ten yards away, he suddenly froze. A security guard was passing through the door. Darren wished there were shadows he could melt into, but there weren't, so he kept walking with a sort of shallow enforced confidence. The security guard, who must have been, at the very least, an octogenarian, seemed to spot him through his failing eyesight. Darren proceeded, unsure of himself, but knowing if it came to a chase he would be able to make a fairly safe escape at a brisk walking pace. The guard glanced up as he approached. Darren stopped. 'Evening, sir,' the guard said as he drew level, before looking back at his feet and continuing on his distracted journey. Darren turned and watched him hobble on towards one of the plethora of huts where security guards huddled together doubtlessly recounting war tales that had become fat after years of telling. He was a little perturbed by the scant level of interest he had aroused by creeping around the building at night, and felt like shouting after him, 'Look, I'm trying to break in here. At least try to stop me, for Christ's sake.'

At the entrance, Darren swiped the security card he had retained in case of emergencies through the metallic slot of the handleless door, which clicked quietly to announce that it could now be pushed open. There was no scientific reason for such security – very few youths are misguided enough to want to steal Petri dishes or Eppendorf tubes – it was just a case of hampering them slightly as they made off with the department's computers at night. During the day, however, the security system gave staff the distinct impression that it functioned more to keep them inside the building than to keep intruders out, given that internal doors could only be brokered by a vigorous and repeated swiping with seemingly ineffectual security cards. Escape from the labyrinthine building could thus be a lengthy process. Entry into it, by comparison, was a breeze, with the front door propped permanently and invitingly open. A large proportion of the Institute's time was therefore taken up attempting to breach the security doors which separated lab from lab, floor from floor, corridor from corridor and person from person.

Darren made his way around the quadrangle on the first floor until he reached his former laboratory, preceded by the echo from his alternately squeaky shoes. None of the labs were occupied. Even the beards had called it a week. Turning the strip lights on, Darren was dismayed to note that Simon had invaded his bench with bottles, tubes and tips. On the plus side, however, it looked as if he had also inherited his solutions, and may well have been adding liberal doses of Darren's P15(s), cUM, BL0$_2$D, 5(Pit) and Ph1(LeGm) to his experimental reactions. Darren smiled to himself, but then frowned as he leafed through Simon's lab notes only to be confronted with page after page of neat gels, clean sequences and voluminous data. Even using his collection of exotic solutions, Simon was getting better data than Darren ever had. He tried not to let it get to him. He had to focus and he didn't have much time. He started a sweep of the freezers for the reagents he would need, and a perusal of the cupboards for the equipment. Fifteen minutes later, he had everything but the starting material. He walked over to the door and closed it, revealing one pristine and one grubby lab coat hanging on the back. The clean one was his own. It had rarely seen any action when Darren had worked at the Institute, as he had decided from the offset that his clothes weren't really worth protecting from the minor chance that he would spill a range of nasty chemicals over himself. This had turned out to be a poor decision in the long run, but Darren had stuck faithfully with it. Simon's coat, on the other hand, did see fairly regular action. Darren took it down from its hook and peered closely at the collar. Holding it up to the light, he found what he was after and took the coat over to his bench. There, he unravelled a short length of Sellotape from a nearby roll and dabbed it on the outside of the collar several times. He examined the piece of tape and noted to his satisfaction the presence of three light-brown hairs which, with the aid of a pair of forceps, he managed to unstick and manoeuvre into a small uncapped tube.

DNA extractions are routine affairs that might distract you from thinking for an hour or so at best. Darren had never taken DNA from hair follicles, but knew the procedure must be similar to any other sort of extraction, only on a smaller scale given the dearth of material. He followed the instructions of the purification kit, and some ninety minutes later he had what he wanted – some of Simon's DNA. As he held the tiny tube with its tiny droplet of clear fluid up to the light, Darren mused that while possession was indeed nine parts of the law, possession of someone's DNA probably counted for at least ten.

Soft Comfort

The stairs are dark and covered with faded swirls of a pattern trodden almost into oblivion. My eyes feel as if they're glued open. I am ready. The fear has gone. I am excited, and this worries me. Every now and then the torch beam catches the scalpel in its path and I feel a surge of anticipation. He is sleeping. There is a faint sound like snoring from one of the rooms above. There are two doors ahead of me, on either side of the stairs. I walk slowly over to the left one, my legs feeling taut through my jeans. The door opens easily and makes no sound. There is a TV in a cabinet, a sofa, an elongated coffee table and two easy chairs. I leave the room and pass through the opposite door. This is of similarly little interest. It is time to go upstairs. I climb as slowly as I can manage. The snoring continues. It is coming from one of two adjacent doors. There are three more doors further down the landing. The first two are empty bedrooms with lace curtains and patterned wallpaper. I guess that one is the bathroom I could see from below, one is his bedroom, and one is his study. I try one of the three remaining doors. The bathroom. Pink and tasteless – an old person's soft comfort hanging in the air. He has been here and I can smell him. I feel a primeval urge for blood. I leave the bathroom.

There are two doors left. I place my ear close to each one in turn and decide which one he is in. I stop for a second, his heavy inhalations sounding alien against my own shallow respiration. I try to inhale more deeply but it just makes my subsequent panting faster. My lungs are trying to maintain an average speed, about twice the rate of comfortable breathing. With the torch and scalpel side by side in my right hand, I examine the finger tips of my left. The glove is intact. I swap hands and repeat the action. It wouldn't be good to leave fingerprints. I turn the door handle, hearing the springs of the handle stretch and groan. I enter the room. I broaden the beam of the torch and run it slowly around the dark edges of the room. I can still hear snoring. I walk forward. This is it. Weeks of planning and deciding. I am no longer scared. I am here to do a job. This is what soldiers say when they kill people in battle. They are just doing a job. I say it to myself, just doing a job, and I like the way it feels inside my mouth. I say it one more time and kill the torch. There is a little light through the pale curtains and I edge forward, scalpel first.

Making DNA

Darren glanced at his watch. Ten more minutes and he could leave the building. He returned the various extraction components to their rightful homes and stored the slim tube housing Simon's DNA at the back of a refrigerator which looked as if it wasn't used much any more, its contents slowly being consumed by an advancing tide of ice. He walked over to a blank-looking machine at the far end of the laboratory which housed four uninteresting bottles. This dull-looking gadget could make DNA. Short stretches, admittedly, but DNA all the same, and important DNA at that, for such sequences could then encourage the amplification and isolation of larger, more pertinent, stretches of DNA. He entered the precise sequences of six, twenty-base stretches of DNA, which he had copied from a computer file at the flat. The modest machine made no obvious flashing or beeping noises as it began the task which would take four or five hours. Darren had a last check around the lab and left it fairly much as he had found it.

As he stood at the end of the corridor listening for the sounds any lingering security guards might make as they shuffled along in sleepy vigilance, he noted that the building didn't creak or groan as a house does when you're alone in it at night. To all intents and purposes, the Institute was dead. Darren made his way quietly through the next set of security doors and paused again at the end of the hallway. The stillness made him uneasy, as if he was trespassing in a graveyard. He had to be careful. To be discovered wandering the corridors of the Institute at well past midnight, as a sacked former member of staff, might not go down too well. He remained stationary at the corner of the quadrangle and listened again. This time, Darren heard a noise like a door slamming. He froze, listening hard. He was now sweating slightly and his stomach wall had clenched. There was another slam, closer this time, which, in the absence of any other sound, echoed unimpeded down the long corridor, hungrily bouncing off walls towards him. The building was still well lit. He peered around the corner. Nothing. He stepped back and waited a second. He ought to be careful and not take any chances. Darren waited as long as he could bear waiting and, hearing nothing, stepped out. There, to his horror, was a security guard, fifteen paces away and as surprised as Darren was. The guard calmed himself and fixed Darren with an unsmiling stare. Darren kept walking. They approached each other. There was just enough room to dash past if the guard wasn't quick off the mark. Darren maintained eye contact, waiting for him to respond. They met face to face. Darren waited to react. The security guard raised his arm. Darren flinched, inhaled sharply and was about to run through him when the guard's arm came to an abrupt halt by his temple. The old bastard was saluting him.

'Evening, sir,' he said, lowering his arm again. 'Gave me a bit of a start there.'

'Oh yeah,' Darren muttered, trying to recover, 'working late, I'm afraid.'

'I'll say. Anyway, mind how you go.'

'Right,' Darren replied, edging past. The guard trundled on, whistling, and Darren made rather more rapid progress on his way out of the building. It was true what they said – you can't teach an old dog new tricks. If an ageing security guard has recognized you once as a member of staff, he will continue to do so until told otherwise, and even then it will be unlikely that he will remember to change his behaviour.

The following evening, Saturday, Darren approached the Institute with a lot less trepidation. He made his way uneventfully to his former lab and removed six small plastic columns housing the freshly made DNA. After a couple of hours of preparation, they were dried, purified and ready for use with the sample he had extracted from Simon's hairs. Later, in the early hours, Darren left the lab and sauntered out of the building. Fatigue had allowed a pleasant kind of cloudiness to settle over his actions. He had felt his concentration and alertness wane and knew it was time to leave before he started fucking things up. The Sequencer would run through the night and come up with its fluorescent answer tomorrow. As he made his way down the lengthy corridors, Darren's bed began to track him down and call to him, beckoning him home.

Disproving Hypotheses

Science. Fucking science. It gets you every time. It builds your hopes up and then swallows them whole, leaving you with nothing but empty pangs of failure. Three nights' work, and for what? Darren sat and stared at his computer, at the blur of overlapping bands which slouched lethargically where sharp, crisp, discrete bands should have stood smartly to attention. Fuck it, he said. He had once again given science the benefit of the doubt, and once again it had fucked him over. He was no further forward. He was still unable to prove beyond reasonable doubt that the profile of Bird, S on the database was indeed Simon's. The image on the screen was a shambles, and no way clear enough to match against Bird, S. He would have to do it again.

As a child, he should have been warned. At school, the slogan 'Physics is Fun' had been touted to persuade pupils like Darren that inertia was dynamic, resistance was electrifying, black holes were sunny, gravity was light and frothy and gases and liquids were solid topics to study. Nowhere had it ever been stated that Science is Shite. No, that was something you only discovered when you had burned all your other bridges, when you had bad-mouthed the languages, drawn a line through art, put history behind you and told geography to get lost. Science was about disproving hypotheses, you had been told. Come up with a hypothesis and then try to disprove it. If you can't disprove it, then your hypothesis must be right, and you can devote yourself to disproving a new hypothesis. You should never try to *prove* hypotheses – that would be far too easy and far too straightforward. But Darren couldn't help thinking that if you were going to start out so negatively in the first place, you weren't going to get a lot of joy out of a career in science. Constantly attempting to disprove the best idea you've had up until that point is a bit like constantly kicking yourself in the bollocks for having an intelligent thought. In all other spheres of your life, you are always likely to give yourself the benefit of the doubt. At work, however, you're likely to doubt any benefit that comes your way. Other professions didn't breed this type of self-doubt. Bricklayers didn't build walls and then try to knock them down. Lorry drivers didn't get up to a fair speed and then do all they could to make their lorries crash off the road. Window cleaners didn't clean windows just to then smear them in dirt. Gardeners didn't grow plants and then try their best to kill them off. Science just seemed so destructive, like carefully nurturing a flower and then throwing toxins at it until one toxin kills it, and then nurturing another plant to see whether the same toxin kills that one, and if not, trying other and successively more nasty toxins. Always killing the beautiful idea. It was this restless lack of satisfaction that irked Darren. It just went on and on and on, never satisfied, never sitting back, feet up, saying, Well, we've found something here, we started out with a nice idea which we managed to prove, so we'll close the box and investigate the next good thought we have. Although Darren understood the logic of completion, and the necessity of thoroughness, and the inevitability of progress, understanding doesn't always mean acceptance. After all, perfectionists rarely get anything constructive done. Progress, true movement forwards, almost always comes through accepting that you will never be able to tie all of the loose ends, and indeed, that a few loose ends hanging about the place are going to make fuck-all difference to anything at the end of the day.

One sphere in which Darren did, however, indulge in disproving hypotheses was the sphere of girlfriends. Darren was a perpetual disprover of girlfriends. His hypothesis with girlfriends was entirely scientific: 'You are perfect until I prove otherwise.' Often, a relationship for Darren meant a protracted quest to unearth imperfection. And if, after six months, he had found nothing intrinsically wrong with a new girlfriend, he would generally dump them on the grounds of being too perfect. It wasn't that he craved perfection, by any means, more that imperfections allowed him to justify his own relationship failings. Darren was restless and sought escape, and rather than look at the reasons for this he chose to look at his girlfriends, reasoning that the blame probably lay with them. It had never occurred to him that if he had managed over time to find fault with an unhealthy number of healthy girls, the true problem might ultimately be his. Rather, he assumed that it was simply bad luck that he had happened across a constant stream of faulty women. The faults didn't have to be particularly overwhelming either. Feet which were a size or two over the norm would do in an emergency. Having extensively and surreptitiously assessed Karen's shoes for signs of over- or under-dimensions, Darren was forced to concede that the prospects thus far were reasonably good, and that Karen was going to take some fairly extensive disproving.

False Negative

A few hours later, Darren once again found himself edging around the Institute's neatly trimmed borders. This felt like one risk too many. He had been able to justify three nights over the weekend as an acceptable risk, but a Monday evening was a different matter. It would only take one over-excitable science type hanging about a few hours later than normal to notice him on the premises and there would be trouble. The guards themselves weren't the real source of worry, given that the hospital had sought as far as possible to recruit its security personnel from diverse minority backgrounds, largely to the detriment of the actual level of security that such a band of ragged misfits could hope to provide. Although admirable in theory, the average youth confronted by shell-shocked war veterans, female geriatrics, disabled people and the partially sighted, was hardly likely to need new under-wear. No, the real problem would arise if the police were called. It would only take a brief search of his flat and a briefer glance at the computer for Darren to really find himself in the shit.

Darren had decided that the error lay in the profiling itself. The DNA extraction was just about foolproof, and therefore, being something of a fool, Darren decided he was probably safe. The short, oligo-nucleotide stretches of DNA he had made were also fine, he discovered after rechecking the Paper database. The actual profiling reaction had proceeded smoothly and Darren had been as fastidious as he could manage. No, the real problem was the Sequencing gel. The bands were there, but were fuzzy. He narrowed it down to a gel which hadn't set properly, in his haste to be out of the building and back in bed. This time he would leave it longer, which would be painful, as it meant hanging around the building for three hours while the gel set and three hours while the machine ran. This was going to be a long night. Twice during the early hours Darren heard a shuffling guard pass the lab, try the door, which was locked, and slouch on to tackle the next one.

He was shaky and a little weak through lack of sleep, but by six forty-five a.m. Darren had begun to tidy away all evidence of his illicit actions and was saving the data to disk. He yawned and stretched and then yawned again. It was beginning to brighten. Darren had one last glance around the lab, then shut the door and sauntered out of the building. Rounding the corner which led to the exit, he saw Simon approaching from the far end of the corridor. Darren looked down at the disk which had his DNA profile on it.

'Darren. How're you doing?' Simon asked as he came close.

'Fine.'

Simon stopped when he was a couple of yards in front of Darren, as if to emphasize the physical space between them. 'So,' he said, glancing at his watch, 'how come you're in the building?'

Simon was smiling, but Darren sensed the question carried more than just an idle curiosity. 'Oh, you know . . .' He could hardly tell him that he was examining his DNA in relation to a criminal case in which Simon had been a strong suspect. 'I forgot this computer disk when I left, that's all. Just thought I'd pop in and collect it.'

'What, at quarter to seven?'

'Didn't want to bump into anybody . . .'

'Graham, you mean?'

'Yeah, you know.'

Simon grinned. 'Yes, I know. He's still useless and still hasn't got anybody in to fill your post.'

'So anyway,' Darren said, feeling some confidence returning, 'what the fuck are *you* doing in at this illegal hour?'

'Got a couple of reactions to set up before I can do anything. Hoping to be out by four – got to take the car to the garage. MOT time, I'm afraid.'

'Jesus, I don't know if mine's even got one. Anyway, good to see you . . .'

'Yes. Look, did you get home OK after that club fiasco?'

'Yeah. Sorry about that, I lost it a bit. Thanks for finding Karen.'

'No problem. Anyway, I'll see you some time.'

'That would be good.'

With that, Darren sloped off towards the exit and left the building.

The flat was cold and Darren shivered uncomfortably in the dawn air. There was just enough light in the room for him not to stumble over Sam, and it was also just dark enough that Darren might be able to get a couple of hours' sleep if he wanted. But he had come this far and there was no way he was going to bed until he had compared Simon's profile with that of Bird, S. on the database. He turned his computer on and Sam stirred.

'What time is it?' he muttered.

'Early,' Darren answered, sitting down in front of the monitor.

Sam swore and rolled over in his sleeping bag, grumbling under his breath. Darren opened the Paper directory and brought up the Bird, S. profile on screen. Then he put his disk in the slot and opened Simon's trace. Darren stared into the screen for a few seconds and then turned the laptop off. Through the gloom he spotted a half-finished bottle of sickly sweet wine. 'Bollocks,' he said, walking over to the bottle, which he took through with him to the bathroom. The profiles didn't match. That ruled Simon out of any misdoing then. As he shut the door, Darren felt another avenue of interest close behind him. Inside the bathroom, Darren opened the cabinet and removed around thirty bottles of diverse colours and shapes. He prised the lids and stoppers off each one and tipped their contents into the sink, before washing the mix of exotic powders down the plughole with a generous splash of Blue Nun. Darren turned and left the sink, and headed for his bed. There was a sudden bang, as uppers met downers and clashed with in-betweeners. The unmistakable smell of 7-choloro-1-methyl-5-phenyl-3H-1,4-benzodiazepin-2[1H]-one-N-acetylmescaline-2, 2-amobarbital-L-amphetamine-bromazo3,7-panol-methylamphetamin hung in the air. Or maybe it was 6-choloro-2-methyl-5-phenyl-3H-1,4-benzodiazepin-2[1H]-one-N-acetylmescaline-2,2-amobarbital-L-amphetamine-bromazo3,7-panol-methylamphetamin-hydride. Difficult to tell. Either way it was one hell of a chemical reaction. Darren got into bed with the suffocating wine.

Half-drunk and half-asleep, he tried to put things into perspective. This was becoming his life. An idea, generally half baked at best, an obsessive need to follow the idea through to its unsuccessful conclusion, a period of self-pity and near-alcoholism, while all the time falling away from normal, contented, safe, rounded life. But things were going to change. He was going to get a sense of perspective back in his life. He was going to delete the Paper directory. He was going to tidy the flat. He was going to kick Sam out. He was going to start looking for a job to get some cash together and get out of the filthy flat, back into his slightly cleaner house and while he was at it delete his theory nonsense, get his hair cut and fix his car and . . . wash his clothes . . . and . . . try not . . . to . . . sleep . . . all . . . day . . .

Conclusions

God-bothering

Sam picked the phone up, said, 'Yes?' and then handed it to Darren.

'Yes?' Darren repeated.

'Darren. Simon. Listen, there's some bad news.'

'Yes?'

'It's Dawn.' Simon sighed and then cleared his throat. 'She tried to kill herself. Yesterday. Thought you should know.'

Darren didn't know what to say. If Dawn had tried to top herself, what hope was there for the rest of the world? 'But she's still alive?' Simon gave a cautious yes. 'How is she?' he asked.

'She's OK, I guess. At the Royal . . .'

'How did she . . .'

'Pills. Paracetamol. She's in the liver unit.'

'Listen, I'd like to see her.'

'I'm going this afternoon, if you want to come.'

'Sure. Where shall I meet you?'

They agreed to meet a safe fifty yards or so from the Institute. Darren spent the morning mulling it over. A God-botherer, an insanely happy God-botherer at that, had tried to cash her chips in. The Lord certainly moved in mysterious ways. Still, if your life's ambitions could be realized by simply poncing around all day on a cloud and strumming a harp, it was a wonder that masses of Christians weren't stringing themselves up on a hourly basis. Putting it off could only be a bad thing. If you spent your life doing good and fully expected to enter the pearly gates and live for ever, surely it was best to do it now, whilst there were still clouds going spare and while science was yet to prove that it was all nonsense and the only rebirth you would experience would be when the worms that ate you reproduced. After all, if the reward was so good, why bother putting up with a shite life of drudgery down here among the unclean, the unfit and the ungodly? Lottery winners, for instance, generally don't sit about for months on end in their knackered flats just staring lovingly at their winning tickets, do they?

Just before he left the flat, Darren had a second call. It was Graham.

'I've just heard,' Darren said, before Graham tried to fit a sentence together. 'Simon rang me.'

'Heard what?' he asked.

'About Dawn.'

'Dawn? Oh yes, Dawn. Very sad. No, what I wanted to say, Darren, to ask, well, to suggest more than anything, was the possibility, the chance . . .'

'Graham,' Darren said brusquely, 'please get to the point.' He had no more time to listen to such nonsense, particularly if he wasn't being paid to do so.

Graham cleared his throat. Darren pictured him frowning and running his fingers along the desk. 'The thing is, the Trust still hasn't managed to fill your post, your old post, as quickly as we would have liked, and we have a deadline coming up and need to get some data together rather urgently.' Graham talked fluently and cogently, like someone who has just been cured of their stutter. 'So, I wondered, and Staffing Services have given their nod to it, whether you might come back into the lab for a month or two, on a rolling one-month contract, just until we've got a couple of small experiments sorted out.' Having made it from the start to the finish of a sentence fairly much in a straight line, Graham paused, not wanting to ruin the effect.

'And I'd be on the same salary as before?'

'Yes.'

Darren was desperate to get out of the flat and back to normality, but in the absence of such an opportunity the Institute might have to do. He decided yes but said maybe, just to irritate Graham a little. 'OK,' he answered. 'I'll think about it.'

Simon was waiting, head bowed, scraping one of his shoes along the pavement as if he was slowly stubbing a cigarette out. Darren was still a little uneasy about having profiled his DNA, and felt as if he had stolen something intangible from Simon, like part of his soul.

'You all right?' Simon asked, surveying Darren's dirty jeans, scruffy shoes and battered jacket.

Darren glanced quickly over his clothes, having watched Simon's eyes do the same. Maybe he should have changed. 'Yeah. Fine,' he said. 'Launderette day. You know.' Simon looked as if he didn't quite understand. Not that it was launderette day. Such non-essentials had long been jettisoned by Darren in favour of occasionally washing clothes in the kitchen sink. 'Anyway, guess who's coming back to work?'

'You?' Simon guessed, a little dismayed. He had, after all, stolen Darren's bench and was in possession of a proud and seemingly exotic collection of his solutions, none of which he'd been able to find reference to in any of the standard scientific books.

Dawn was sitting up in bed, looking drained and miserable. She was pale and the drip which entered her body looked as if it was leaching the colour from her veins rather than infusing nutrients into her bloodstream. Her posture suggested cumulative defeat: her lower back was fairly upright, but sagged the further up your eyes journeyed, so that her shoulders hunched forwards and her neck arched down, leaving her head to hang limply, her chin jutting into her sternum. She lifted her head momentarily in recognition as Simon and Darren approached.

'What are you doing here?' she asked, her head falling gently back to its flaccid position, her eyes staring into the bleak whiteness of her bed sheets. It was a statement of utter defeat.

'We came to see how you were,' Simon answered calmly, as if he had been expecting to see Dawn so utterly broken.

Dawn glared up at him. 'How do you think I am?' she spat. Darren looked nervous and fidgeted with a small flap of skin which had detached itself from its home at the base of one of his fingernails. There were no flowers around her bed, and, unusually for Dawn, no sign of any religious paraphernalia. Darren wanted to ask her why, but couldn't even look her in the face. He had never seen someone in such abject misery. Darren felt a curious empathy for Dawn, of the sort that had never been called upon before. As he fidgeted and Simon tried to think of something comforting to say, a stethoscoped medic approached the bedside and was about to speak when he was overcome with a look of curiosity, which quickly melted into a thin smile.

'Simon Bird,' he said.

Simon appeared fairly taken aback. 'Jim,' he answered, shaking the hand which was proffered. 'Jim. How are you?' Dr Jim said he was fine, good in fact, really good. 'Look, Jim, could I have a word with you?' Simon asked, taking Jim aside and away from the bed.

Darren stood and stared at the small flap of skin on his finger, before pinching it between the nails of his index finger and thumb and tugging smartly. He winced as it detached, leaving a tiny red furrow where it had dragged some neighbouring skin along for the ride. Dawn watched him, and conscious of the scrutiny, he looked up and into her eyes. 'Why did you do it, Dawn?' he asked gently.

Dawn paused, and then said through flat tones, 'I've been thinking about something you said, something that preyed on my mind since I heard it. Something about science and religion.'

Although Darren was religious about science, albeit with fundamentalist tendencies, he was seldom scientific about religion. Sure, he had thought things through a couple of times when Dawn was God-bothering while cloning genes at the same time and without seeing any apparent contradiction, but he was having difficulty remembering any specific occasion when he might have said anything out loud. Then again, his memory was slowly drowning in a swamp of clammy, soggy, waterlogged thoughts, and so anything was possible. He tried to think. Dawn looked up at him.

'You have no idea what you said, have you?'

Something in the bitterness that her eyes betrayed jogged his memory. Darren glanced back at his damaged finger. He had made a speech. She had irritated him with her undented optimism. He was feeling raw and on edge. She had been patronizing. She had pitied him as an unbeliever. Darren had attacked her religion as an easy target. He told her that she had put all of her worries in one basket, a basket that you couldn't hear, see or touch, a basket which therefore could never let you down, a basket which shielded her from the cold harsh actualities of life. It's God's way. He moves in mysterious ways. It is all for His purpose. If something bad happens and you can justify it, and something good happens and you can justify it, and something indifferent happens and you can justify it, you are at least halfway to being happy. Not knowing, that is true misery. But Darren hadn't stopped there. He was struck suddenly by the hypocrisy of what she was doing. OK, science and religion have similarities. The deeper you look into both, often the more questions you unearth rather than answer. Parts of science and religion try to understand how and why we are here. But this is precisely when the two lock horns. You can't believe both, though evidently some do. A slim but all the same prevalent number of geneticists co-believe Genesis and evolution, and have devised tricky paths through the maze of common sense in order to do so. Talk to Christian scientists and they will tell you that God created a lower form of life, which then evolved into humankind. But with the best will in the world, it's hard to picture Adam and Eve as two slime moulds. *Digesting* an apple might have been possible, but where the fuck would the spare rib have come from exactly? A spare flagellum maybe, but a whole bone? So, a few weeks before he left the lab for good, Darren had accused Dawn of hypocrisy.

'Was it the science-religion hypocrisy thing?' he asked, presently, 'because if it is, I'm really—'

'You're the hypocrite, Darren,' she said, in raw, stinging tones that Darren had never witnessed before. 'Call yourself a scientist? You stop and actually think about science for a few weeks and you lose it completely. What sort of faith do you call that?'

Darren stood and stared out of the window. He was angry, largely because she was right, and to retaliate would be in poor taste given Dawn's current state. He looked around for Simon who was twenty yards away, chatting to the doctor about Dawn.

'You still haven't said why,' he said at last.

Dawn straightened, fighting as she did so the fanatically tucked-in sheets which seemed to be trying to pin her to the bed. 'I'll tell you why. Eighteen months, since my rebirth, and I kept my occupation at the Institute secret from my church. Only my family knew. And then one day the sermon is about living a lie, and the guilt is bearing down on me, and I'm thinking suddenly about what you said, and people are confessing left, right and centre to anything, trivialities, and I can't help it, God is watching me, urging me to be clean in front of him, and so I let it all out, I'm a hypocrite, I say, believing in science, working in genetics and living as a Mormon, and all of a sudden the focus is on me, and my church are praying for me, and the church leader tells me I can no longer do both, that it's heresy to tamper with genes and yet worship God as the mighty creator of everything, and suggests I give up my job, which I can't, because it's my life outside the church and I need to feed my children, and so he's telling me to choose between my God and my job . . .'

Darren felt sick and gazed desperately in the direction of Simon, who was still deep in conversation with the doctor. He couldn't look at Dawn. The doctor and Simon at last approached the bed.

'Well,' Simon said, unwholeheartedly, 'Dr Stevenson here says you're going to be OK.'

'That's right,' Dr Stevenson said, 'no real need to worry. You won't be drinking for a few months though.'

'I don't,' Dawn replied, miserable nonetheless. As a Mormon, Dawn couldn't even drink coffee. Alcohol, cigarettes, swearing, taking the Lord's name in vain, beverages containing caffeine, sex outside marriage and any other potential avenue of pleasure had all been closed down for her by the Mormon church. Darren wondered whether he might also have tried to top himself under such a regime.

'Look, I've got to get back to work. Darren – I'll be in touch. Bye.' Simon made his departure. Darren, with no similar excuse, felt obliged to stay with Dawn and wallow in his unhappy conscience.

After a few seconds, the doctor asked, 'You two friends of Simon?'

'Workmates. Well, Dawn is and I used to be.'

'And where's that?'

Darren told him. Dr Stevenson reassured Dawn, made his excuses and left. Darren tried to think of a convincing reason to leave. Dawn refused to make it easy for him. After a couple of minutes of tutting and humming and aborted attempts to start conciliatory sentences, Darren said he had to get back. To where? she asked. Just back, he replied and left.

Convolutions

It seemed like lunacy now. Four days back at work and already an alarming sense of perspective was returning. Darren smiled to himself and turned his computer on. Another wild-goose chase. He highlighted the Paper directory and his finger hovered over the Delete key. What a twat he had made of himself. Insinuations, phone calls, creeping round the Institute at night, profiling DNA from the hairs on Simon's lab coat . . . Darren changed his mind. He had assessed about ninety per cent of the directory's files, but had left around forty which, through habitually lethargic and fragmentary patterns of labour, remained unopened at the end of the long, tiresome list. He worried suddenly that it would be wrong to delete the whole of the Paper files without at least having a cursory look at the stragglers. After about fifteen minutes of routine file-opening, scrolling, reading, copying the information into a word processing document, closing, opening the phone directory, scanning, and comparing, Darren stopped and screwed up his eyes. He was very near the bottom. Viner, G. He unscrewed his eyes again. Darren opened the phone directory and ran his fingers down the Venables, the Vickers and the Vincents to the bottom of the page. There were two Viners, one B., one

G. A single Viner, G. And a Dr Viner, G. at that. It was Gavin. No multiple entries this time. The address was in Broomhill, which was Gavin's neck of the woods. Gavin Viner, the Gavin Viner he worked with, was on the police profile list as well. Darren opened the associated notes file. Viner, G. He cross-referenced the number, finding it after a couple of false starts. Viner, G. He read the entry. Category of risk: High. One of only three. And one of which, Simon, he had already discounted. Darren rubbed some sharp crystalline sleep from the inside corner of his eyes. He opened and closed the file and checked again. He had been known, of course, to make the odd mistake. There it was, though, in all its glory, Viner, G., High. The devious bastard. Now this was news.

Darren walked into the bathroom and had a long look in the mirror. He tried to focus simultaneously on both of his pupils, suspecting that one was actually larger than the other, but was never quite able to hold the image of one eye long enough to accurately compare with the other. As he thought about Gavin he became distracted, staring down at his nose, examining it for blackheads which might be worth trying to coax from the protection of their deep, subcutaneous pores. The blackheads of Darren's nose had been a source of intermittent joy since he was fifteen or so. If he got one right, a long, off-white column of solidified pus would surge forth to the surface of his skin like a train through a tunnel. The great thing, however, was the intricate structures of the resulting columns, which seemed to mirror the convoluted pores they had been hiding in. Having had a couple of such joyous successes, Darren sauntered back into the living room, pleased with himself. Then he had an idea. He picked up the phone, made a quick call and then left the flat. He was going to visit the very source of Paper.

Air-conditioning

The car was really starting to piss him off now. There was no way he could afford to have it fixed, and no way he could do it himself, so it had him over a barrel. Outwitted by a one-litre Polo. As far as Darren could tell, which wasn't particularly far, the cooling system was shot. This was the irony of being at the cutting edge of one scientific discipline – you are almost certainly going to be an idiot in every other scientific discipline you come across. Being a top geneticist, for instance, guarantees that you probably don't understand a word of physics. So the root cause of the inadequate cooling of Darren's engine remained a mystery. Still, he was able to apply one firm principle of thermodynamics. With the engine perpetually having to be nursed back from the brink of meltdown, heat had to be lost from somewhere, and so Darren had to drive with the heater full on, blasting hot engine air into his face regardless of the outside temperature. Generally, this meant driving with the windows down, the heater on full, and the occupant in a dazed state of temperature disequilibrium. Another knock-on effect of the lack of engine cooling was that Darren couldn't use the gears to slow down, and so he had to unlearn changing down from fourth to third, and down to

241

second at the last minute when approaching junctions and roundabouts. Instead, he generally braked in neutral, and then had to fish around with the gear lever to try to find a suitable gear to accelerate with again. Due also to funding inadequacies, Darren couldn't afford to have his brakes looked at, brakes which were bearing the brunt of any change in momentum, and which were becoming decidedly spongy. All in all, he thought to himself as he focused variously between the *A to Z*, the temperature gauge, the gearstick and, occasionally, the road, if one thing falls down then everything leaning against that one thing falls along with it, and he was just congratulating himself on this metaphor for the state of his life, when he pulled up behind a row of cars at a junction and noticed a girl in his rear-view mirror, who was singing to her heart's content. He tried to lip-read in reverse to catch the song. This was important. She was attractive, from the steering wheel up at least, and Darren hoped she wasn't singing something shite. She was certainly enjoying herself. He turned the radio on and tuned through several stations. She wasn't singing Radio One – *News Beat* was on, or rather some poor sod was desperately struggling to read the news over the sound of some other sod fiddling about with a drum machine. Radio Hallam was out as well – there was a string-bending Oasis guitar solo plodding through the speakers. It wasn't Piccadilly 103 either – it also carried news, though this time without the beat. Radios Three and Four were out, for obvious reasons, which left Virgin or a host of minute local channels which hung around the street lamps of bigger stations hoping to draw in people who couldn't tune their radios properly, and then presumably couldn't be arsed to retune to the stations they were looking for in the first place. Darren kept watching the girl in his rear-view mirror, a type of reverse voyeur, and continued to flick through stations. It could of course be a tape, but it was a battered car of similar neglect to his own, and he doubted whether it would have a cassette player. In desperation, Darren switched to Radio Two. That was it! She was listening to Radio Two and singing her heart out to a Bacharach song. Dionne Warwick singing 'Walk on By'. It was official – the girl had taste. The cars in front started to move a little, and Darren edged forward, still intent on the rear-view mirror and now singing along himself. The song headed for the fade and the cars ahead of him shuffled forwards once more. Darren wanted the entire road system of Sheffield to cease up for ever, and to be trapped in the bitter-sweet chorus with his rear-view woman. The music began to sublimely drift away. He imagined that they were singing opposing phrases – her telling him to walk on by and Darren asking his rear-view woman to stay. It was a rare moment of harmony with someone in his life, and almost inevitably it was with someone who was oblivious to it. A gap presented itself and Darren edged out onto the main road, feeling flushed, maybe from the perpetual and defeating heater, or maybe from the feeling that, if only for a brief moment, he had been in love.

Darren drove slowly, aware that he was early. The South Yorkshire Dept of Police Forensics was listed coyly in the *A to Z* under Police Services, Crookes Moore. It was the sort of building that was easy to find but spectacularly anonymous, so much so that your curiosity wasn't even grazed by passing it, and you would hardly be aware of its existence unless it had been pointed out to you. It had an air of grey-stone and smoked-glass remoteness which, once inside, was further emphasized by its air-conditioning, a relative rarity in never-tropical Sheffield. There was a quiet hum of activity about the place, which Darren put down to the climate control. In the absence of cool air, the place might well have felt more honestly lethargic, for air-conditioning often seems to be more a form of employee conditioning than temperature maintenance, always being just a few degrees too chilly to sit around and do nothing.

Dr John Sammons was quiet but engaging, with a soft, self-deprecating sense of humour, a civilian scientist in a police institution. Darren felt a degree of empathy – another square peg working in round-hole science.

'So you're interested in switching to forensics? Bit of a jump, don't you feel?' he continued.

'Not scientifically . . .'

'No, I mean from diagnosis of the living to diagnosis of the dead.'

'I'd never really thought in those terms,' Darren answered, side-stepping the attempt at a scientific joke, which are rarely worth troubling with even a smile. 'But anyway, the point of coming to see you was really to find out what sort of a jump it might be, whether I might have the right skills, what sort of vacancies come up, that sort of thing.'

Vacancies happened, he said. Scientifically Darren wouldn't have any problems. Wouldn't be too much of a jump, unless of course he had a criminal record, in which case there would be no jump to make. Darren sat and fidgeted a second. He needed to turn the conversation around to specifics. Dr Sammons, was, after all, the name he had on the Paper database of genetic profiles.

'So what sort of crimes do you investigate?' Darren asked.

'You know, the whole lot really, from A to Z. You name it, if it's on *Crimewatch* we look at it.'

'Murder? Arson? Rape?'

'Everything,' he confirmed, smiling.

'I mean, I once read somewhere about a crime that appeared in the newspapers.'

'Yeah?'

'But they never said exactly how the crime happened, only that it was being investigated forensically.' He paused, a lengthy pause in the cool humming air, a goose-pimple pause which Dr Sammons failed to fill. 'I suppose it was that sort of aura of mystery that first pricked my interest in forensics,' Darren continued, hoping to draw him in.

'I see,' he said.

This wasn't going to be easy. Dr Sammons regarded Darren expectantly, waiting for him to proceed. He decided to take the plunge. 'Yes, it was called something like Paper, as I remember. I kept wondering, you know, just out of curiosity, what sort of a crime that might actually be?' Darren had been bold, maybe too bold, but he wanted to see the reaction.

Dr Sammons looked across at Darren for a couple of seconds. 'Paper? What do you mean?'

'A crime called "Paper".'

'Doesn't ring any bells, I'm afraid,' he answered.

Darren wanted to mention Gavin's name, to see if that sparked any recognition, but decided against it. Instead, he persevered with the only other piece of information that had made no sense to him. 'What about Thorn? Maybe I made a mistake and the crime was called "Thorn".' Desperate curiosity called for desperate tactics.

Dr Sammons screwed his face up and pushed his thumb and middle finger into his eyelids like he was trying to bury his eyeballs into his skull, and then said, 'There was that cardiologist thing out at Dore, Professor Thorn I think his name was . . .'

'Professor Thorn?'

Dr Sammons stopped what he was about to say, cutting a word off before it even got started. 'I'm sorry,' he said, beginning again, 'one of the preconditions of forensic diagnosis is not discussing specific cases with members outside the department here, as you'll discover if you move over to this line.'

Darren strung the conversation out for another ten minutes or so with some fairly mediocre questions and a host of commendable generalities, all the time excited that Thorn was a name, a professor's name, a cardiologist from Dore, and that at last he now had something tangible to work from. Eventually he indicated that he had learned all he needed to know and they stood up. Dr Sammons wished him luck and gave him his extension number in case Darren wanted to have a more formal discussion about potential employment. Darren walked briskly out of the cool air of the building and into the slow lethargy of his permanently heated car.

Lucky Dip

I remember as a child, my mother taking me to a local fair. I was feeling lucky and made straight for the Lucky Dip, handing over my 5 sweaty pence and thrusting my stick-arm up to its elbow in expanded polystyrene. I had a good grope around, but didn't hit upon anything solid. It was getting late in the afternoon and I imagined all the good prizes had already been found. 'Didn't get anything,' I said, withdrawing my arm and turning away from the stall, disappointment welling. 'Hang on, son,' the stallholder said, 'it's not a competition, you know. You put your arm back in there till you find something.' I was shocked. 'What, you mean everybody wins something?' I asked. 'Yes,' the man replied, smiling. I walked away and went home with crushed expectation. Lucky Dip. There was absolutely no luck in it. It was fixed. And if everyone won, and everyone paid 5p, then it made sense that every prize must be worth substantially less than 5p. It was the first time in my life that I had felt conned, and it was fairly much downhill from that day onwards. And here I was, conned now more than ever, about to indulge in a lucky dip of my own.

The lights of the ground-floor lab were on. They were always on, whether illumination was required or not. During the day, the blindless windows of the room were slightly tinted, so that you could study your reflection in them as you passed outside, if you so chose, which was always good to watch from the inside. At night the balance shifted, and all you could see as you strained to look out of the lab into the darkness beyond was your own dazzled reflection having a nervous breakdown as yet again you ballsed up some tricky technique or other.

As I approached the building, I could see even from a distance that no-one was still at work. This was good. When I had worked on the inside of the tinted windows for one long, reflective year, this would not have been good. It used to bother me as I tried to sleep, the unblinking lights glaring at me through the blindless windows as I tossed and turned in bed, beckoning me back to the bench, the cold relentless stare of science keeping its beady eye on me. A long, long year. As I looked through the window now though, the lab was just bathed in an impotent dim glow.

All the best medical students take a year out to do a B.Sc., I had been told, and had duly signed up for a tour of duty in a DNA lab. And it had been fine. A bit difficult at first, isolated from the rugby scrum formed by the interwoven lives of my medical-school colleagues, but I had coped, and had even, at times, enjoyed it. Four months of DNA extractions from blood, four fairly easy months of lectures and writing up, and three extra letters after my name. All in all a bargain. And it might just save my life. I had a quick casual walk around the outside of the building. It was nearly ten o'clock and no-one was around. Even the omnipresent security guards had made an honourable retreat. Around the back, there was a small window, if the worst came to the worst. I was suddenly nauseous, echoes of a night spent in Dore a few months ago, stomach acid trying to climb up the back of my oesophagus and into my mouth. I swallowed hard. This was different, I whispered to myself through a burning throat. I stood still and settled myself, and then took the slender key out of my pocket and approached the side entrance. The bolt turned and I pushed the door open. Despite the lack of people, I worried that I was exposed in the blindless windows, exhibited for all to see like a picture in a frame. I made straight for the unmarked minus-eighty freezer in the corner of the lab. I wouldn't have time to hunt around, and was relying heavily on the principle that, if they could remotely justify it, people would never go to the trouble of throwing anything away. As the heavy freezer door swung open my name stared out at me from one of the icy metallic drawers like an old faded friend. I was in luck. I pulled the drawer as far as it would come and surveyed the enclosed Eppendorf racks that were huddling together for warmth inside. One rack was marked simply with the date, May 1992. I recognized the writing. It was my own. Seeing the date, written on a day several years ago by a very different me at a very different period of my life, made me stop for a second. Cold air skulked out of the open freezer and dropped to the floor. I removed the box, pulling the lid off with difficulty, the flesh-gripping cold forcing me to alternate the fingers holding the metal rack. Inside were six small plastic tubes. I examined them in the palm of my hand, condensation quickly obscuring their labels, and selected two at random. I put them in my pocket, replaced the lid, replaced the rack, replaced the drawer and finally shut the freezer door.

Three Hairs

'Oh hello, is Professor Thorn there please?'

A pause of five seconds. An elderly female. 'Who is this?'

'I'm sorry. My name is Dr Peter Abnett.'

'And how did . . . do you know Robert?'

'Professor Thorn taught the cardiology section of my degree, must be seven or eight years ago now. Is he in? I just wanted to say hello.'

'Where did you get this number?'

'The phone book. I've been abroad . . .'

'Oh, I see. Must do something about that.' A deep inhalation. 'In that case, I'm afraid I have some rather bad news. Robert passed away some five years ago now. I'm sorry for the questions, Dr . . .'

'Abnett. Peter Abnett. No, not at all, I'm just terribly sorry . . .'

'But, what with the police and everything . . .'

'The police?'

'My poor boy, I don't suppose you would have heard. Where did you say you were stationed?'

'Hong Kong.'

'Well, seeing as you're an old student of Robert's and we don't get many visitors over here in Dore, why don't you come on over for tea and we can talk about it then . . .'

'I'd love to, really, Mrs Thorn . . .'

'*Marjory.*'

'But I only have a few hours before I have to head back to Heathrow. It's why I was ringing, to tell the truth, though I feel terrible about it now, given the circumstances, but I literally had a couple of people to visit and thought while I was at it I would give my old professor a call. So I'm a bit pushed for time really.'

'It would make *such* a difference if you could come over.' There was almost a tremor in the voice. 'Please could you?'

Fingers drumming the table. A quick glance at the time. Lower lip bitten gently between incisors. A deep breath. 'Yes, sure, I'd be delighted. I won't be able to stay for very long though.'

The laughingly entitled Sprinter train, which had made several false starts and had stopped at almost every half-opportunity along the way, moped into the village and came to a lazy halt. A short taxi journey and he was in the driveway of the Thorns' house. Mrs Thorn, surprisingly sprightly, opened the front door.

'Dr Abnett,' she said, genuinely pleased to have a visitor.

'Mrs . . . I mean Marjory . . . I'm terribly sorry about your husband. A great loss.'

'Yes . . .'

'Anyway, it's Peter. Please call me Peter.'

'It was such a terrible shock,' she said, almost absent-mindedly, before ushering him inside. 'But time does heal, you know. What makes it worse though is the not knowing.' They sat down at a fussily draped and decorated table and Mrs Thorn poured two cups of Earl Grey tea. 'Of course, I couldn't talk about it for a long time. A long long time. I just felt so angry about it all. In our own house, of all places, the place that I still live.'

'What happened?'

'Oh I'm sorry. Rambling again, as usual. An intruder. A burglar.' Mrs Thorn stared into the gloom of her tea.

'Mrs Thorn?'

'The police said that Robert had disturbed a burglar. I was away at my sister's for the week. Only a week . . . But that's how these things happen, isn't it? I was away, Robert disturbed a burglar, a struggle . . . Myocardial infarction, that's what you doctors call it, isn't it, Peter? Spent his entire life studying M.I., publishing papers, and then . . .'

'But the police, did they catch the person?'

'No. They were very thorough, did everything, looked everywhere. Even found some of the . . . of the intruder's hairs . . . a weapon . . . he'd mutilated some of Robert's papers . . . there was evidently a struggle.'

'Jesus.'

'No, these are all things the good Lord has helped me deal with,' she said, sighing. 'Are you religious, Peter?'

'A little,' Darren replied dishonestly.

She nodded sympathetically. 'That was the funny thing. Three hairs, found between Robert's fingers, pulled out of the intruder's head as they fought. They even did DNA testing. Former colleagues, students of Robert's past and present. Hospital staff. Said the attacker may have been medical. Dropped a scalpel, you see. They believed he knew his attacker. Never convinced, myself. Came to nothing, of course.' Mrs Thorn again gazed into the cloudiness of her tea for long second after long second. 'It all came to nothing,' she said eventually.

Mullet

On his way home from the train station, Darren was increasingly aware of the lurking presence of a white Astra, which had been behind him for the twenty or so minutes since he had left the station's car park. Each time he checked his mirrors, the Astra remained stubbornly a couple of cars behind, despite several junctions and roundabouts. He was probably being paranoid – it wasn't the first time, and by no means would it be the last – but the car lingered until he turned into the small, litter-strewn car park at the base of the flats, where it continued past the entrance and on up the hill. Darren strained to catch a glimpse of its driver, but was only able to see the driver's head in profile.

As he entered the flat, Darren greeted Sam with the recent enthusiasm that being away from him all day had encouraged. 'Hello, honey, I'm home.'

'Nice day, dear?' Sam responded.

'All right. Tell you what though, I reckon I was followed home from work.'

'You're losing it again,' Sam said. 'Anyway, followed by who?'

'A nasty-looking bastard in a white Astra.'

'Didn't have a curly mullet by any chance?'

'Yes, looked like it. Who is it?'

'No idea. But there was a bloke hanging around the car park this morning with a fucking awful haircut and a white car. Saw him on my way to the offy. Still there when I came back. Assumed he was some sort of debt collector or bailiff, after that money I owed on my credit card. Left me well alone though.'

If Mullet Man wasn't interested in Sam, and you couldn't blame anyone for that, and had been hanging around the flats and generally following Darren's car, it was a fair bet he wanted something. Darren grabbed some toast and sat down at his computer. Maybe he had been followed to Dore, or even from Mrs Thorn's house. He shrugged. A private investigator? Maybe employed by Mrs Thorn to check out anyone with an interest in her late husband. That didn't sit well as according to Sam, the man had been hanging around before Darren even set off. He tried not to let it aggravate him, and focused instead on what he now knew. A cardiologist is killed, a police sweep of suspects singles out, among others, Gavin and Simon as likely candidates. Simon's DNA doesn't match the suspect's. Gavin was a failed medic, whose training had obviously gone awry at some stage. A motive? Darren sat back in his uncomfortable metal chair. It all seemed too simple. He was painfully aware that rarely, if ever, did he make it from hypothesis to results and conclusions without some sort of series of catastrophic U-turns, cock-ups, miscalculations, oversights or false assumptions along the way. For the purpose of confirmation, Darren tried to disprove his hypothesis. He couldn't test Gavin's DNA, but had tested Simon's and that hadn't matched. Gavin had been considered to be high-risk. And Gavin was a bit of a wanker . . . After a few minutes, Darren realized he was going round and round in circles, and decided instead to watch

Celebrity Squares. He joined Sam, who was on the sofa already well into shouting abuse at the quadratic assembly of desperate and fuzzy minor celebrities.

The next morning, Darren took the bus to work. He hadn't slept well, and couldn't face driving. He dreamed the hair at the back of his head had suddenly grown in the night and had permed itself for good measure, and felt tentatively up from the back of his neck as he awoke, just to make sure. Fortunately though, he hadn't been mulleted. Under normal circumstances, Darren would have spent the bus journey reading, but instead he monitored the rear windows for any signs of a white Astra. None were forthcoming, but as he left the bus and walked into the hospital grounds, Darren was half sure that he spotted Mullet in the passenger seat of a passing Cavalier.

At coffee, Darren felt distinctly uncomfortable. To avoid a potentially fatal pincer movement involving Winning System and Tea Break Terminator, both of whom were seated on one side of the coffee room, he had been forced to sit next to Gavin, who had edged away slightly as Darren sat down. Although Darren was glad of the distance, a little more would have made him feel more comfortable. Gavin continued to snide his way through coffee, chatting about the previous night's television as if he had never done anything wrong in his life. Darren was silent, watching, listening and wondering. What he needed of course was a sample of Gavin's hair. Maybe he could get hold of his lab coat when he had gone for the evening. This would be the proof he needed to sort things out one way or another. And he already had the techniques more or less up and running. Gavin finished his drink and left the room. Darren sat back, more at ease, before noticing a distressing glint in TBT's eyes. He had been down this road before and had no desire to suffer again, and so got up and left, saving his eye contact strictly for the carpet.

Back at his desk, Darren thought about the man in the white car. He was unsettled. Finally, he realized it was no good. How could he possibly work? He was in danger of once again slipping off the point and into distraction. Gavin. Right here, drinking coffee, chatting. Maybe capable of murder. Laughing and joking. Gavin fucking Viner. How could he even think about working? And Mullet Man seemingly following him around. He wondered whether there was any connection between them. And then he had another nasty thought. Suppose Mullet was the third high-risk name on the list. Jesus. Darren rubbed his face with the palms of his hands. This was useless. He might as well go and hand his cards in now and save Staffing Services the trouble. But what to do? Sequencing Gavin's DNA wouldn't be easy, and he could hardly confront him, at least not one to one. Maybe, though, there was another way. At lunch, Darren sauntered over and sat with him.

'What do you want?' Gavin asked, smiling thinly.

'Nothing,' Darren replied. He strung out some meagre conversation for ten minutes or so, while Gavin sporadically yes-ed and no-ed. He seemed preoccupied. Presently, Simon came over to join them. Darren took a deep swig of ice-cold Coke, which hurt and felt good at the same time, as if he had been swimming and water had gone up his nose, but dribbled down the back of his throat with sugary gratification. He resolved to put the cat amongst the pigeons and see how Gavin reacted, with Simon to back things up should any kind of independent confirmation be needed. 'I forgot to say that while I was on the dole I went over to see about a job in police forensics – you know – genetic testing.' No reaction. 'Anyway, I was talking to this guy there about unsolved murders and such. Really fascinating.' Nothing. 'The stuff they can do – profiling from human hairs and single cells.' Similar lack of interest. 'He was on about some doctor, a prof. I think, who died a few years ago.' Both appeared unconcerned. 'Thorn, I think his name was. Professor Thorn.' Neither said anything. There was a tangible impression of disinterest. 'Did you hear about it?' he asked. Both said half-heartedly that they did. The conversation quickly petered out. Gavin remained silent. Simon looked at Darren with slightly raised eyebrows, doubtlessly confused about his motive. Darren could think of no way of being any more direct and so made his excuses and returned to the office, where he sat and gazed out of the window. This was daft. He was getting nowhere. A gardener below was trimming extraneous grass away from the concrete path surrounding the Institute. There had to be a way of accusing someone without doing it face to face. The gardener switched to sweeping up the clippings and dumping them back on the remaining grass, as if giving the remaining foliage a warning not to grow too far. And then Darren thought of a way. He took two pieces of headed paper and slotted them into his printer. After a couple of false starts, he typed eight short words, printed them twice as separate letters, addressed them and placed them in the internal post. It was Thursday. With a bit of luck, they would be delivered tomorrow morning.

Blood Simple

It was after I'd parked my over-excitable Fiat in the garage and was thinking about peering under the bonnet to have another unhappy, head-shaking conversation with the engine that Sarah came out.

'The police were here,' she said. 'Wanted to talk to you.'

'What about?' I asked.

'They wouldn't really say. Want to take a blood sample though.' I abandoned my attempt to locate the bonnet catch and tried to appear calm. 'Gavin,' she enquired, 'is there anything I should know?'

I said nothing, but all the time a nasty thought kept coming to me and wouldn't let me alone. And this on top of the note I received this morning.

When Sarah went out to her exercise class, I knocked back a couple of tablets of emergency Valium. I also started drinking, but gently. I was shaking through the sedatives. To occupy myself, I sat and stared deeply into a book, any book, I didn't even know the title, focusing on the shape of the letters and the patterns of the words, following the spaces between words like the route through a maze. I stared deeper and deeper and receded further and further. Some indeterminate time later the bell went and I struggled to my feet. There was a WPC and an older looking man, CID maybe, smiling at me. I was groggy, but not in a just-got-up sort of way, more a hazy, slow-motion mode of being. He did the introductions and then confirmed my name. Gavin Viner, I mumbled, before wandering into the kitchen to make a pot of tea. I had, at least, stopped shaking.

'The reason we're here,' CID says, when small talk has filled the seemingly enormous vacancy of time while the kettle boils and the tea stews, 'is just a routine follow up of an old case that you will have probably forgotten all about.' He looks at me as he says this with the suggestion in his eye that I certainly haven't forgotten about it. He reminds me of the details, just in case I can't remember them. The WPC sitting by his side nods from time to time. After two or three minutes of nervously sipping my tea, they get to the point. They want a DNA sample, another DNA sample. They say their inquiries are still ongoing and due to a freezer malfunction they have lost many of the original specimens they took seven years ago. This doesn't seem particularly likely. I put my coffee down as my cup is starting to rattle slightly against its saucer. I am legally obliged to give a sample, they tell me. The WPC pulls out a swab and receptacle from a small plastic box, and also takes out a syringe and needle. I thought I was safe from all this. I start to sweat. I imagine it is obvious to them and this makes me sweat more. They are looking suspiciously at me. I have to use the bathroom, I blurt out. This will only take a minute, sir, the officer says. The WPC steps forward. I stand up. Look, please just let me use the toilet. The officer walks forward and puts a clamping hand around the top of my arm. It will just take a minute, I assure you, then you'll be free to do what you want. I have to think of a way out of this. Look, I want to go now, I tell him. I'm sorry, sir, he says, sarcastic on the sir, you have to be observed at all times when giving a DNA sample. Home Office regulations. The WPC is fiddling around with something just out of my line of view. I turn my head slightly. It is a canula. Just in case we can't get any blood out of your arm, she explains. I have to get out of the house. I feel trapped. There must be something I can do. Now if you'd just like to sit down, the WPC says, holding the syringe ready. This is bad, very bad. I have to think of something, anything. Fear is hacking its way through the warm hazy under-growth of the Valium, stripping away the thick layers of insulation which lie in its way. This can't be hap-pening to me here in my own home. I thought I was safe after all this time. The WPC has a plastic tourni-quet in her other hand. The officer is in my face trying to distract me. This is the last thing I remember.

Don't Ask

Karen visited Darren at the flat after work on Friday. They watched videos, drank wine, smoked and made love, before eventually crawling into bed at 01:43. Darren knew it was 01:43 because the video display said it was, having recently and eventually been set to the correct time. Before they slept, Karen seemed to want to talk. Darren tried to at least appear to be awake. ' "Let's get nakid." Every night. And I'm already fucking naked,' she said. 'The light is out, I'm naked, and it was always "Let's get nakid." It was his password, his way of asking. I mean sometimes I wanted someone who was going to push me up against a wall and, you know, just fuck me, because he wanted to, whether I liked it or not . . . not just, do you want to get naked, I mean, would you permit me to have sexual relations with you? Are you still awake enough not to preclude the chance of intercourse?' She stared intently at Darren through the half-light. 'Promise me you will never, never ask.'

'What, never?' Darren yawned.

'As soon as you've asked, it's like you've declared your intentions, it's over, no adrenalin, no surprise, no nothing. It's like, we're going to do this thing, if you agree.'

'Fair enough, but *never* though?'

'Well, OK, sometimes . . .' Karen conceded.

'When?'

'You know, period, PMT, stressful day, my entire family has just been killed in a ballooning accident, just-discovered-I've-got-cellulite day . . .'

'So I'm supposed to know when to ask and when not?'

'It should be fairly obvious.'

'Oh yeah, and how exactly?'

'You know, just obvious.'

Darren kept quiet for the moment. He desperately wanted to sleep, but had warmed slightly to the theme. He had once read an article in a women's magazine, with the less-than-scientific byline, 'How do *you* show you want it?' Various partners owned up to how they asked the unaskable, and Darren had been appalled at the paucity of romance involved. He had vowed then and there that he would never ask future girlfriends for sex, and this had been fairly easy given his subsequent born-again virginity. Rather, he pledged, he would just look permanently available and let nature do the rest. And as things were, this was working well, though it was, admittedly, early days. 'OK,' he said, 'it'll be obvious and I won't ask.'

Karen was intent on continuing. 'I mean, it all starts out OK, because you're at it like rabbits in the early stages . . .'

'Great,' Darren enthused. This was good news. A positive statement of intent.

'. . . it's just when you settle into . . . into *comfort*, you know, when feeding your stomach becomes more exciting than feeding your fanny, when you start *counting*, like I've been down on you more times this month than you've been down on me, like when shagging almost becomes a chore, just one more thing to do before you go to sleep . . . that's what I'm talking about, that's when asking just becomes *fatal* . . .'

'Yeah. I know.' Darren decided to share what he had gleaned about such matters from the magazine article. 'I once read this thing in *Cosmo* or somewhere and people had to list what they said to, you know, tell their partner they were in the mood.'

'Yeah? Was "Let's get nakid" in there?'

'No. Far worse. Some of them struck me as tragic and funny, and I remembered them. But it wasn't just stock sentences, there were actions, and most of them were even more dismal than the "I'm feeling tense" or "Are you feeling tired, darling?" or "I'm off to bed, then" or even my favourite, "Have you flossed your teeth?"'

'No!'

'Yeah, and worse. But it was the actions that were really bad. They said that they hid their girlfriend's pyjamas, or paced around distractedly, or put condoms by the bed . . .'

'What a passion killer.'

'Or, there were loads of them . . . or . . . or they just turned the telly off – like, there's fuck all else on, how about it? Or they skipped their nightly exercises and just got into bed. I mean, talk about fucking oblique.'

'Jesus, yes,' Karen said, appalled. 'Makes my experiences sound positively racy.'

'Anyway,' Darren muttered, rolling over in one last show of enthusiasm, 'how would you feel about getting naked?'

In the morning, Karen went out to do some shopping and Darren sat and stared at the opaque television. Monday morning was going to be interesting. The telephone rang, and Darren answered it. No-one replied, so he replaced the receiver. Maybe Gavin would answer the note by not turning up for work. That or he would be fucking edgy. He congratulated himself on his experiment. For once, he had been thoroughly scientific. He had even included a negative control, sending Simon a letter as well, so that he could judge Gavin's actions against the background of Simon's less panicky, though probably slightly spooked, behaviour. Darren stared out of the window and down over the untidy car park below, continuing to wonder what the following week might bring. Despite only having been back at work for a short period, the five-days-on, two-days-off regime of the working week had already overwhelmed the nameless, structureless days of his unemployment. Throughout his years in the lab, as much as he could hope for during his weekends was to forget about work, because he suffered acutely from Sunday Fear – the fear of Mondays, the fear of the rest of his life. For Darren, weekends were like coming off at half-time and sitting in a warm dressing room, not wanting to go back out into the numbing cold, with its impenetrable terrain and stinging air. Weekends gave him just enough time to work out where everything was going wrong, before having to get out there and do it all again. It wasn't so bad when he was actually in the middle of it all, running around with no time to think. To sit back from it, however, was to see things as they were, and this was what Darren hated about Sundays – it was discovering that Monday to Saturday was actually a real struggle.

Karen would be back soon with the shopping. Darren would have gone with her if he could have been bothered, which he couldn't, but had offered half-heartedly anyway, for the sake of appearances. He strained his eyes in the direction she would return from, head bowed no doubt, straining away from the desolate huddle of single-storey shops with flat roofs, which were almost permanently battered by the wind-tunnel consequence of having several closely spaced blocks of flats for neighbours. Even on calm days, the flats channelled great gusts of wind between them like some sort of monumental experiment into aerodynamics. As he continued to think and watch, Darren tracked a car from the edge of the estate, turning left and left again, before pulling into the car park and stopping smartly. It was a white Astra. Two men got out and looked up at the flats. One was Mullet. Darren had no doubt they were coming up to him. He glanced quickly around the flat and at the bookcase, and wondered whether he had time to block the door. He thought about a knife, but a recent memory stopped him. Darren grabbed his keys, looked at the laptop, swore, threw a blanket over it and ran out of the front door. The flats opened out onto a communal landing, which emptied into a grim concrete stairwell. Darren sprinted down the corridor and made for the stairs. He stopped. The lift. Slow, but it never looked as if it was working. Probably, they would take the stairs. Fuck it, he pressed the button. Four floors. The lift could only take seconds to arrive, surely. He punched the button. Come on, you fucker, come on. The lift failed to show. Maybe they were in it. Darren changed his mind and dashed for the stairs. If he could get down a storey, he could dodge down the fire escape. Halfway down the first flight, he froze. Mullet was tearing up towards him. He turned and launched himself back up the stairs, three at a time, sprinting for the lift. Mullet was nearly on him. The door of the lift was open. He dashed in and reached for the control buttons. The man inside took a firm hold of his upper arm. Darren tugged away from him. Mullet reached the lift opening and grabbed him from behind, arm around his neck, cutting off the air.

Bruise Pristine

Darren smiled thinly as he entered the coffee room, and tried to recall the last time he had even half-smiled on a Monday morning. Given the events of the weekend it had been his intention just to observe Gavin's behaviour, to see whether anything was different now that he had received his anonymous note, but one change was immediately apparent and Darren couldn't help but be distracted by it. 'Dear oh dear,' he said, almost compassionately, 'what happened to you over the weekend?' Gavin looked sullenly up to meet his eye. 'Bit nasty that.'

'Yeah,' Gavin mumbled quietly.

'Door, was it?'

'No,' he answered flatly.

'Pissed?'

'No,' he answered again.

'Sport?'

Another 'No.'

Having ruled out three of the four most likely causes of a black eye, he concluded that Gavin had at last had his come-uppance. 'So come on, what was it?' he asked.

Gavin went to rub his eyes involuntarily, but stopped as soon as his fingertips touched the swollen eyelid, wincing as he did so. 'Look, Darren, I didn't get punched, if that's what you think.'

'No?'

'No.' The coffee room was just about dying with curiosity but no-one said anything. Gavin took slow thoughtful sips of his coffee. He looked a mess. His right eye was swollen badly, and in conjunction with his already scarred cheek, Gavin made for less than comfortable viewing. People began to bury their curiosity under mundane conversation. Darren's interest, however, was feverishly alive. After a couple of minutes, Gavin stood up. 'Look,' he said, in a rare moment of solemnity, 'the truth is I passed out and hit my face on the corner of a table. OK?'

A general nod went around that yes, it was OK, with members of the department generally feeling a little sheepish for prying. Darren, however, had to know the details and sparing himself any such feelings of conscience asked, 'And you weren't pissed?'

'I was giving blood . . .'

'What, weren't you lying down?'

'I was giving blood . . . giving a blood sample, at home, when I . . .' He paused, staring into the floor.

'When you what?' Darren enquired.

'When I passed out.' Gavin sat down again and seemed a little uncomfortable. He said nothing for a couple of minutes, but appeared to be on the verge of wanting to speak. The coffee room took the opportunity to leave in dribs and drabs, having heard what they wanted to hear.

'What? Just like that?'

'It's needles,' Gavin said, miserably, 'bloody needles. All my life, needles.' He stared into the floor. 'I mean, have you ever thought to ask me why I work here, as a failed medic, instead of bossing patients around in the Royal?' In the absence of a reply, he continued, 'It's fucking needles.'

Darren had no idea where this was leading. 'Yeah?' he asked, hoping to coax some more information out of him.

'When I was a student, OK, the anatomy and physiology was a doddle. I loved it. Medicine – that was my life. And then we started doing general medicine, and that was fine. I could take blood, I didn't enjoy it, but I could do it all the same. But the more blood I took, and the more I convinced myself it was painless and easy, the more I dreaded having blood taken from me.' He looked almost pleadingly at Darren. 'And then all the practical classes began, and we started to use ourselves as guinea pigs, and practised giving injections and taking blood from each other. But I couldn't do it.' Gavin shook his head slowly as if he still couldn't believe it.

'I don't understand what you're trying to say. I mean, surely you were surrounded by people, medical people, who could help you out?'

'That was the thing. We were having lectures on detailed anatomy all the time and I had these images in my mind of the needle tearing skin cell from skin cell, gouging its way through flesh, ripping through my nerves, piercing blood vessels and passing out the other side of them, blood leaching into the wounded tissue, all done by this cold metal spike. I couldn't shake it, no matter what I thought about. It was becoming obvious in practical classes.'

'So what happened?'

Gavin sighed. 'People were noticing and teasing. Eventually the lecturers became aware that here was a medical student who could barely stand the sight of blood, and for whom the very thought of a needle left him virtually convulsing.'

'But needles . . .'

'Right, so you're going to tell me they're sharp and

painless. But I have this other image, and this is what fucks it up for me. When you see a needle or a pin magnified under a microscope, the sharper and more magnified the picture, the blunter the point of the needle becomes. It starts off razor-sharp under no magnification and that's fine. It's just when you look more closely it becomes this, this blunt instrument which gets forced through your flesh . . .' Gavin was sweating slightly. Darren glanced at him, not sure what to say or indeed why Gavin had opened his heart to him. He wondered whether Gavin might be on the verge of some sort of confession.

'You said you were giving a blood *sample*,' Darren prompted, in the prickly seconds following Gavin's disclosure.

'Yeah. The police were taking a sample for DNA profiling. Something to do with that prof. from the medical school you were talking about the other day. All routine, they said. Think the cheeky bastards even took a swab from my mouth when I fainted.'

Relatedness

Darren ran out to his car and drove home as quickly as the one-litre engine would allow. Inside the flat, he turned his computer on, and opened up Simon's profile one more time. A nasty thought was rattling around his head. Surely Gavin was now in the clear. But Simon had failed to turn up to work and it was approaching lunchtime. Maybe Darren had made a mistake. He opened the database's Bird, S. file. He lined the two profiles up next to each other, for the purpose of one final confirmation. They were certainly different, very different. But, as he peered more closely into the monitor, he became increasingly aware that there were some similarities between the two traces. The database Bird, S. seemed noisier, somehow. It was almost as if there was a background of random bands on the profile which was absent from that of the hair DNA. Darren started to trace individual red, yellow, green and blue bands from one profile to the other. Many, maybe a third, were shared. This was extremely unlikely through chance alone. There was a degree of relatedness apparent which he hadn't spotted when he had examined the profiles for the first time. And relatedness must be the key word. There was no chance about this. People don't have similar DNA profiles. This is the very point of their use in forensics. No, people have very different, effectively unique, DNA fingerprints. Unless, that is, they are related.

Darren stood up and paced around the flat as he had done so many times before. Clearly, the police profile wasn't based on Simon's DNA. It was similar, but must have come from someone else. This was interesting. A profile with a similar name and a similar pattern of banding. This could mean several things. Darren tried to think. How could he have missed this likeness between the two traces? He cursed himself for not being more thorough, and wondered whether Simon had a brother or sister. It was conceivable that a close relation had given a DNA sample in place of Simon. Surely though the police would have checked ID. Or else a relative had perpetrated the crime, but given his name as Simon Bird. That didn't make too much sense either. He sat down again, but was too excited to sit still, and so stood up and paced about some more. The only other explanation he could muster was that Darren had accidentally taken one of Simon's hairs from the collar of his lab coat together with one or two of someone else's, and had effectively profiled two people. This didn't seem particularly plausible. He had been careful, as careful as he could be, and they were all, as he remembered, short, light-coloured hairs. So, for the first time, Darren realized he was definitely onto something. Simon was implicated, if only through someone else. Somewhere along the line there had also been some form of deception. And deception and innocence rarely appear together in public.

Darren closed Simon's file and made his way back to the car, muttering to himself. He had ruled Simon out of the equation on the grounds of forensic evidence. But clearly his assumptions had been precarious, at best, for any certainty built on the quicksand of Darren's sporadic incompetence was likely to flounder eventually.

Motorways of Acceptance

The toilet seems suddenly small, as if the walls have decided they want to get to know me better. I read it again. And then triple-check the envelope is addressed to me. An internal envelope, addressed in capital letters. Headed notepaper. I walk into one of the two flimsy cubicles and slide the flat aluminium bolt across the deliberate gap in the door, into its housing on the other side. I am sweating everywhere and my hands feel cold. I read it once more.

```
Re: Professor Thorn

I AM ON TO YOU
```

I screw the paper up as if that will make the problem smaller and easier to handle, and think about flushing it down the toilet. It will probably float though, which just about sums up the state of things. It won't go away. It will never go away, no matter how I try to get rid of it. However hard I swallow, it is still there, a bitterness at the back of my throat. I decide that despite all my precautions so far, I have to get away from the Institute, and soon. But who? Who in the building could possibly know anything? Who could have known me before? Who could have any idea? And then, as I unlock the door and leave the toilets, a name comes into my head. Just looking into his eyes will give me the answer. But maybe it will give him an answer as well.

I walk out of the building and towards my car. I have to get away for a couple of days. I swing out of the car park and head out, away, beyond my troubles, gliding swiftly down narrow slip roads and onto wide open motorways of forgiveness and acceptance. As I drive, I stare back into the rear-view mirror as if afraid that the past is coming up fast behind me and I start to notice a car, occasionally at first, more now I'm looking for it, a white car which stubbornly won't go anywhere I'm not going. I slow down and it slows down. I thrash the engine and it thrashes as well. Paranoia is consuming me from the inside and spitting me out through damp palms, a running forehead and a cascading back. Who is it? I strain to see, driving now on peripheral vision, having to brake suddenly, trying to focus on the bright future of the flat straight road laid out before me. Who? I can't see well, but I can see enough to know it isn't anyone I have met before. He is permanently four or so cars back and I wonder whether he wants me to know he is there. Certainly, if he is trying to follow me surreptitiously, he is making a poor job of it.

Exits are signed, appear, and fade away into the mirrored distance, and he is still there. I can think of no clever plan of action. My Volvo is too sedate to try speeding off. I look at the fuel gauge. Nearly full. My car is by no means economical, but statistically, it is likely that I will be able to travel further than whoever is trying to track me. I could therefore outrun him. Sooner or later, he will have to stop for fuel and I will be able to lose him. It seems a bit of a self-defeating answer though. I don't want to have to drive 200 miles just to be rid of someone who probably knows where I work anyway, particularly when I've only planned to go forty or so miles. No, I will let him do his worst. I put the radio on but it annoys me so I turn it off again. Two more junctions and I will be there. It will be a form of sanctuary. My parents don't know I'm coming, or even that I'm bringing a guest along for the ride, but I feel suddenly like a child coming home, expecting to be wrapped in thick, warm, welcoming arms of protection. I leave the motorway with my escort in his Astra, who drops back as we hit A roads and pass through dissected villages. Ten more minutes of perspiration and mild palpitation and I pull into my parents' drive. My brother's motorbike is there. This is good. The Astra slows and then passes. I do not see the car again all weekend. And then, as I leave my parents' house on Monday morning, after a weekend spent losing myself in home cooking, cats and memories of pleasant times, I am sure for a minute that I see the car again. This time, it doesn't follow me, but I check all the way anyway, until I at last reach the Institute, three or four hours late for work.

Betrayal

In my office, I start to calm down, and dial my home number. It rings twice and I check my messages. There is a healthy number of beeps. Eventually, I hear:

'Mr Bird? Ah, this is Detective Matthews from Sheffield Crookes station. Would you give me a ring on extension four three five as soon as possible, please. We need to arrange taking a routine sample from you. Thanks. Oh, it's Friday four p.m. Bye.'

Beep.

'Mr Bird? Detective Matthews again. Please would you give me a ring as soon as possible?'

Beep beep beep.

I put the phone down slowly. This is very bad. First, a note. Second, I'm sure I have been followed over the weekend. Third, and most fatally, they want to test me. They are doing precisely what they always do – they are putting the word around, watching for panic. Otherwise why would they be ringing me at home? Do they have something new? I try not to get too hysterical. I am safe, I remind myself. But who sent the note? Who is on to me? I walk up to the lab, trembling slightly. Darren is talking to Gavin on the other side of the room. Darren and Gavin. Shit. This could be trouble. Darren has been dropping hints, asking strange questions. But how could Darren possibly know anything? Darren and Gavin and me. I try to put it all together. Darren has found something out and has told the police. But what about Gavin? Surely Gavin knows something about this. Darren doesn't like Gavin, but they are talking intensely. Maybe I am just being paranoid. Darren keeps looking over. I am being overly suspicious, I tell myself. But whatever has happened, I am in real trouble. Especially if the police want another sample. I need to find out what Darren knows. If he has told them something then it's all over. It is time to confront him. And there might not be much time. But why now, after all these years? And then I think of Darren. Maybe it's anxiety working overtime, but he has been different recently. The bastard. There are betrayals, and then the betrayals of your friends. But how could he possibly have any idea about anything?

Discussion

Extraction

'Darren,' I say, verging on panic, 'I have to talk to you. Now. Somewhere private. The Seminar Room, maybe?' I try to sound calm, but can't imagine it comes across very composed.

'Sure,' he says. He looks a little apprehensive. 'I'll just finish up in the laboratory.'

I go up to the top floor, through a couple of unnecessarily reluctant security doors and into the empty room. I sit down at a small table housing an overhead projector and wait for him. The table is dusted with a fine layer of chalk which has settled out from the room's prevailing air of erudition. A tatty white screen hangs limply over the top half of a blackboard, neither fully extended nor fully retracted, and looking none too desperate about seeing any action either way. Darren presently struggles through the two sets of doors and sits down a couple of yards away. I glance at him, unsure of what to say. I have no idea where to start or what I might gain from confronting him.

Presently Darren says, 'So it was you, then?'

I say nothing. What could it possibly have to do with him — an obsessive-compulsive scientist who has lost the plot. Maybe he will take my silence for guilt, but nothing matters now, except finding out how he knows and why he has told the police. 'Darren,' I start, 'why? I mean how . . .'

'It *was* you?'

I am aware for the first time that Darren has something in his hand. It is a small brown bottle, 100 millilitres maybe. He has loosened the metal top so that it is merely resting on the mouth of the bottle. 'Look, just tell me what you are accusing me of.'

Darren fingers the loose cap of the bottle. 'You know perfectly well,' he says, frowning down at his fingers.

It is no good stringing this out. I have to discover what he knows. 'OK, so I know what you are accusing me of. And if you want to call that guilt then that's up to you.'

Darren looks a little satisfied and then puzzled. I peer more closely at the bottle in his hand, and eventually understand what it is. He has brought it from the laboratory. Brown bottles are few and far between. There is only one fluid routinely kept in brown glass and that is the fluid used for DNA extractions. It is phenol. This is not good news. A modest splash of phenol on my skin will be enough to kill me. Darren has come prepared. I am suddenly aware that he holds all the cards. 'Look, Darren, I have no idea how we came to be here in this situation,' I blurt, 'but I want you to believe me that whatever you think I may have done isn't the whole truth. I don't know who you've talked to . . .'

'Dr John Sammons.'

'Who's he?'

'Police forensics.'

I have no idea who John Sammons is, but obviously he must know about Professor Thorn. 'What did he tell you?'

'Nothing much,' Darren replied. 'But that isn't really where I got most of my information from.'

'So where did you get it?'

'From a computer, indirectly. That's not the point though.' He is more insistent now. 'I want to know what the hell you did.'

I run my fingers along the dusty surface of the table, my damp fingertips picking up a layer of chalk as I do so. Darren seems excitable and is staring at me as if I am about to reveal one of the last remaining secrets of the world. He continues to mould the palm of his hand around the circumference of the bottle. I take a deep breath. 'This is how it was. I've never told anyone, so I don't know how it will come out. Maybe it will sound as awful as you probably imagine it to be, I don't know.' From the inside the door looks delicate, and so, despite Darren's phenol, I walk over to it and wedge a pound coin in the adjacent security slot. Darren watches me closely. I give him a wide berth. He looks edgy and dangerous. I haven't seen him like this before. 'Jams the door,' I say, as if by locking the door I can keep my words away from the reality of the world outside. 'Look, I was a medical student.' Darren raises his eyebrows and nods quickly, as if I have just confirmed something that he had suspected. I have to talk my way out of this. I speak rapidly and lucidly. 'I was doing well. I took a year out after my first two years, to do a B.Sc., an extra three letters, I thought. Worked in a clinical sciences lab doing routine DNA extractions from blood. When I came back onto the course, we started our medicine proper – wards, patients, specialities, firms. So one stint I ended up doing at the end of my third year was coronary medicine, and I was on a good firm. Except, that is, for the consultant bastard who taught us. Took a complete dislike to me from the moment he saw me. I never knew why.'

'Professor Thorn?'

I ignore the name. 'This was personal and malicious.

And nothing I could ever do stopped him from wanting me out. I was stuck with him – he had to pass my course at the end of four months so that I could move on to the next speciality. Well, things got worse and worse, I lost all confidence, the rest of the firm cottoned on that I was the weak link, and if they alienated me as well, then so much the better in the eyes of Thorn.' I can hardly believe I am saying all this. It all sounds so natural, as if I'm recounting someone else's story. 'It was pitiful. Playground stuff. Thorn was the bully and the others put me down to further their own selfish causes.' I pause, thinking, and watch Darren fidget, screwing and unscrewing the bottle top. Another betrayal. I wonder whether I might be able to overpower him. I am bigger than he is, and probably stronger.

'So then what?' he asks.

I keep talking, all the time trying to figure my way out of this mess. 'It was one long nightmare, a year of darkness. He hated me and set about undermining every positive thing I did. I began to lose my nerve. At the end of the four months, I failed my course exam. The only one to fail. And so I had to start over again. Another four months of hell. I failed again, almost unheard of. And that's when I started losing it, spent more time in the bar than on the wards, drank myself to sleep every night, dosed myself up on slimming tablets and anything else I could get my hands on to see me through the day . . .' I stop. I feel an anger which has long been dormant flexing its muscles. 'I dropped out. I had to. I saw the dean a couple of months later to discuss my problem with Thorn, and he took one look at the state I was in . . . And in that instant, I lost nearly all my friends, my self-esteem, my parents' respect, my hopes and most of my ambitions. And all because some wanker took a pathological dislike to me.'

Discussion

'So you killed him?' Darren says quickly, a little too quickly, and then sits there looking sheepish. I am aware for the first time that he may be scared of me.

'Killed? What, like murdered?' I snort. 'Nonsense. He killed himself.'

'What? There was a break-in, a knife . . .'

'A scalpel,' I correct him. 'And there was a break-in, but that hardly constitutes murder.'

Darren looks agitated, and screws his eyes up slightly. 'Neither, as far as I'm aware, does that constitute suicide.'

'Look, I didn't say it was suicide.' Someone tries the door, which remains solidly shut. During a long and mainly unwelcome conversation a couple of weeks ago, Tea Break Terminator had told me that a coin in the swipe slot fucks the mechanism. These hadn't been his exact words, and Christ knows what he'd been doing to make such a discovery, but for the moment at least this is invaluable information. 'Thorn killed himself', I continue, 'because he got me thrown out of medicine.'

'So like a girl wearing a short skirt gets raped and it's the girl's fault – she was asking to get raped?'

Another try at the door. 'We're busy,' I shout, hoping they will leave us alone. 'You don't understand what I'm saying.'

Darren is slightly perturbed, and very on edge. 'Well, what are you saying?'

Spyhole

I try to get my words out slowly and carefully, as if I'm speaking English to someone foreign and want each word to stand out from the rest, proud and intelligible, thinking, desperately, while I talk. 'I went to his house. His wife was away and I broke in. I took a scalpel and searched around the rooms downstairs and then the rooms upstairs. I was going to teach him a lesson.' Another push at the door followed by a couple of knocks. 'Finally I found the room I was looking for in the dark. I went in, got my scalpel out, the scalpel I had used for so many dissections, and made my way over to the end of the room. Jesus, I was angry. I had to make the bastard pay for the misery he had inflicted on me. I had it all planned out.' This time the knocking on the door is louder, and totals maybe eight or nine sharp bangs.

'We're having a meeting in here,' Darren shouts. 'Come back later. Go on,' he says in my direction.

'So I know what I'm going to do to the heart surgeon. Every professor has one sacred thing that they keep hidden and treasured. A file of their publications, not reprints, but the actual papers taken from the journals they appeared in. Their life's academic achievements in black and white. I was in his study, hunting around, and finally I found the wanker's hallowed file.'

'What? You weren't going to kill him?'

'Just listen. I was there to cut the heart out of the *esteemed* cardiologist's collection of published papers. I was going to rip the heart out of his life just as he had ripped the heart out of mine. I opened up the folder – there must have been forty or fifty of them – and got my scalpel ready to gouge the very heart out of the middle of the stack. But just as I was tearing into them . . .' This time there is real urgency about the door. Darren walks over to it, leaving the bottle of phenol on the table. I think about grabbing it. He peers through the spyhole and then turns around and sits down. I curse my impotence. This may have been my only chance.

'So what then?' he asks, reacquainting himself with the phenol.

'Who is it?'

'No-one. Go on.'

I have to let this out, have to finally get it off my chest. 'So I suddenly turn around, and there he is, the professor in his pyjamas, with the light on, pale and rigid with fear, eyes transfixed by the scalpel in my hand. And he comes towards me, slowly at first, and I back off, and he's coming more quickly, staggering forwards, and I'm thinking that I'm going to have to defend myself, and he's still coming, but falling now, falling headlong, grabbing a chair as he falls. He is on his back, fitting, going blue, thrashing, having a fucking infarction, staring up wildly at me, deflated, indecipherable words said with no air in them, probably pleading with me to help him, and I'm standing over him, putting the scalpel down, and . . .' My mouth is making funny shapes of its accord, and I realize I am crying like a guilty schoolboy. 'And . . . I kneel down to try and help him, but I panic, I don't know what to do, and I'm thinking this is all your fault, you old bastard. If you'd taught me well I'd know what to do now. Instead, you've taken all of my fucking confidence and replaced it with fear, and all my diagnoses and replaced them with indecision, and so I'm paralysed – the one person who can help you and you've made me too weak to be of any use to you. He is looking very unhealthy, and is thrashing less and looking more and more blue and cadaverous, and so I put my ear on his chest to see if he is still alive, and he grabs my hair between his fingers, pulls my hair and fits one more time, and then . . .' My sentence dies.

'And that's how they got the DNA sample – from the hairs in his hand?'

I rub my eyes and stare at the floor. 'Yes. It was the only mistake I made. But whether you—'

'It was your brother, wasn't it, who gave the DNA sample in your place? I figured it out.'

I look at him, puzzled. 'What do you mean?'

'Your DNA profile was similar to the one . . .'

'What do you know about my DNA profile?'

'It's a long story,' he says, 'but there must have been something funny about your DNA test. You were all assessed, weren't you? Hospital people and students. Gavin . . .'

Darren seems to know everything. I don't quite understand how. 'I did something,' I tell him, 'something to conceal my identity.'

'What?' he asks impatiently.

'I went back to the lab I worked in.' There is another determined pounding of the door.

'And?'

'I stole a couple of DNA pellets from a freezer. Then, just before I was tested, I rubbed the pellets around the inside of my mouth. They took cheek swabs, and so the profile they got for me was a combination of my cheek cells and two other random people's DNA.'

'Jesus,' Darren says, letting the word out slowly, his brow furrowing. 'Jesus.' There is another bang at the door. 'But, surely they would have blood-tested?'

'Yes,' I say, rather pleased with my scheme as I think back. 'Yes, they would. But I had a letter. A hospital letter on hospital paper from a supposed hospital consultant, indicating that I wasn't to give blood under any circumstances. Haemophiliac, you see.'

'So they couldn't take your blood.'

'I said I'd prefer if they didn't, and they seemed fairly happy. I mean, it was five or six years ago, maybe things were a bit laxer then, and they did have three or four hundred other people to screen.'

'Devious bastard,' Darren says. More hammering at the door. 'So what, after medicine?'

'I had a B.Sc., so I did a Ph.D. to rescue a bit of doctoral pride. And here I am.' I look squarely at him. 'But I want to know something now. Why the fuck did you do this to me?'

'Do what to you?' he asks.

'Get the police involved.'

'That was nothing to do with me,' he replies. I imagine I appear unconvinced because he continues, 'Look, the police came round to my flat and tested me – a big nasty-looking guy with a terrible haircut – they wouldn't do that if I'd simply grassed you up. And anyway, you're a mate.'

The knocking resumes, hard and insistent, and the handle continues its futile waggling. 'Who is it?' I ask Darren again.

He shuffles a little uneasily in his chair. After a pause he answers, 'The police.'

The Milk of Human Kindness

This is it. All previous panics are nothing. All I'm late for work, I'm overdrawn, I've left the gas on, I'm a failure, my hair is falling out, my house is subsiding, my arm feels broken, nobody likes me, my glands are swollen, the sell-by date has expired, she is having an affair, what if I die before my parents, my car has been stolen, there's someone downstairs, I haven't reproduced yet, the engines are slowing down . . . These panics are, in an instant, nothing. And how I wish I had had a true frame of reference in my life to count all these miserable half-worries against. No scale, that has been my problem. If little things are the only things then they become big things because no-one wants to believe they are troubled by nothingness. In the absence of big problems, therefore, we will magnify small problems to fill their space. The one true frame I have has failed me because Thorn was just far too big a frame to measure anything else by. Nothing else would make any sense. Every normal worry would appear too trivial to bother basing a life around. No, I had to disassemble Thorn into small fragments which could be absorbed and forgotten and dismissed. Small worries that could be easily swallowed with only a mild indigestion. If I truly sat down and thought about it, I would collapse. But it had taken time to break it down into manageable chunks, and in the long weeks after Thorn's death everything else had seemed pointless by comparison. And now, the fear is back, and bigger than ever, having reassembled itself into something more swollen and massive than it had ever been before. It is coming back to life and filling me up, crushing the life out of my organs, squeezing the hope out of my soul.

We are cut off. I am in the one place that can save me, and I am trapped. There is freezer after blank freezer piled high with icy DNA in anonymous tubes lurking in the basement, and no way of getting to them. Just two tiny pellets of DNA and I could repeat my trick and camouflage my profile against a fluorescent background of otherness. But no, I am stuck in the top-floor seminar room and the police will be inside in minutes. Think. It is not all over, surely. There must be a way. Somehow. I look at Darren.

'You're fucked,' he says.

'I know,' I reply, slumping against a wall, my arms and legs trembling. I feel weak. Defeating gravity is sucking me to the floor. I am one step from lying down and just closing my eyes. Minutes, that is all. I will be in a car, in a courtroom, in a cell. I wish I had the strength to kill Darren. It is his fault. His fatal curiosity. I close my eyes and see something that I have swallowed somewhere along the line. A picture of a blank wall in Poland. As I stare into its enveloping whiteness I see fingernails embedded in the unforgiving surface. There are scratches and blood, but most of all, there are fingernails. It was horrific but made no sense when I saw the photograph as a child. And then I read the caption. 'Wall inside an Auschwitz gas chamber.' I open my eyes and stare into the wall in front of me. Darren speaks.

'Look, if everything you've told me is true, we've got to do something.'

'It is true,' I say. Not that it matters. All I can see are fingernails being ripped out by sheer fear, futile last desperate efforts taken through final airless closing breaths. Mice gnawing their legs off to escape from traps. Daddy-long-legs losing wings in a vain struggle to flee. I am receding, retreating. Darren is shaking me.

'For fuck's sake,' he says, 'get up, Simon. Come on, let's sort this out.'

I get reluctantly to my feet and look at him. Maybe I should lunge at him. He has left the phenol on a table on the other side of the room. They are working at the lock. I can't help feeling that this is all his fault. And as if he could help me even if he wanted to. 'Whatever you think, Darren,' I so want to hit him, 'whatever you think . . .'

'It doesn't really matter what I think,' he says. 'What matters is whether I'm going to help you.'

I start to shout. 'Help? You've done more than enough of that.'

'Getting upset isn't going to get you out of this,' he says. He is calm and sensible and this makes me more angry. *He* isn't going to get dragged off by the police and buggered in prison. 'We've got to get organized. And fast. They will be in here soon.' He pauses while seconds drip away and then says, 'I've had an idea.'

'Yeah? What? As far as I can see, the only idea is to climb out of the window and make a run for it.'

'On the third floor? Let them flush you out? Come on, you're acting like they know you're guilty.'

'They do.'

'No. They think they do. They can't prove it. Unless you try and climb out of the window.'

There is the occasional muffled shout through the heavy door. 'So I'm fucked. If I run I'm guilty. If I stay and they take a DNA sample I'm guilty. Jesus.' The true extent to which I am well and truly fucked becomes clear.

'But there is a solution,' Darren said again.

I sit down in defeat. 'Let's hear it,' I say.

'You need someone else's DNA, right? So if they take a sample they can't prove that your DNA matches the stuff they've got from the prof. Obviously there will be similarities, but that's not how they work. Forensics is yes or no, not maybe. This is your chance.'

'I don't want to spend my last seconds of freedom in a fucking discussion here.' I am getting desperate. 'What's your idea? Now. For Christ's sake.'

'I give you some of my DNA.'

I look up. 'How?'

'I'm thinking,' he says.

'Blood?'

'No. Dangerous. Messy. Detectable.'

'Cheek cells.'

'Wouldn't be enough in my mouth to make any difference. We're talking a lot of DNA.'

'Hairs?'

'Ditto cheek cells. Bit obvious.' Darren goes quiet. There is the sound of what is probably a drill. 'And of course there's no reason why they don't still believe your haemophilia yarn.' He looks down at me. There is a nasty glint in his eyes. I don't catch on immediately. He stands up and walks over to the blackboard and pulls the retractable screen all the way down until it almost reaches the floor. 'If you so much as look in my direction I will open the door and let them have you,' he says, stepping between the screen and the blackboard.

Summary

Swallow Two

The policeman confirms my name. He wants to see some ID so I show him my driving licence. Darren leaves the room. 'Bit annoying about the door,' I say, after I have removed the coin.

The policeman looks doubtfully at me and grunts. 'That's computers for you,' he says, half-heartedly. There is a tinge of sarcasm, but only a tinge. He takes a cotton-wool swab out of a self-sealing plastic bag and tells me to open my mouth.

Having had two DNA samples taken on separate occasions, I am confident that any solicitor worth their salt will be able to prevent me having to give a third. Also, I am confident that when my sample is compared with the original hair sample it will differ sufficiently from it to rule me out; as Darren is now on his way home to delete the entire Paper directory from his computer, and then to format the hard drive to make sure, it is unlikely that the forensic team will ever know that the sample I am about to give today is different from the sample I gave six years ago. After all, forensics is yes or no, not maybe.

My mouth, though, remains bitter, more bitter than even I would have imagined. I try hard not to swallow. I now understand what girlfriends have been complaining about all these years. The policeman, nasty haircut with an overhang at the back, like an Eighties footballer, scrapes the inside of my cheek with the swab. I am fairly certain that this is the man in the white Astra. From what Darren and I had been able to surmise before the door finally yielded, he must have been tipped off by Dr Sammons after Darren's visit, and put two and two together, when he discovered not only Darren's unhealthy interest in the Paper case, but that he also worked with two of the key suspects. He had tracked all three of us down, Gavin, Darren and myself, and I am the last to give a sample. The policeman removes the swab and replaces it in the bag. I take the opportunity to swallow, finally, and try hard not to retch.

Radio Girl

'Talk me through it again,' Darren said, returning from the bathroom with a glass of water and getting back into bed.

'It's like my alarm clock,' Karen said, taking a sip and then lying back. 'You can select beeps or the radio. I select the radio. That's a conscious choice. But it's the only one, and when it wakes me up, I just decide to be like the very first record I hear.'

'But I still can't see how that works,' Darren said.

'Look I told you, if it's a happy song, then I'm happy. If it's a sad song then I'm sad.'

'And if it's neither?'

'I listen to the words.'

'So you're either happy or sad? It just doesn't make any sense.'

'Well, there's a little more to it than that. It's not just the mood of the record,' Karen explained. 'OK, so the music gives you a clue as to temperament, but there are happy songs with sad words and sad songs with happy words. Overall, I'd say it was more the words.'

'It just seems so random.'

'I don't think it's random exactly. Somewhere, a committee decides a radio station's playlist. Somewhere

299

else, someone decides on the order of the records. It isn't just random. In many ways it's a lot more predetermined than just waking up and letting the day take you where it will.'

Darren was appalled. 'So someone somewhere has probably already decided, on your behalf, what your day is going to be like.'

'Yeah,'

'That's terrible.'

'But that's what life is like.'

'Not for me it isn't,' he said.

'Exactly.'

'And what do you mean by that?'

Karen remained silent and Darren lay next to her and thought. He had hoped that life might be logical, quantifiable, containable, describable by numbers. Maybe it was, but he had clearly failed to sum it up in such terms. As he deliberated he realized that he had been nowhere near. And as he continued to reflect, he realized that the more he had searched for order in life, the more his own life had become disordered. The more he had searched for rational explanations, the more his life had thrown up irrational questions. The more he had sought to understand, the more he had missed the point. The more he had sought logic, the more he found himself drowning in chaos. When things had still made sense, Simon had come to work alongside him, a veritable beacon of common sense. When things became shambolic, Sam had come to stay, a man as inherently random as any ever born. And when everything was in danger of finally falling apart, Karen, a girl who decided her days by songs on the radio, arrived to tell him in the nick of time that life isn't logical, and that living it illogically is every bit as valid as living it logically, only more fun. Karen rolled over to face Darren.

Summary

'What are you thinking?' she asked.

Darren closed his eyes. 'You know . . . science and all that.'

'What about it?' There was a long pause. 'What about it?' Karen asked again. From Darren's side of the bed came only the sound of his breathing.

Karen reached over and flicked the switch on top of the alarm clock to radio mode.

THE END

INK

John Preston

'PART MYSTERY TALE, PART BLACK COMEDY, IT IS A SPLENDID
FUSION OF TWO GENRES . . . A THRILLING READ, DEFTLY
PLOTTED, FULL OF TWISTS AND TURNS'
Literary Review

In the depths of a winter's night, a man throws himself into the River
Thames. When his body is pulled from the water, there are no clues
to who he was, no distinguishing marks, nothing . . .

It is 1989 and Fleet Street is in crisis. So too is Hugh Byrne, a
journalist on one of the few remaining papers left there. Suffering
acute writer's block, he is sent to cover the story of the drowned man
before being ignominiously banished to the bowels of the building to
update the Queen Mother's obituary.

As the newspaper prepares for its move to another glass palace along
the river, Hugh is drawn into uncovering the identity of the drowned
man and begins to wonder, is it possible for someone to die twice?

'A DELIGHTFUL, HILARIOUS NOVEL WHICH WILL MAKE YOU
WONDER IF ANYTHING IN LIFE MATTERS'
Sunday Telegraph

'EXTREMELY FUNNY . . . WITH A RARE GIFT FOR BOTH
HUMOUR AND DESOLATION, PRESTON IS A BRILLIANT NEW
PLAYER IN THE FIELD OF SERIOUS COMEDY'
Sunday Times

'A TEASING, MYSTERIOUS WHOWOZZIT OF A TALE . . . THE
COMBINATION OF READABILITY AND INTRICATE PLOTTING
RECALLS JONATHAN COE . . . AN ENTERTAINING, DEXTROUSLY
WRITTEN NOVEL'
Independent on Sunday

'COMPLEX AND CAPTIVATING . . . AN EXCELLENT THRILLER'
The Times Literary Supplement

'A MORDANTLY SATIRICAL WIT TO DIE FOR . . . SHARP SATIRE,
ABSURDIST RELISH AND THE ELEGIAC DESIRE FOR MORALITY
IN A SORDID WORLD COULD HARDLY CONVERGE MORE
SATISFYINGLY'
Independent

'EXCELLENT . . . A GREAT STORY . . . IT MAKES YOU THINK BUT,
ABOVE ALL, IT MAKES YOU LAUGH'
Evening Standard

0 552 99817 6

BLACK SWAN

Things Can Only Get Better

Eighteen Miserable Years in the Life of a Labour Supporter

John O'Farrell

'Like bubonic plague and stone cladding, no-one took
Margaret Thatcher seriously until it was too late. Her first
act as leader was to appear before the cameras and do a V
for Victory sign the wrong way round. She was smiling
and telling the British people to f*** off at the same time.
It was something we would have to get used to.'

Things Can Only Get Better is the personal account of a
Labour supporter who survived eighteen miserable years
of Conservative government. It is the heartbreaking and
hilarious confessions of someone who has been actively
involved in helping the Labour party lose elections at
every level: school candidate; door-to-door canvasser;
working for a Labour MP in the House of Commons;
standing as a council candidate; and eventually writing
jokes for a shadow cabinet minister.

Along the way he slowly came to realize that Michael
Foot would never be Prime Minister, that vegetable
quiche was not as tasty as chicken tikka masala and that
the nuclear arms race was never going to be stopped by
face painting alone.

'VERY FUNNY AND MUCH BETTER THAN ANYTHING
HE EVER WROTE FOR ME'
Griff Rhys Jones

'VERY FUNNY'
Guardian

'EXCELLENT . . . WHATEVER YOUR POLITICS *THINGS
CAN ONLY GET BETTER* WILL MAKE YOU LAUGH
OUT LOUD'
Angus Deayton

0 552 99803 6

BLACK SWAN

A SELECTED LIST OF FINE WRITING
AVAILABLE FROM BLACK SWAN

99830 3	SINGLE WHITE E-MAIL	*Jessica Adams*	£6.99
99822 2	A CLASS APART	*Diana Appleyard*	£6.99
99842 7	EXCESS BAGGAGE	*Judy Astley*	£6.99
99619 X	HUMAN CROQUET	*Kate Atkinson*	£6.99
99824 9	THE DANDELION CLOCK	*Guy Burt*	£6.99
99853 2	LOVE IS A FOUR LETTER WORD	*Claire Calman*	£6.99
14698 6	INCONCEIVABLE	*Ben Elton*	£6.99
99751 X	STARCROSSED	*A. A. Gill*	£6.99
99760 9	THE DRESS CIRCLE	*Laurie Graham*	£6.99
99847 8	WHAT WE DID ON OUR HOLIDAY	*John Harding*	£6.99
99848 6	CHOCOLAT	*Joanne Harris*	£6.99
99796 X	A WIDOW FOR ONE YEAR	*John Irving*	£7.99
99758 7	FRIEDA AND MIN	*Pamela Jooste*	£6.99
99887 7	THE SECRET DREAMWORLD OF A SHOPAHOLIC		
		Sophie Kinsella	£5.99
99569 X	MAYBE THE MOON	*Armistead Maupin*	£6.99
99762 5	THE LACK BROTHERS	*Malcolm McKay*	£6.99
99803 6	THINGS CAN ONLY GET BETTER	*John O'Farrell*	£6.99
99718 8	IN A LAND OF PLENTY	*Tim Pears*	£6.99
99817 6	INK	*John Preston*	£6.99
99810 9	THE JUKEBOX QUEEN OF MALTA	*Nicholas Rinaldi*	£6.99
99122 8	THE HOUSE OF GOD	*Samuel Shem*	£7.99
99846 X	THE WAR ZONE	*Alexander Stuart*	£6.99
99809 5	KICKING AROUND	*Terry Taylor*	£6.99
99819 2	WHISTLING FOR THE ELEPHANTS	*Sandi Toksvig*	£6.99
99780 3	KNOWLEDGE OF ANGELS	*Jill Paton Walsh*	£6.99
99834 6	COCKTAILS FOR THREE	*Madeleine Wickham*	£6.99